"Kathi Macias has done it again. She has once again told a story ripped from today's headlines . . . a story about human trafficking and the people who fall victim to this modern-day evil. As you read this book, you might be tempted to look away because she tells the unvarnished truth on every page, but I encourage you to read on and be changed by what you read."

—CHARLES POWELL, founder, the Mercy Movement, and coauthor of *Not in My Town: Exposing and Ending Human Trafficking and Modern-Day Slavery*

"Kathi Macias draws us into the world of sex trafficking, showing how it sometimes, believe it or not, is right under our noses—in our own communities. She sheds a bright spotlight on the emotional and spiritual effects of not only the victims but those called by God to help victims and be a source of deliverance to them. A timely book."

—C. S. LAKIN, author of *Someone to Blame*

"In *Special Delivery*, Kathi Macias explores the troubling realities of human trafficking in a powerful and emotional new novel that puts a face on the women and children involved in this all-too-real world."

—LISA HARRIS, author of *Blood Covenant*, a Christy Award finalist

"*Special Delivery* by Kathi Macias handles a tough subject with compassion and an intriguing story that sweeps you from the United States to Thailand. The three-dimensional characters make you care what happens to them in this hard-to-put-down book."

—MARGARET DALEY, author of *Saving Hope* (Abingdon Press, March 2012), and American Christian Fiction Writers president

"*Special Delivery* continues Kathi Macias's important and captivating series dealing with human trafficking and sexual slavery in which she highlights the reality and inhumanity of a very real world issue. As a survivor of long-term childhood sexual abuse, I have a small sense of what these 'slaves' suffer and I applaud Kathi for her willingness to tackle this topic, enlighten readers with truth, and offer the hope of our Rescuer and Healer, Jesus Christ. Thank you, Kathi!"

—GINNY L. YTTRUP, author of *Words* and *Lost and Found*

"Kathi Macias really cares about the victims of sex trafficking. If you didn't know that before, you will after reading *Special Delivery*. Interwoven stories from Thailand to Mexico to the USA show the horrific plight of girls caught up in this vicious web. Their combined story is sure to move your heart."

—KAY MARSHALL STROM, award-winning author of 40 books, including two fiction series: "Grace in Africa" and "Blessings in India"

Special Delivery

Kathi Macias

NEW HOPE
PUBLISHERS
BIRMINGHAM, ALABAMA

New Hope® Publishers
P. O. Box 12065
Birmingham, AL 35202-2065
NewHopeDigital.com
New Hope Publishers is a division of WMU®.

Library of Congress Cataloging-in-Publication Data

Macias, Kathi, 1948-
 Special delivery / Kathi Macias.
    p. cm.
 ISBN 978-1-59669-307-4 (sc)
 I. Title.
 PS3563.I42319S64 2012
 813'.54--dc23

                                    2011045861

ISBN-10: 1-59669-307-X
ISBN-13: 978-1-59669-307-4

N114141 • 0312 • 5M1

Dedication

This book and series is humbly and heartbreakingly
dedicated to all who are held in modern-day slavery.
We stand together with you with the united cry of
"Abolition!" And we look to the One who died
to set us all free.

On a more personal level, I dedicate this book and series
to my partner and best friend, Al, who daily supports
and encourages me as God calls me to
"write the vision . . . and make it plain"
(Habakkuk 2:2).

Prologue

It was good to be back in San Diego, though Mara made it a point to avoid going anywhere near the area where she'd once lived as a modern-day slave. The memories were too ugly, and she did everything possible to block them out. When the topic came up—which it did all too often these days as the general public became more aware of its prevalence—Mara immediately changed the subject or walked away. It was an evil best left for others to combat.

The early summer sun shone warm on her dark hair, cut short now in a modern style that complimented her dainty features and accentuated her large hazel eyes. Her good looks and trim figure often drew whistles and comments, but she ignored them all. Having a man in her life didn't even rate at the bottom of her priority list.

Mara closed her eyes and let the mild breeze toss her hair and caress her skin. There was nothing she liked better than coming to the beach and finding a deserted spot to sit and listen to the waves rush in and break on the packed, wet sand. It was nearly impossible to find such a private place on the weekends, but this was midmorning on Monday, and the place wouldn't start filling up until closer to lunchtime. By then she'd be at work.

She smiled at the thought of her new job. She was a waitress now, making enough in wages and tips to rent a room and meet her basic needs. Though she'd taken advantage of UI benefits, specifically designed to help people from other countries who had been victims of crime while in the United States, it had still taken her nearly two years to get all the necessary paperwork cleared so she could not only come to the States legally but do so as a US citizen. But she'd been persistent, determined to leave her homeland of Mexico, with all its violence and corruption and poverty, behind. Even with all that had happened to her here in Southern California during her youth, she knew that America held more promise for her than the country of her birth. And besides, what did she have to hold her there? It was her parents who had sold her into slavery, and her own uncle, her *tio*, who had stolen her innocence, held her captive, and served as her pimp until at last he was captured and sent to prison. So far as she was concerned, her family was dead to her. She had no desire ever to see any of them again.

Mara opened her eyes and watched a tanned, bathing-suit clad couple stroll along the sand in front of her, the waves lapping at their bare feet. Arms wrapped around one another's waists, they seemed oblivious to anything or anyone else, talking and laughing together as if they were the only human beings on earth. The thought skittered through Mara's mind that she might have a relationship like that one day, but just as quickly she excised it from her realm of possibility. At barely twenty years old, she'd already had enough of the male population to last her for several lifetimes.

Affirming that thought with a quick nod of her head, she grabbed the towel she'd been sitting on and stood to her feet. She didn't have a car yet, but it was only a ten-minute walk to the seafood café where she was now employed.

Gainfully and respectably employed, she reminded herself. *Tio used to tell me I'd never be anything but a prostitute, and that he'd kill me before he'd let me leave. But look at me now — free as a bird while he rots in prison. Maybe there really is a God after all.*

Chapter 1

So, what do you think, Sis? I'm halfway through four years of Bible college and you're officially out of high school now. Where do we go from here?"

Leah, eyes closed and head tilted back to enjoy the noonday sun, felt her smile move up from her heart before she let it take over her face. It was so good to have Jonathan home for the summer! The excitement of his coming home in time for her graduation the previous Thursday was more overwhelming to her than the graduation itself. True, the ceremony had been nice, as had the family dinner and the overnight trip to Disneyland with the rest of her class afterward. But on a scale of one to ten, the importance of those events scarcely registered in comparison to having her only brother home for the next couple of months.

Leah used her bare foot to nudge the porch swing back and forth. She could feel her brother's presence, even though there were several inches of green and white striped fabric between them. The modest home where they'd grown up in the San Diego suburb of Chula Vista had always been a haven to the two siblings, the hub out of which flowed all their activities and dreams and plans for the future. What more appropriate place could there be for the two of them to envision what was yet to come?

"Sometimes I think I'd like to know what's around the next corner," Leah answered, not moving but opening her eyes to glance at Jonathan, who stared at the fenced lawn in front of him as he listened to her answer. Focusing on his finely chiseled features and short auburn hair, shining like fire in the midmorning sun, combined with his six-foot-two frame and broad shoulders, made Leah wonder what was wrong with the girls at that college he attended. Either they were awfully slow on the uptake, or he was really playing hard to get. Leah imagined it was the latter. She remembered how many girls had crushes on her big brother throughout his high school years, but other than an occasional date, he scarcely gave them a second look. Leah's smile widened. Sooner or later the right one would come along, and he'd be a goner for sure.

"Other times," she continued, "I think it's better not to know, don't you? I kind of like letting God surprise me."

Jonathan grinned as he turned toward her, his brown eyes dancing. "Absolutely. I used to think I knew what I wanted out of life—a professional baseball career, period. That was all I thought and dreamed about. Then God got hold of my heart and showed me how small my dreams really were." He paused and sighed, his smile fading a bit. "I just wish that realization hadn't come with such a high price for someone else."

Leah sat up straight and laid her hand on her brother's bare arm. It was warm from the sun and muscular beneath her touch. "You're not still blaming yourself for Jasmine's death, are you?"

Jonathan dropped his eyes before raising them again and shaking his head. "No. I'm not. Not really, anyway. I know it probably would have happened, one way or the other, whether I'd run into them at that motel that evening or not. But the memory of her face, the fear in her eyes . . . I'll never forget that. And I don't think I'm supposed to. God had a purpose for planting that memory in my mind."

Leah nodded. She had no doubt Jonathan was right. The

events of those few weeks just two years earlier, when it was her brother and not she who was graduating from high school, had been indelibly imprinted on her memory as well. Each time she considered how close Jonathan had come to being hurt, or even killed, she experienced a fresh appreciation for God's divine timing and protection. That God had used Jonathan to help break up a human-trafficking ring that forced teens and even young children to be sex slaves—right here in the San Diego area—was nothing short of miraculous. God had also used the situation to draw Jonathan into a deep, personal relationship with Himself, and for that Leah was exceptionally grateful. Though she and Jonathan had always been close, their brother-sister ties had been limited to the temporary status within their immediate family. Once Jonathan moved from having a head knowledge of Christ to inviting Him into his heart, the bond between brother and sister had become eternal.

13

"Do you ever think about the other girls?" Leah asked. "I mean, I know you remember Jasmine, but . . . what about Mara? Do you ever wonder what happened to her after the authorities busted up that ring?"

Jonathan's gaze moved away then, and he stared into the distance before looking back. When his eyes were once again fixed on her face, Leah saw his jaw twitch before he spoke. "I think about her a lot," he admitted. "I only saw her a few times—the first time at the motel with Jasmine, and then the night we ended up calling the cops and seeing those scumbags that prostituted those poor kids arrested. And, of course, during the trials when we both had to testify. But yeah, I think about her and wonder what she's doing now. Dad said he heard from Barbara at church that Mara went into a rehab ministry just south of the border while she waited to get US citizenship through UI benefits, but I don't know anything about her after that."

"Neither do I," Leah said. "I should ask Dad. He probably knows or at least could find out, since Barbara has ties with that ministry in Mexico. Do you want me to ask him?"

Jonathan paused before shaking his head. "Nah. Probably better not to. The girl needs to make a life for herself. I'm sure the last thing she wants is to be reminded of what her uncle did to her. I wonder about her and pray for her—the other kids that were involved too—but I think it's best to just leave it alone."

Leah nodded. Jonathan was right. Mara had undoubtedly moved on with her life, as had they. But she was glad that the events of two years earlier had thrown their entire family into the ministry of rescuing human-trafficking victims and helping them recover and get established in new and productive lives.

It's enough, she told herself. *Mara and the others were all sent somewhere to get help, and we really don't need to follow up on them. There are plenty of others who need our help. For now, like Jonathan said, we'll pray for Mara. It can't be easy trying to adapt to a normal life after living as a slave for so many years. Still, I can't help but wonder where she is and what she's doing.*

14

The lunch crowd was thinner than usual today, and Mara knew that meant less in tips. Good thing she lived in Southern California where the weather was almost always decent, making walking a viable option for getting around. Occasionally she splurged and rode the bus or trolley when she had to traverse large sections of the greater San Diego area, but fortunately that didn't happen often and she was able to get around on foot just fine.

She smiled in greeting at the two middle-aged women

who had just settled into a booth in her section. "Welcome to Mariner's," she said, placing a glass of ice water in front of each of them. "Our specials today are clam chowder and fresh cod fish and chips."

The women glanced up and smiled, though neither responded to her greeting. Then they returned their attention to their menus. Good. Mara preferred the no-frills customers to the chatty ones. If her tips were going to be light, she didn't want to spend any more time than necessary conversing with the clientele.

An elderly gentleman at the next table motioned to her. "Can we get our check, please?"

Mara nodded. "Sure thing." She pulled out the ticket she'd been planning to deliver anyway and laid it in front of the old man, who sat across from a gray-haired woman who was still working on her chowder.

"I'm not quite done yet," the woman commented between slurps. "He's always rushing me."

The man frowned. "I am not. You're just slow, that's all. Sometimes I think you poke along on purpose."

The woman set her spoon down in the bowl. "Now why would I do that?"

Before he could answer, Mara interrupted. "Just take your time," she said, immediately wanting to defend the woman from what she imagined was her unreasonably impatient husband. She smiled at them both and walked back toward the kitchen. Would she ever get to the place where she didn't automatically blame men for every problem in the world? She doubted it.

She grabbed another couple of glasses of water, balancing them carefully in one hand, ready to deliver them to the two men she'd just seen walk in, and snagged the coffee pot with the other. The guy at the counter was making a point of draining his cup as he watched her from his perch, so he no doubt was ready for a refill. She sighed. She might still be making a living by giving people what they wanted, but at least now she got paid for it—and she could quit any time she wanted.

Lawan's tenth birthday had come and gone, and she was no closer to escaping the brothel than when she'd been kidnapped and tossed into the dark, filthy room two years earlier.

When Chanthra was still here, she thought, tears stinging her eyes at the memory of the older girl who had helped her survive those first terrifying days. Chanthra. How she missed her! They'd had only a few short weeks together before the teenager had succumbed to an infection brought on by a forced abortion, but it had been long enough for Lawan to be nearly certain that the girl named Chanthra had been her older sister.

A girl called Kulap, who was slightly older than Lawan, had taken Chanthra's mattress and most of her customers, but though she and Lawan shared a room, they had never become close. *It is easier that way,* Lawan told herself. *It hurt too much to lose Chanthra. If Kulap dies before I do, I do not want to feel that kind of pain again.*

Of course, she realized such a loss would not be as deep as what she experienced with Chanthra, simply because she had come to believe Chanthra was her sister. Two years later, she was even more certain that was true. Would they soon be reunited with *phra yaeh suu*—with Jesus Christ—when Lawan died? For Lawan knew no one lived long in this place. A few lived into their twenties, but then they were thrown out onto the street to fend for themselves. Lawan shivered at the thought. She tried to hold onto her faith in *phra yaeh suu*, as her Christian parents had taught her—a faith that had been shared by Chanthra—but it was so difficult to believe in One who died and rose again so many years ago when all Lawan knew from one day to the next was more pain and darkness. From the time Lawan had foolishly ventured too far from home and been kidnapped and dumped into this horrible place, the only happy memories she had were the hours she had spent with Chanthra.

"I miss you, Chanthra," she whispered into the predawn light that peeked through the room's only window. "I wish I could be with you. Is it really as beautiful there as our *maae* used to tell us it would be?"

The only answer was a moan from the girl on the other mattress, just a few feet away. Soon the sun would rise above their little Golden Triangle corner of Thailand, and it would burn hot and merciless, turning the room into a steamy oven as the girls rested until the cooler evening temperatures brought their first customers of the night.

Lawan closed her eyes. She knew from experience how hard the approaching hours could be. Until then, she would sleep and try to forget.

Chapter 2

Rosanna Flannery smiled as she sliced fresh fruit and mixed tuna salad for sandwiches. Was there anything better than having her entire family home for lunch together? The familiar kitchen, sunny and bright with colors that teased Rosanna with memories of the one trip she and Michael had taken to Hawaii a few years earlier, was undoubtedly her favorite room in the house. After all, she had logged a lot of hours in there, chopping and sautéing, mixing and blending. She knew some women didn't consider being a stay-at-home wife and mother a worthy occupation, but she was so grateful that her husband had agreed from the beginning that he would be the breadwinner and she the keeper of hearth and home.

Peering through the window above the sink, she caught sight of Jonathan's ancient once-blue VW Beetle, the car he'd saved up for since his twelfth birthday and bought on his sixteenth. Though he often threatened to "dump it" and buy something newer and more reliable, he always seemed to patch up the old car's problems and nurse it along just a bit longer. Rosanna imagined he would continue to do so until he graduated from Bible college in a couple more years.

She sighed as she reached for a head of lettuce and peeled off a handful of crisp leaves. Running them under the cold water, she felt her smile fade as she thought ahead to the fall months when not only would Jonathan return to college, but Leah would join him as she began her own four-year trek through the halls of higher learning.

Thank goodness they both decided to attend Bible college, she reminded herself. *I have to stay focused on how blessed I am to have two such committed Christian children, rather than wandering off on some pity-party trail, feeling sorry for myself because my babies are growing up and moving into lives of their own.*

Setting the lettuce down on the drain board beside the freshly peeled and sliced apples, she dried her hands on the dishtowel hanging on the oven handle and stepped over to the back door, where she could gaze out the window at the two young adults sitting side by side on the porch swing. She had rejoiced at their high school graduations, and yet she still struggled to accept that they were old enough to have reached that point in their lives.

Rosanna started as hands slipped around her waist and the familiar warmth of her husband pressed up against her back. "I know what you're thinking," he whispered, his chin resting on top of her head. "How did they grow up so quickly? Weren't they just starting school and learning to ride bikes?"

She nodded. "You know me far too well, Michael Flannery. But don't tell me you don't have the same thoughts at times."

He kissed her hair. "Of course I do. How do you think I know exactly what you're thinking?"

Rosanna smiled. Her children might be nearly grown up and ready to move out on their own, but God had blessed her with the best husband ever. How could she possibly waste her time and energy feeling sorry for herself?

She turned and allowed him to pull her against him, as she tilted her face up and received his kiss. "You're a good man," she said. "I'm blessed to have you."

Grinning down at her, his green eyes sparkling beneath the red curls that he'd so obviously passed on to their daughter, he said, "So you finally figured that out, did you? I've been trying to tell you that for years."

❧

It had been a long day, but weariness was never a problem for Mara—at least not now that she had what she considered a "normal" job. Her experience as a child growing up in forced prostitution made any other employment seem easy and even enjoyable by comparison. Getting paid for her labors was a bonus she never imagined in her former life.

The sun had already set over the Pacific Ocean by the time she hung up her apron and snagged her purse to head for the café door and home, but even walking in the dark seldom alarmed her. Darkness had been her nearly constant companion as a child; the only time it bothered her now was if she imagined someone was following her or if the darkness included confinement.

The hole, she thought, shivering only slightly in the light breeze that blew in off the Pacific as she tugged at her sweater and stepped up her pace. Of all the terrible memories—and there were many—her times of punishment in the darkened, securely locked closet where she could scarcely turn around let alone lie down or stretch out were the worst. She'd been beaten, raped, starved, and threatened with worse many times over. She'd even witnessed murders and knew her captors' threats were not idle words. But it was the isolation in complete darkness in such a cramped space that had nearly driven her mad. There were times she still wondered how she had managed to keep her sanity.

But I did, and that's all that matters, she reminded herself, spotting the tiny porch light in front of the big house where she rented a room. She was almost home now, and the fresh knowledge that not only did she actually have a home—small as it was—but that she worked and paid for it herself caused a surge of adrenaline to speed up her heart rate. *It isn't much, but it's mine. Until a couple of years ago, I had nothing to claim as my own—absolutely nothing. If it hadn't been for that pizza guy . . .*

Her mind drifted off as she reached the steps that led up to the wide, sprawling porch. She unzipped the side pocket of her purse and pulled out her key, slipping it into the lock and letting herself inside to the dimly lit entryway, a vision of the handsome young delivery man who had rescued her danced through her mind, as it did so often. How many times had she tried to blot it out? But always it came back—his face, smiling at her as if she were his equal and not some damaged prostitute. It was ridiculous, she knew, to think that he might consider her his equal, but at least for a few moments, as they'd waited together for the police to come and arrest her *tio* and his bodyguard, he'd made her feel special. And that was a very foreign emotion for someone such as Mara.

Jonathan, she said to herself as she climbed the stairs to her room. *Jonathan Flannery. I wonder where you are now. You said something about going to Bible college. Did you? Are you still there? And why? You're handsome and smart . . . and probably from a good family with enough money to send you to medical or law school. Why would you choose Bible college? Why would anyone choose something like that? What's the point?*

She shook her head and stepped into the comfort of her own room, dismissing her pointless musings about someone she would never see again. Monday was over, and she was home now — safe and sound and alone — and that was really all that mattered.

❧

Nyesha Johnson held her daughter's hand tightly in her own. How was it possible that Anna could be old enough to start kindergarten in the fall? It seemed she and Kyle had just adopted the precocious little Thai girl, and yet it had been more than three years since they first encountered the eighteen-month old toddler, her almond eyes wide with fear as tears rolled down her pudgy cheeks. Mali, as she was known then, had been given up for adoption by parents who were unable to care for her, and the imagined pain of that decision had torn at Nyesha's heart.

23

She glanced down at the little girl who had seemingly made such a healthy adjustment to her new home and family. The noonday sun shone down on her short, silky black hair. As if she felt her mother staring down at her, Anna lifted her head and smiled hesitantly. Nyesha had tried to explain to her that they were going to school today to register her for kindergarten in the fall, but it was obvious that Anna had no real idea about what was going on — or why. Nyesha and Kyle had opted not to place Anna in preschool, reasoning that she learned social skills and interacting with other children through their many church activities. And Nyesha had devoted much of her stay-at-home time teaching her only child to read, so she was well ahead of many of her peers. With Leah Flannery as a devoted babysitter and a second tutor, spending endless hours reading to the child and helping feed the girl's growing love for books, Nyesha was confident that Anna would do well in school.

Still, her heart constricted at the apprehension and confusion in her daughter's expressive eyes. Until Anna came into her life, Nyesha had never truly understood or appreciated her own mother's protectiveness with her brood of five. Now it all made sense.

She knelt down beside Anna and looked her in the face. "I love you," she said, watching a bit of the concern melt away from the child's eyes. "And Jesus loves you even more. Remember, wherever we go, Jesus is there with us. Do you understand, sweetheart?"

Anna smiled and nodded. "Jesus loves me," she said, her voice taking on a singsong quality as she added, "The Bible tells me so."

Blinking away tears, Nyesha nodded in return. If her daughter learned nothing else in her lifetime, she already knew all that really mattered.

Chapter 3

The man known as Jefe, or "boss," not only to the young innocents he had once held captive for so many years but also to the other inmates, quietly finished the slop the prison served as food. He fumed as he shoveled the unidentifiable, lukewarm meat product into his mouth, remembering the tender steaks and rich lobsters he had eaten so many times at his favorite waterfront restaurant in San Diego. How had he been reduced to this—living as a common criminal when, in fact, he had been such a successful businessman?

Mara. That's what had happened. His niece. His own flesh and blood. The very girl he had taken under his wing and smuggled out of Mexico to give her a better life. But after all he had done for her, after all the years of putting a roof over her head and food in her stomach, she had turned on him. Betrayed him and left him to rot with a life sentence while she went on her merry way, ignoring his pleas to testify as a character witness on his behalf.

He used the dull fork to stab the last piece of meat on the plate, wishing he could inflict the same pressure—and more—on the ungrateful girl he had cared for as if she were his own daughter. Hadn't he paid good money to her parents to buy her way out of the nowhere life she was destined for in Mexico? Hadn't he taken a chance smuggling her across the border and then breaking her into the business himself before introducing her to their regular customers? What more could he have done to give her a better life? If only he'd known what she would one day do to him, he would have killed her the first time she disobeyed him.

That's what I should have done, he thought, mopping up the gluelike gravy with a mushy slice of bread and shoveling it into his mouth. *I should have strangled her with my bare hands when she tried to help that little one escape. Instead I showed mercy and threw her in the hole. I thought sure she'd learn, but I was wrong. She was trouble from the beginning. I should have known she wouldn't change. And now she thinks she's won.* Jefe washed the horrible meal down with a swig of tepid water. The only thing that kept him from upending the entire table and roaring out his rage was the thought that even though he was locked up for life, he still had connections. And one of them was going to find that girl. When that happened, Mara too would wish her *tio* had killed her long ago.

⁓≫≪⁓

Jonathan felt as if he'd gone back in time—not far, just a couple of years—to the summer when he was delivering pizzas in this very area in this very VW Bug. But so much had happened since then that it seemed much longer than two years.

With the late afternoon sun slipping down toward the Pacific, Jonathan placed the heat-retaining delivery container full of six large pizzas into the back of his car and climbed into the driver's seat. It was his first day back at Slice of Italy Pizza since he left home at the end of summer nearly two years earlier to head for Bible college. Though he'd come home after his first year away at school, there had been no opening for him at his old job, so he'd hung out at his parents' house and done odd jobs around the neighborhood for gas money. He was glad the delivery spot had opened up this year because he sure needed to dump some money into the faithful old heap that passed as a car.

He tapped the accelerator twice before gunning it, and the engine sputtered to life. Jonathan smiled. Some things never changed, while other things changed so drastically they were nearly unrecognizable. One of those things was the seedy motel where he had first laid eyes on Mara and Jasmine. He would never forget it. At the top of the stairs at the motel's second floor, as he glanced around for the right room number so he could deliver a pizza, he had nearly been knocked over by a young, half-dressed girl, racing from one of the rooms. Her eyes were wild with fright, but before Jonathan could find out what was going on, a man claiming to be her father had come to retrieve her, offering an explanation about her not wanting to take her medication. Another girl — the one he soon came to know as Mara — came out of the room and corroborated the man's story, so Jonathan had let it go, a decision he had come to regret deeply and thought about often.

Heading down the street on his way to his first delivery, he yielded to the temptation to once again detour past that fateful spot. Though he'd already seen the changes that had taken place there, it still startled him to drive up and see how the motel that had once been used to force children and teens into prostitution had now been purchased by several churches in the area and turned into a homeless shelter.

Jonathan slowed his Beetle to a crawl and smiled. "You're amazing, God," he whispered. "Not only did You rescue those people and lock up their captors, but You turned this place to good use. Bless all those who come here for help, Lord. May each one of them find You, just as I pray for Mara and the others who suffered here for so many years."

Blinking back the wetness that stung his eyes, Jonathan again tapped his accelerator and drove away. He had work to do, and everything here was now in good hands.

~∞~

It had been a long and terrible night for Lawan. Though she approached each night with dread, this one had been especially difficult. She had even wondered for a time if she might not survive it. But now her last customer—the one who had abused her so badly—had gone, and with the first thin sliver of daylight peeking its way through the room's tiny window, she listened to Kulap's even breathing. It was impossible that the older girl hadn't been aware of Lawan's mistreatment by her last customer, but Lawan understood that there was nothing her roommate could have done to help, even if she'd tried. In fact, her interference might have gotten them both killed.

Lawan lay on her back, staring at the familiar ceiling. Even in the muted light, she knew every crack and dirt smudge. How many early mornings had the miserable girl lain on her filthy mattress, staring at that unchanging ceiling after enduring yet another night of pain and degradation? Some nights, like this one, were worse than others, but all were terrible. Lawan wondered how many more she would have to endure before *phra yaeh suu* finally released her from her misery and took her home. Would her parents be there to meet her? Lawan had no idea if they were dead or alive, but she imagined that after losing the last of their three children, they might also have lost the will to live.

28

So sad that they gave up their oldest, believing she was being adopted by a wealthy family and would have a good life, Lawan thought. *Maae used to hold me on her lap and tell me how it had broken her heart to give up her firstborn, but when the chance had come to give Chanthra a better life, she thought they had no choice.*

Lawan swiped at the tears that trickled from her eyes, more from the pain in her heart than the lingering pain in her body. Having been reunited with Chanthra in that very brothel and then watching her die after a botched abortion, Lawan knew only too well that her parents' sacrifice for their oldest child had been in vain. But at least Chanthra was now safely with *phra yaeh suu.* Lawan could only hope and pray that it wouldn't be long until she joined her.

That leaves only Mali, she mused. *My baby sister. You had just learned to walk a few months before you were adopted by a family far away in a place called America. I hardly remember you, but Maae said America was a wondrous place, where everyone has a lot of money and no one is ever hungry. Oh, Mali, I hope our maae was right!*

Another tear plopped down from her cheek into her hair, as she whispered a silent prayer that little Mali had indeed found a good home and a blessed life, unlike either of her older sisters.

Chapter 4

Leah soaked in the morning sun as she walked the few blocks from her own home to the Johnson's place. Now that her high school graduation was behind her and she had a couple of free months before heading off to Bible college in the fall, she was happy to spend as much time as possible with little Anna. Leah had been Anna's primary babysitter since the Johnsons' adopted the child, and Leah knew it would be hard to leave her at the end of summer.

With the Johnson home in sight now, she smiled to herself, remembering how pleased she was when Nyesha called her a couple of days earlier to tell her that she and some of her friends had decided to have a regular "girls' day out" every Wednesday. When she asked Leah if she would be able to take care of Anna each Wednesday for the next couple of months, Leah hadn't hesitated to accept. Not only could she use the money, but she couldn't imagine a better way to spend part of her otherwise leisurely summer.

She turned up the walkway and rang the bell. Immediately she heard Anna's excited squeals and chatter behind the door.

"Leah's here!" the girl cried. "Come on, Mommy. Hurry! Leah's here!"

Leah's smile widened as the front door swung open and Anna scooted past her mother and threw herself at Leah, wrapping her arms around her legs. "You came," she cried. "You came! You came!"

Leah laughed and bent down to lift Anna up and plant a kiss on her chubby cheek. "Of course I came," she said. "I wouldn't miss the chance to spend a day with you, ever!"

Nyesha too was beaming as she led Leah, with Anna still in her arms, inside the house. "I'm so glad you could do this," she said, aiming for her brightly colored kitchen as Leah did her best to keep up. Nyesha's energy level seemed never to ebb, and Leah thought that was one of the many reasons she so enjoyed being around her. Of course, the entire family was delightful—the "rainbow family," as Nyesha referred to themselves. Nyesha, with her milk-chocolate coloring and sparkling dark eyes, her passion for loud colors and joyous noise, her zest for life and passion for people, so complemented her quiet, reserved, blond-haired, blue-eyed husband. The addition of their little Thai daughter completed what Leah considered the most perfect family imaginable.

Leah plunked down at the kitchen table, holding Anna on her lap. She knew from experience that Nyesha wouldn't go anywhere until she'd served Leah something to eat, or at least drink. She wasn't in the least bit hungry, having downed a bowl of cereal and bananas just before leaving her house, but the walk had made her thirsty.

"Lemonade?" Nyesha asked, opening the refrigerator door.

"I'd love some." Leah smiled and kissed the top of Anna's head, the girl's nearly blue-black hair glistening under the overhead lights and smelling of baby shampoo. Leah marveled yet again at the fact that she not only got to have such an enjoyable day but also got paid for it. She couldn't imagine how life could get any better than it already was.

Nyesha poured lemonade from a pitcher into an ice-cube filled tumbler and set it in front of Leah, along with a half-full plastic cup for Anna. Without getting any for herself, Nyesha sat down across from the girls and smiled as she folded her hands on the table in front of her.

"So," she said, "you are officially a high school graduate, heading off to Bible college." She smiled. "I think that's wonderful. But now what? Any specific plans?"

Leah swallowed a cool sip of lemonade and set her glass down. "I've been asking myself the very same questions," she admitted, keeping one eye on Anna, who was slurping from her own cup. "I'm afraid I haven't come up with any clear answers yet. Do you think that's unusual?"

Nyesha reached across the table and laid one hand on Leah's. "Not at all. In fact, I'd be surprised if you'd said you knew exactly what you were going to do when you graduate. No, I think you're going to the right place, where you can listen for God's direction while you prepare and equip yourself for wherever that direction may take you. I've known you for many years, Leah, and I know you have a heart for God and others, and I can hardly wait to see how God will use that."

Leah smiled. The warmth of Nyesha's hand seemed to flow right up her arm and into her heart, reassuring her that she was indeed on the right track, even if she didn't yet know where that track would take her. The important thing was that she was trusting God in the process, committed to whatever He had purposed for her. She was already seeing that process begin to play out in her brother's life, and she had no reason to doubt that she would soon see the same thing happening in her own.

Mara was midway through her afternoon shift on Wednesday when a man and a teenage girl walked in and sat down next to one another in the farthest booth from the counter, their backs against the back wall as they faced the front door. People sat there all the time, and Mara didn't think anything of it. This time it was different.

Her eyes narrowed as she wiped the counter and prepared to take water and menus to the newcomers. Though she couldn't remember ever seeing the man before, there was something about his slimy ways and proprietary manner toward the girl sitting beside him that elevated her heart rate and put her on high alert. Not only had she seen that condescending attitude in men before, but she'd seen the frightened, defeated look on the girl's face as well. In fact, she'd worn that look many times.

Forcing herself to take deep breaths, she wiped her now sweaty palms on her apron and picked up the water and menus before heading toward the back booth. Because it was between lunch and dinner crowds, there were only a couple of other patrons in the café at the time, so she had a little more time than usual to study this odd couple.

Odd to some people, she thought, setting the glasses in front of them and laying the menus on the table, *but not to me. No way is this guy her father or boyfriend. He's just another creep, like my tio, using a young girl for his own profit. I can smell the evil on him . . . and the fear on her.* The fact that he sat next to her and boxed her in where she couldn't even get out to go to the bathroom without his permission just confirmed her suspicions.

She wanted to spit in the man's face, but instead she forced a cool smile and said, "Welcome to Mariner's. Our special today is fried calamari. Can I get you anything else to drink while you check the menu?"

The man, who appeared to be in his late thirties or early forties, lifted his eyes and fixed them on Mara. The familiar feeling of being undressed by a look washed over her, and she suppressed a shudder. The man's upper lip lifted on one side in what Mara recognized as a sneer of contempt, and she had to force herself to remain standing and not turn and run for the kitchen. Was there anything she could do to help this poor girl, or would any effort on her part just worsen an already awful situation?

Mara swallowed and stood her ground, shifting her gaze from the man's unshaven face to the girl sitting next to him, her head bowed over her menu as if reading it were the most important thing in the world. Mara knew better. She had sat in that girl's seat far too many times over the years. Mara understood the girl was too paralyzed to respond, even if Mara did say or do something to try to help.

"Just bring us a couple of burgers," the man said, his gruff voice pulling Mara back. "With everything for me," he added, and then nodded toward the girl, "but no onions for her." He smirked, and the girl cringed, appearing to draw deeper within herself in an attempt to become as small and invisible as possible. How well Mara knew that need to disappear!

Her heart aching, she turned away, pretending to scribble their order on her pad as she hurried back to the kitchen. She had every intention of taking advantage of the downtime in the restaurant to memorize everything she could about those two customers, but from the safety of a spot behind the counter.

Michael Flannery sat at his desk in his church office, preparing for the midweek service. Though the turnout on Wednesday evening never came close to equaling that of the Sunday morning services, Michael was always pleased when the senior pastor asked him to lead the group. He enjoyed the more intense study time of a Wednesday night gathering, as well as the deeper commitment level of most of those in attendance.

He pored over his notes, praying and jotting down tidbits that came to him in the process. But no matter how hard he tried to concentrate, his mind continued to drift to the events of two years earlier, when Jonathan had nearly spearheaded their family's involvement in the rescue of human-trafficking victims. Though their son had not yet come to a place of personal faith that put serving God first, he had a compassionate heart and couldn't bear the thought of anyone being used or abused — particularly children. When he had nearly singlehandedly broken up a human-trafficking ring and rescued two of the young girls involved, it had seemingly catapulted him into a deeper faith walk than either Michael or his wife, Rosanna, had imagined or dreamed — though they had prayed for it for years.

Michael smiled. Amazing how they claimed to be people of faith, praying continually for a specific outcome and yet reacting in near shock when God answered their prayers. Now Jonathan was halfway through Bible college, aiming toward some sort of missionary work either abroad or right here in America, rescuing modern-day slaves, feeding the hungry, helping the homeless. And there was little doubt that Leah would quickly follow in her older brother's footsteps. Could there be anything better than knowing that your entire family was committed to serving God?

Michael sighed and shook his head. No, there could not. Just as He promised in His Word, God had given Michael and Rosanna the desire of their heart. With gratitude and joy, Michael returned to his notes, determined to honor God as he led the congregation later that evening.

Chapter 5

It was obvious to Mara that the girl had been ravenous, just by the way she eyed the food when it was set before them. And yet she hesitated to eat until the man ordered her to do so.

Keeping an eye on the pair as she polished the counter and busied herself filling salt and pepper shakers, Mara grew more and more certain of the slave/owner relationship between the two as she watched. Through mental observations, Mara noted that the girl had long black hair, slightly wavy and thick, definitely healthy. Her olive complexion caused Mara to conclude that the girl had been smuggled across the border from Mexico, much as she had been so many years ago. Was the girl sold into slavery by her parents the way Mara had been? Was the man with the heavy mustache and various tattoos on his neck and arms sitting beside her a once-trusted relative, the way Mara's *tio* had been to her? There was no way to be sure of the details, but they weren't necessary to come to the conclusion that the girl was being trafficked—and she was terrified and miserable.

I can't get involved, Mara told herself. *I just got free myself a couple of years ago. I know how hard it is to even make contact with these girls. Even if I try, if her owners find out, she'll pay a terrible price.* She shivered at the memory of the many punishments she had received during her own captivity, and she didn't want to be responsible for someone else suffering in the same way. Yet how could she ignore the situation and not at least try to do something?

Barbara Whiting. The name came to her unbidden, and she remembered the middle-aged woman with the pale blue eyes and graying black curls, the one who had worked with her and the others after they were rescued, finding safe places for them while they waited to testify in the trials and to find permanent placement. Did she still have her card somewhere? The woman had told her she could call anytime. Was it possible this Barbara Whiting had meant what she said and would help again if she could?

Then again, if the woman were willing, what would Mara tell her? Just seeing the two people here in the café didn't provide the information necessary to find them once they left the place. Was there some way to connect with them before they left and somehow snag a piece of information that might give a clue to their names or where they lived — or something?

Mara doubted it. She knew how carefully her *tio* had guarded his personal information, as well as that of his stable of slaves. Still, if she didn't at least try, the two might pay their bill and walk out of here, and Mara would probably never see them again. The memory of those who had been in captivity with Mara, and those whose lives had been snuffed out so mercilessly, called out to her to at least try and do what she could.

Stuffing the pair's meal ticket in her pocket, she approached the booth where they now sat, finishing the last of their meal. "Did you save room for dessert?" she asked, doing her best to smile naturally.

The man squinted at her, and his sneer returned. "Nah," he said. "I'm full. And she doesn't need any. Don't want her getting fat, if you know what I mean."

He smirked, as the girl dropped her head even lower. But

even beneath her bowed head and the long hair that hung forward, hiding much of her expression, Mara didn't miss the girl's flaming cheeks.

Yeah, I know what you mean, you scumbag, Mara longed to spit out. *You want her thin and frail and helpless, the way the clients like them best.* But instead she kept her mouth clamped shut and slapped the ticket down in front of the man. She probably wouldn't get a tip with that attitude, but who wanted one from someone like him anyway?

Before she could move her hand from the top of the bill, the man laid his hand on hers, exerting just enough pressure that she couldn't pull away easily. Mara felt her stomach lurch and her eyes widen, as she looked from their hands on the table to his cold gray eyes zeroed in on hers, his nearly shaved head glistening under the overhead lights. "If you ever want a job that pays better than hustling tables for a few bucks, let me know," he said, his voice low and sultry. "I can make it worth your while."

When Mara jerked her hand away, causing the half-empty water glasses to shake, he smirked. The girl dared to glance up then, and Mara caught the frightened brown eyes with her own. In that wordless exchange, Mara knew she would follow through with trying to find Barbara Whiting. She had no idea what the lady—or anyone else, for that matter—could do to help, but she had to at least alert someone to this girl's situation. She only wished she could do more . . . but of course, she couldn't. She was, after all, just one person with nothing to offer except understanding—she had walked in the girl's shoes for many years.

Ignoring the man, Mara took a chance and smiled at the girl, wishing she could telegraph hope or encouragement with her eyes. And yet, what real hope or encouragement could she or anyone offer someone in the poor girl's situation? The likelihood of ever being rescued from the torturous life she now lived was very slim indeed.

Turning her back on the heartbreaking scene, Mara hurried past the counter and into the kitchen, asking the cook if he could please ring up the customer who was about ready to leave, as she wasn't feeling too well.

Rushing for the bathroom and locking the door behind her, Mara leaned over the toilet and lost what was left of the lunch she'd eaten a couple of hours earlier.

Jonathan had been pleasantly surprised when the schedule for his first week at work in nearly two years showed that he had Wednesday evening off. He'd be back on Thursday and would work every evening after that until Monday, but that was fine with him. Weekends were the biggest tip nights, and Wednesday was the one evening he liked to have free so he could attend the midweek service at church.

Sitting in the third row back, with his sister and mom to his left, he leaned against the end of the pew on his right, his eyes fixed on his dad as he came forward to open the service following a lively time of praise and worship. It was like the perfect ending to his first week home from college. The week had begun with watching his little sister graduate from high school, and now he would get to hear his dad lead the Bible study.

He grinned at the thought of all the Wednesday night services—Sundays too, for that matter—that he had endured before giving his heart and life to Christ. He knew even then that his parents wanted only the best for him, but his priorities were not in order, and all he wanted was to escape forced church attendance and devote his time and energy to playing baseball.

How shallow was I? he wondered. *Seriously! Life was so all about me it was ridiculous. But I couldn't see it then.* He shook his head. *Thank You for opening my eyes, Lord. What a difference it makes to see things from Your perspective.*

His mother laid her hand on his arm, and he glanced at her. She was smiling, and her brown eyes were misty. Jonathan imagined that her thoughts had been running in a similar direction as his own.

He returned her smile, as they both picked up their Bibles and then turned their attention back to the front, ready to follow along in the weekly study.

Barbara Whiting was late arriving at church that evening. She'd been just about to rush out the door when her cell phone rang. She nearly ignored it, but at the last moment yielded to the urgent need she felt to answer it.

Mara, she thought, slipping into the sanctuary and settling in a back row as the associate pastor opened the Bible study with instructions on where to turn in order to follow along. Barbara couldn't help but wonder what Pastor Flannery and his entire family would think if they knew she'd just been contacted by one of the young women Jonathan had helped to rescue a couple of years earlier. It was the first direct contact Barbara had experienced from Mara since the trials, though she'd often wondered how the lovely yet severely wounded young woman was doing.

Thank goodness I never changed my cell phone number, she thought. *And people like Mara are exactly the reason I don't.*

When I gave her my card with my office and cell numbers on it, I meant it when I told her to call me anytime. But most people never do. I can't believe she kept that card all this time. For her to break down and call tells me she was deeply disturbed by what she saw today.

And well she should be, Barbara reminded herself. *From what she described, there's little doubt that the situation was exactly as she suspected. We may have broken up one human-trafficking ring and sent the bad guys to prison, but there is always another crop of those creeps waiting to take over where the others left off. And as always, it's the innocents that suffer.*

Pastor Flannery was beginning his teaching, and she pulled her thoughts back to his words. She needed to focus on the Scriptures right now, rather than allowing herself to dwell on the evil that seemed to be winning on every side. Ultimately, she knew that wasn't true, but if she didn't concentrate on God's promise of faithfulness, she'd slip right into the abyss of depression that pulled at her from every corner. Rescuing victims of human trafficking was her passion . . . but she knew it was also the greatest threat to her sanity and well-being.

Chapter 6

Thursday morning dawned bright and warm, without the usual coastal fog that sometimes hid the sun until at least noon. But Mara didn't even notice. Her eyes felt as gritty as the sand under her feet, as she forced herself to walk along the beautiful coastline in an effort to clear her head.

Why did those two have to come in to eat while I was there? If one of the others had been working, they wouldn't have even noticed what was going on. They probably would have thought they were just a father and his pouty teenage daughter—if they thought anything about it at all. But I know better. There's no way to deny what's going on there.

Once the two left the restaurant, Mara had tried to convince herself to wait until she got off to try and contact Barbara Whiting. But when she'd peeked in her wallet to see if she just might have saved the woman's card, she knew it was no accident that she had. When it was time for her break, she'd stepped out back behind the café and used her cell phone to make the call, fully expecting to leave a message. But Barbara had answered and quickly affirmed that she not only remembered Mara but was happy to hear from her. After a quick catch-up conversation, Mara had haltingly told her what she'd seen, and Barbara had agreed that it sounded very much like a trafficking situation. Of course, with no names or other information to go by, they would be hard-pressed to help the girl, but at least they could alert the police to their descriptions.

Kicking at a pebble, Mara relived the nearly sleepless night that followed that conversation. Had she started something she would deeply regret? Most likely. After all, she now had to go to the police station with Barbara to find out if her story would be enough to open an investigation. Barbara didn't think it would be, but she knew people on the force who would at least take a report and possibly even include descriptions of the pair Mara had seen in Mariner's. For now it was all they could do.

To be honest, it was a lot more than Mara wanted to do. She would have preferred to do nothing at all. Since the night at the motel when Jonathan had helped her break free of the horrible lifestyle she had endured for so many years and then the subsequent trials where she'd had to testify, Mara had done everything in her power to blot out every memory of those years—and that included not thinking or talking about it with anyone. Now she would have to dredge it all up when she talked to the police, in order to give some sort of credibility to her story.

The memory of the frightened girl's large brown eyes tugged at the edges of her conscious thoughts, and she nearly yielded to the temptation to fall to her knees in the warm sand and weep. To imagine what the girl must already have experienced and was even now going through was nearly more than Mara could stand. Every ugly shred of the past that she had tried so hard to bury came flooding back, torturing her with negative thoughts of her own degradation and lack of self-worth, as well as fear of what could still happen if she wasn't very, very careful. After all, who knew better than she what a tenuous hold she had on her fragile freedom?

And yet she knew she had no choice. Once her eyes had connected with those of the terrified captive sitting in the

44

booth, Mara was committed to help her, regardless of the price that might be required of her. She only hoped it would not include ever again being held by merciless owners who used her for their own profit and pleasure.

⋅∾⊱ઉ⊰∿⋅

If the man who had so cruelly abused Lawan the night before was the meanest of her many customers, her first—and as it turned out, only, since he paid enough to stay the entire night—customer on Thursday night was the kindest. Lawan's stomach always relaxed when the man known as Klahan came to see her. He had first paid for her company nearly a year earlier, and since then he had come at least once a month, always insisting on seeing only her and reserving her for himself until morning. Lawan had no idea why, but she was grateful.

She was also confused. Klahan was one of the few men who ever divulged his name to the girls. Lawan had often wondered if it was because his name meant brave and perhaps he wanted Lawan to think of him as a courageous man. Whether or not that was true, Lawan knew he was a kind and gentle man, who always came just to lie beside her and hold her in his arms. Though he certainly could have, he never took advantage of the favors he had paid for, and he was careful to treat her with consideration, never hurting or insulting her in any way. Lawan wished there were more men like Klahan, but she was also grateful that he had chosen her as his "special girl," as he often called her.

Lawan was especially grateful to see Klahan's smiling face when he entered her room that night. She was still hurting from her last customer the night before, and she knew Klahan would not add to her pain. As it turned out, he somehow recognized her discomfort and quietly asked about it. Careful not to allow her roommate, Kulap, and her customer to overhear, Lawan had whispered a brief explanation into Klahan's ear. The man's eyes had widened and grown moist as he listened, and then he had pulled Lawan into his arms, carefully laying her head on his shoulder as he soothed her by rubbing her arm. His hands were rough, and Lawan imagined he was a common laborer, but he was the first man who had treated her with such care and respect since she was last with her father before she was kidnapped. In Lawan's eyes, Klahan was no common laborer; he was royalty who made her feel like a princess. How she wished she could leave with him when his time with her was over! What would it be like to live with such a man? She could only imagine, but it had to be many times better than where she lived now.

And so it was that on that very night, as the battered child who had yet to see eleven birthdays lay sheltered in Klahan's arms, she imagined what it might be like to be married to the kind man whose name meant brave. She knew better than to hope for such a miracle, but already her heart felt bound to his. Was this what it meant to be in love? Lawan had no idea, but it was the first positive feeling she'd had in a very long time. It was also the first time since Chanthra died that she dared to think that she might be able to trust someone.

Michael Flannery sat in his office, going over his schedule for the day. It appeared he had one spare hour that Thursday morning; every other slot was filled with meetings and counseling sessions. Even lunch would be cut short, so that meant he wouldn't be able to go home and share it with Rosanna.

He sighed and raked his hand through his short red curls. At least he had this early hour to do some studying before he jumped in with both feet. But before he could crack open his Bible, he heard a confident knock on his door.

Michael frowned and once again scanned his schedule, glancing at his watch. Had he missed something? The staff knew that when he was in his office with the door shut, especially early in the day, he was probably spending time with the Lord and preferred not to be interrupted. Of course, there were always exceptions, which usually translated into some sort of emergency.

Sighing again, he rose from his chair and went to the door, opening it with no idea of whom to expect. He raised his eyebrows in surprise when he saw Barbara Whiting standing there, a no-nonsense look on her face as she nodded in greeting and stepped inside without waiting for an invitation.

"I heard from Mara yesterday," she said, heading straight for one of the two chairs that sat side by side in front of Michael's desk.

Michael frowned, following Barbara toward the desk and settling down across from her. Why did the name sound familiar? "Mara?" he said. "The name rings a bell, but I can't place it."

Barbara nodded, her short, salt and pepper curls bouncing. "Mara Jimenez," she said. "Though when we first met her she wasn't certain that was her name. She was the older of the two girls Jonathan rescued at the motel."

Michael nodded. Now he remembered. Mara. Of course. How could he forget the beautiful young girl whose name meant "bitter"? After what she'd been through in her lifetime, it wasn't surprising that she resembled her name.

"She called you?"

Barbara nodded again, and Michael noticed the gray that was spreading through her once dark curls. As many years as she'd been involved in the ministry of rescuing and rehabilitating human-trafficking victims, he was amazed she hadn't turned completely gray long ago.

"Yesterday," she said. "Just as I was leaving for the service last night. She apparently kept my card and had something she wanted to tell me." Barbara paused. "I knew it was something important because these girls seldom get back in touch with us once they've been placed somewhere. They tend to want to forget as much of their past as possible."

"I can imagine. So what did she tell you? Are you free to share it with me?"

"I don't see why not. She didn't swear me to secrecy, and though I wouldn't tell just anyone, I figure you and your family already have a vested interest in this girl." Barbara leaned back and crossed her legs. "I think Mara has run into another captor/slave situation. And who better to recognize something like that than one who spent so many years in that very place?"

With that Barbara spilled out Mara's story, while Michael listened with an aching heart. Though he and his family had been involved with a ministry to human-trafficking victims for a couple of years now, he never ceased to be shocked and heartbroken each time he heard of another such tragedy.

"So what can we do?" he asked when Barbara wound up her report.

"Not too much at this point," she said. "I'm going with Mara in a couple of hours to talk to the police. We haven't much to go on — no names or anything else, for that matter. But I know several people at the station, and Mara's experience gives her more credibility than most." She shrugged. "All we can do is make them aware of it, maybe give them some descriptions so they can watch for them. Other than that, not much at all. But at least Mara has reached out. That she was willing to do that much says a lot for her. I'm hoping to reestablish a connection with her now that she's living and working here legally."

Michael nodded, a picture of Mara teasing his memory. Her eyes had haunted him from the moment he first saw her. How was it possible that a child could be so abused and damaged for so many years — and by someone who was her actual blood relative? The depth of evil involved was almost more than he could fathom.

"I'll keep this to myself unless you tell me otherwise," Michael assured her. "And I'll certainly be praying. To think that young girl — and so many others like her — are out there, forced into such an awful life, with nowhere to turn." He shook his head. "If it weren't for God, I couldn't handle even knowing about this."

"I feel exactly the same way," Barbara admitted. "But because of God, and because we do know about it, we have no other choice but to do everything we can to expose and stop it, do we?"

"No choice at all," Michael said. "Absolutely none."

49

Chapter 7

It had been a busy night for a Thursday, and tips had been generous. Jonathan pulled into the driveway at just past midnight, hoping to do as well or better over the weekend. Then he could put some much needed money and work into his ancient Beetle and maybe even have a few bucks left over.

That would be a welcome relief, he thought, unfolding his six-foot-two frame from the cramped front seat and jiggling his keys as he headed for the front door. The night was pleasantly warm, with only a light breeze to carry the hint of salt inward as far as his Chula Vista dwelling place. Jonathan loved his dorm life at college, but there was nothing like the familiarity of home.

He let himself inside and was surprised to find the light on in the family room. It wasn't like his mother to forget any part of her routine before heading to bed, and that included leaving on the porch light and a small nightlight in the entry way, but turning off everything else.

Jonathan ignored the pull of the kitchen, where he usually diverted on his way from the front door to his room as he looked for a last-minute snack. Instead he turned to the right to check out the family room. Either his mother had forgotten to turn out the light, and he'd do it for her, or someone was waiting up for him.

Sure enough, his father sat at one end of the couch, in his robe and slippers, his head leaning forward on his chest. His even breathing told Jonathan that he'd fallen asleep waiting, so whatever the reason for staying up it must be important.

"Hey, Dad," he whispered, touching his shoulder lightly. "Dad, I'm home."

Michael Flannery awoke with a start, jerking his head upright and blinking a few times before focusing his green eyes on Jonathan. Recognition came slowly, and Jonathan realized his dad had been sleeping much deeper than he'd realized. A twinge of guilt reminded him that his father had worked all day and had to get up early the next morning to do the same. All the more reason to find out why he'd waited up.

Jonathan sat down beside him. "What are you doing up?" he asked, his heart racing as he wondered for the first time if something might have happened to either his mother or Leah. Then again, if it had, his father wouldn't be sitting here on the couch. "It must be something important to keep you up this late. Is everything all right with Mom and Leah?"

"They're fine," his father assured him, all vestiges of sleepiness gone now. "But there is something I wanted to talk to you about before you went to bed — or before you heard it from someone else."

Jonathan frowned. "I'm listening."

"It's Mara," Michael said. "The older of the two girls you helped rescue. She's . . . she's apparently here in the San Diego area, and she's contacted Barbara."

Jonathan raised his eyebrows. Mara? How many times had he thought of her and wondered how she was doing. So she was here after all. He wasn't sure how that made him feel, but it certainly did stir up a conglomeration of emotions.

"What about?" he asked.

"It seems she's working in some waterfront café, and just yesterday some guy came in with a young teenage girl. The way they were acting, Mara was certain the guy was holding her against her will."

"You mean . . . human trafficking? Forced prostitution?"

Michael nodded. "We have no proof, of course, but that's what Mara told Barbara."

"So what are they going to do about it?"

"Barbara took Mara to the police station today to see if they'd at least take a report and circulate the pair's description. Not sure how that worked out because Barbara came to talk to me before they went, but I thought I should mention it to you now. I didn't want you running into Barbara and having her say something without your knowing about it ahead of time."

Jonathan nodded. He appreciated the heads-up. Knowing that Mara was nearby was unsettling, though he wasn't sure why. The girl's sultry good looks had risen up to tease his memory more than once, but always he'd been able to ignore them — until now. Suddenly the girl's effect on him had become more personal, and it disturbed him more than he wanted to admit. That she might have stumbled across a human-trafficking situation only made it more complicated.

"Thanks," he said. "I really appreciate you letting me know."

He hesitated a moment, but when his dad didn't continue the conversation, Jonathan stood to his feet, suddenly anxious to get to his room to do some thinking . . . and praying.

"I think I'll head to bed," he said, looking down at his father and giving him one more chance to chime in with more information. When he didn't take him up on it, Jonathan added, "You should do the same. You've no doubt got an early morning again tomorrow."

Michael smiled. "Sure do. But don't you want to stop in the kitchen for a snack before you go to bed?"

Jonathan shook his head. As much as he'd wanted to grab

something to eat when he first came home, he wasn't in the least interested now. "Nah. I had a couple slices of pizza before I left work. That'll hold me till morning. Good night, Dad. And thanks again for filling me in."

Klahan had slipped away early on Friday morning, just after placing a feathery kiss on the sleeping Lawan's forehead but not before he was certain he had stayed long enough to prevent any last-minute customers from coming up to take advantage of the sweet young girl. It had taken Klahan nearly the entire month to put aside enough money to buy the full night with Lawan, and though he had restrained himself from taking advantage of her sexually, he had enjoyed holding her in his arms throughout the long night. He only wished they could have been completely alone and not had to share the room with the other girl and her customers. How he would love to spend time with Lawan away from that awful place where he knew she was forced to perform all sorts of lewd acts for customers. Unlike himself, the others didn't care for Lawan; they cared only for themselves. Klahan loved Lawan. His dream was to one day fulfill their physical union in a gentle way that would seal her heart to his forever. But he would never allow that to happen until he could somehow buy her from her owners and take her away to live only with him.

Where would I ever get that kind of money? he had asked himself, time and again since first discovering the young girl whom he considered so much lovelier than any of the others available for his buying pleasure. He knew he would certainly never earn enough as a fruit-and-vegetable vendor or digging in the fields, though the two combined jobs enabled him to keep a roof over his head and food in his stomach—not to mention setting aside just enough to visit Lawan once a month. The only other option was to get involved with the illegal drug trade that thrived in the Golden Triangle. It was easy to get into that sort of business, but nearly impossible to get out. As much as he longed to have Lawan for himself, he had seen too many foolish men lose their lives in run-ins with drug lords. He would have to think long and hard before taking such a chance.

At the same time, the thought that other men would continue to use Lawan for their own passions and lusts for the next several weeks while he struggled to save enough money to go back and claim her as his own, even if only for one night, nearly drove him mad. Lawan might have a woman's experience when it came to pleasing a man, but she was still a child at heart, and for Klahan, that was what drove his desire. A lovely young thing like Lawan should not be abused by those who didn't appreciate her beauty. Only he would treat her as she deserved, but first he must find a way to spirit her away from the brothel.

Had anyone ever tried such a thing and succeeded? Klahan made his way down the crowded, narrow streets, oblivious to the rancid odors of unwashed bodies and fly-infested meat that hung from the poles of outside vendors. He scarcely saw the beggars that sat or sprawled along the way, calling out for food or money. Even if he had, he would have had none to give them. Every spare bit of money he earned must be set aside for the purpose of finding a way to either buy or kidnap Lawan and get her out of that horrible place.

He spotted his shack in the distance. It was obvious he couldn't sneak Lawan out and hide her there. If he couldn't find a way to legitimately purchase her and had to kidnap her instead, he would also have to find another place to take her where they wouldn't be found. That presented a problem, but certainly not an insurmountable one. He might even have a contact who could help make that happen.

With that thought in mind, the young widower whose wife had died giving birth to their first child, a stillborn son, now smiled to think that perhaps he would soon have Lawan by his side and would no longer have to spend the remainder of his life alone. That she was a frightened child of no more than ten years did not seem a problem to the obsessed man. Klahan cared little about the girl's age; he knew only that he must have her for himself, whatever the cost. And the sooner he could make that happen, the better.

⁓⦾⁓

"Did you talk to him?"

Rosanna's whisper in the darkness startled Michael, and he stubbed his toe on the foot of the bed.

"Ouch," he mumbled, remembering to keep his voice down as he hobbled toward the bed. "What are you doing awake? I thought you were asleep a long time ago."

"I was. But you know I always wake up when you get out of bed."

Michael sighed. It was true. He'd tried to be so quiet and careful when he slipped out of bed and practically tiptoed out of the room a couple of hours earlier, determined to waylay Jonathan on his way in. No doubt Rosanna had awakened soon after he closed the bedroom door and started down the stairs. It spoke volumes of their mutual trust and respect that she had waited here in bed, knowing that he obviously had something he felt he must do and so had allowed him to do it uninterrupted.

He removed his robe and laid it at the foot of the bed, then kicked off his slippers and climbed under the covers beside his waiting wife, lying on his back beside her. "I wanted to tell him about Mara. I didn't want to risk having him hear it from Barbara."

He felt Rosanna roll toward him and place her hand on his bare chest. "I figured that's what it was," she said. "Ever since you told me about Barbara's visit, I knew you'd want Jonathan to be aware of it." She paused and then asked, "How did he take it?"

Michael sighed. "About like I'd expected. No visible reaction, but I think I know him well enough to know it set off a real emotional reaction inside. That entire experience was pretty life-changing for him."

"It sure was," Rosanna agreed. "For all of us, but more so for him. God used it in a powerful way, and I'm so grateful, but it's still got to stir up some difficult memories and questions for him."

"It'll be interesting to see what comes of all this," Michael commented.

"It certainly will." Rosanna kissed his shoulder. "But for now we'd better get some sleep. That alarm will be going off before we know it."

Chapter 8

Mara walked the length of the Imperial Beach pier — not once but twice, back and forth all the way, each time. And still she felt restless, as she had since she first awoke that morning and decided to utilize public transportation to get to the nearest beach with a pier.

After her second return trip down the expansion of concrete and wooden planks, she forced herself to sit on a bench near the entrance of the pier. She watched three early-morning tourists pause just a few feet away to position themselves behind the cardboard cutouts of a handsome surfer dude and a shapely bathing beauty and smile through the holes where the faces were missing. A laughing woman snapped their photos and then insisted on trading places with the other girl for her turn.

What a waste of time, Mara thought, though a part of her envied the easy camaraderie they seemed to have with each other — not to mention the carefree lifestyles that enabled them to experience such enjoyable moments. Mara wondered if she'd ever come to a place in her life where she too could be so lighthearted as to frolic with friends in such a way, but the thought was too foreign to entertain seriously.

Work is all I need right now, she told herself. *And as soon as my paperwork is approved, I'll take some classes this fall. I sure don't want to be a waitress all my life, even though I have no idea what I really want to do.* The memory of Barbara Whiting accompanying her to the police station the previous day flitted through her mind, and she briefly entertained the possibility of getting involved in some sort of counseling or charity-related profession where she could help people the way Barbara had helped her and the others after the trafficking ring was broken up. Then the realization that few people would be interested in going to someone like her for help of any kind drove the thought from her mind.

The memory of the visit to the police station remained. Mara realized that if Barbara hadn't known two of the officers on duty, they probably wouldn't even have taken down her information or agreed to distribute the descriptions Mara had given them. But as a favor to a woman they respected, they had listened politely and agreed that it was indeed a possibility that what Mara had seen had been some sort of trafficking-related situation. They also stressed that it could be something else entirely.

Mara knew better. As the trio of tourists tired of taking one another's pictures and moved off to explore a different area of the beach, Mara told herself there was no way she'd been wrong about what she'd seen. That girl was being held as a slave, just as she had been for years. She only hoped someone would find and rescue her before it was too late.

Leah didn't have any special plans that Friday morning, so she'd slept in later than usual. By the time she dragged herself down to the kitchen, her father had long since gone to work and her mother had gone with him to attend a women's meeting at church, leaving a note that she would return before lunch.

Jonathan was already seated at the table when Leah walked in, freshly showered and her wet hair wrapped in a towel. Her brother's eyes were puffy, and his red ringlets were matted. She raised her eyebrows in surprise. Jonathan was known for his neatness and almost never showed up at the breakfast table before taking a shower and getting dressed.

"So what's up with you?" she asked, pouring a cup of coffee from the half-full carafe on the counter. Loading it with cream and sugar, she waited for Jonathan's usual smart-aleck remark about "having some coffee with your sugar," but it never came.

She carried her full mug to the table and sat down across from him. "Rough night?"

Jonathan nodded. "Sort of," he mumbled, sipping his own black coffee as he spoke. "I actually had a really good night at work. We were totally busy, and I made some serious tips. But . . ." He paused and took another swig. "But then I got home and found Dad waiting up for me."

Leah frowned. "Must have been something important. He doesn't do that much on weeknights when he has to get up early the next day."

"Exactly." He leveled a bleary gaze at her. "Do you know? About Mara, I mean?"

Leah raised her eyebrows. "What about her?"

As Jonathan told her what he'd learned from their father, Leah forgot about her coffee. She'd often wondered what had happened to Mara, and she was certain Jonathan had done the same, if not more so. But somehow it had never occurred to her that the girl might pop back into their lives at some point, even if remotely. That she was living and working right here in the San Diego area was especially surprising. Somehow Leah had thought Mara would want to get as far away as possible from the place where she had spent so many miserable years.

"I'm not sure what to say," Leah admitted when Jonathan stopped speaking.

Jonathan shrugged. "Me neither. I don't even know what I think about all this—not that it really matters, I suppose. I mean, it's not like she came knocking on our door or anything. We probably won't even see or talk to her. But . . ." He shrugged again and refocused on his nearly empty coffee mug. When neither of them spoke for several seconds, he got up and went to the counter for a refill.

"So you stayed awake and thought about it last night," Leah commented, turning to look at him as he leaned against the counter, watching her.

He nodded. "Most of the night. Gonna be a long shift at work."

Leah smiled. "I don't have any plans. Would your boss mind if I tagged along and kept you company? It's not like he has to pay me or anything, and you don't have to share your tips. But I could help you stay awake."

Jonathan grinned. "How crazy am I to like the idea of my kid sister riding around with me to deliver pizzas on a Friday night?"

"Pretty crazy," Leah teased. "So is that a yes?"

"Sure. Why not?"

Leah nodded. "Good. Now I have something to look forward to for the rest of the day."

Jonathan laughed out loud. "You must be as crazy as me, Sis." He shook his head. "What a pathetic pair we are. You'd think we could come up with something a little more fun for a Friday night. But if this is the best we can do, then I guess we'll run with it."

Jefe was pleased. He sat on the edge of his lower bunk and tried to picture the Friday afternoon sun sliding down the western sky toward the Pacific, igniting another weekend of partying in the beautiful city of San Diego where he had spent so many exciting and profitable years. Those years were behind him now, with little to look forward to—until this very day.

It had cost him plenty, but at last he'd accomplished what he'd been working at for weeks. He'd had to trade nearly two weeks of food rations from the canteen and his hidden stash of hooch to get a message to his guy on the outside, but he'd done it and it was worth every sacrifice. True, he still missed the days when he could summon Destroyer or Enforcer to do his dirty work, but for now he'd settle for whoever he could get. And he knew his contact would be perfect for the job. Already he'd heard that Mara had been seen in the San Diego area, and though it was hard for him to believe she'd be so stupid to come back there, he couldn't help but smile at the thought that soon the one who had betrayed him would pay for that betrayal beyond her wildest imaginations. He despised the girl every bit as much as he had once loved her, though apparently she hadn't appreciated or reciprocated his feelings. Now she would learn what happened to people who crossed El Jefe. Few lived to tell about it, and none got away without extreme and extended suffering. Mara would die for what she'd done, but not until she begged for death to release her from her prolonged torture.

The only thing that bothered Jefe was that he wouldn't be there to see her agony and witness her ultimate demise. In fact, there was nothing he'd like better than to be the one to personally dump her body into the ground and cover it with dirt, but he'd have to settle for a videotaped version from the executioner he had hired. But at least it shouldn't be long. If Mara had already been spotted at least once in a specific area, she would certainly be seen again. It was just a matter of time. And then, at last, the man who had treated his niece as if she were his own daughter would have his much-deserved revenge, making the remainder of his life sentence so much easier to bear.

With that delicious thought in mind, the middle-aged prisoner who even behind bars commanded respect and authority over many of the lesser inmates picked up a deck of cards and sauntered from his open cell to find a partner to help pass the dull, endless afternoon that was just like every other in this miserable, monotonous life. If it weren't for the anticipation of Mara's pain, he doubted he could make it through another night.

Chapter 9

Jonathan smiled as he exited his somewhat blue Bug to deliver an order of two pizzas with everything. Leah had sat beside him all evening, speaking on occasion but overall remaining relatively quiet.

That had surprised him. Despite the fact that she'd offered to accompany him to help keep him awake through the long night of driving and delivering, he had wondered if she might have an ulterior motive. He knew Leah loved to get him alone and pick his brain—such as it was.

He handed the still warm pizzas to the man who answered the door, and pocketed the payment, including the generous tip. It had been a profitable Friday night so far, and it was only half over.

Ignoring the familiar squeak of his car's front door, he scrunched his oversized frame inside and glanced at his sister, who was staring out her side window into the darkness. "What are you thinking about, Sis?" he asked. When she didn't respond, he raised his voice a notch. "Leah?"

She jerked her head around toward his voice, her green eyes wide. "Oh, hey," she said after a moment. "Sorry. Guess I was distracted."

"Ya think?" Jonathan chuckled. "Seriously distracted. What's on your mind?"

Leah dropped her eyes before raising them again and

locking her gaze with Jonathan's. "This Mara thing got me thinking again . . . about all she and the others went through before you ran into them. And now she thinks she saw someone else in the same kind of situation." She shook her head. "It's hard not to get discouraged, don't you think? I mean, we got involved with the outreach to human-trafficking victims nearly two years ago. Do you think it made a difference? Seriously, have we helped anyone at all?"

Jonathan resisted the temptation to jump in with a reassurance that even if they helped just one person, it was worth the effort. He knew in his heart that was true, but he too had questioned himself many times as to their scope of effectiveness. He couldn't dismiss her questions that lightly.

"I've wondered the same thing," he admitted. "Many times. What we do is like the proverbial drop in the bucket or needle in a haystack." He reached out and laid a hand on her arm, squinting in the semidarkness at what he was certain were tears in her eyes. "But that doesn't mean we quit. We can't give up. You know that, Leah. We have to try—and try again and try some more. We know we're not the only ones fighting this thing, right? I mean, since we got involved we've found out about groups all around the world who are doing everything they can to stop this and set the slaves free." He squeezed her arm lightly and leaned closer as he continued. "It's why we insist on abolition. Nothing less will do, remember? It's bad enough that we know this kind of stuff goes on all over the world, with millions of people enslaved and no hope of escape unless we continue to fight. But the worst part is that some laws protect the very slime bags that kidnap and torment these poor people. It has to be stopped, and it will be a long, hard fight. But if we don't do it, who will?"

Leah nodded, and this time Jonathan was close enough to see a tear roll down her cheek. "I know you're right," she whispered. "It's just . . . it's just that sometimes it hits me that girls—and even some boys—who are my age or younger are caught up in that horrible life and can't escape. How can anyone possibly grow up like that?"

"Many of them don't live that long," Jonathan reminded her. "That's all the more reason that we have to do everything we can to try to help, even if we feel like our efforts aren't making a dent."

He waited, giving Leah time to respond. At last she raised her eyes to his and nodded. "I know you're right," she said. "I truly do. But sometimes . . ."

Her voice trailed off, and Jonathan put an arm around her shoulder and pulled her close. "I know," he said, resting his chin on top of her head. "Believe me, I know exactly how you feel."

67

Mara's Friday afternoon shift had been so busy that she'd ended up working a few hours over. Now it was nearly midnight and she'd have to walk home alone—again. She told herself she didn't mind, that she'd done it many times before, and that she'd survived a lot worse in her younger years. Still, she preferred it when she got off early enough that there were at least a few tourists and families still out and about. Now she was pretty much relegated to sharing the streets with the bar crowd and a handful of homeless people.

She held her purse close to her as she headed out the café door and turned in the direction of her room. At a fast clip she could walk it in just over five minutes. What could happen to her in five minutes? Memories of what she'd endured in various instances of five minutes danced through her memory, and she walked even faster, careful not to trip over occasional cracks in the sidewalk.

"Got any spare change, miss?"

The voice seemed to come out of nowhere, and Mara gasped. She hadn't seen the old man leaning up against the deserted storefront, but quite obviously he'd seen her. The realization did not offer her the assurance she needed.

She pushed ahead, refusing to respond to the man's continued pleas. By the time his requests had turned to curses, she was nearly half a block away, reminding herself that she had just enough money to get by on for herself; she certainly couldn't give it away to every homeless bum who asked.

For surely that's what he was. Mara couldn't allow herself to think that he might really have been hungry. No. He undoubtedly wanted the money to buy himself a bottle of some cheap booze so he could once again drink himself into unconsciousness. Now that was the one part of the man's plight she could relate to, as she had spent many nights wishing for something that would dull the pain and blot out her own suffering. But nothing had come along—until Jonathan.

The image of the handsome deliveryman once again danced around the edges of her memory, begging to be allowed in. But she refused. She had to keep her focus on working, saving her money, and going to school so she could improve her future. That future had no room for a man, however nice or handsome he might have been.

Besides, she argued with herself, *what would he want with someone like me? It's one thing for those do-gooders to help rescue people like us, but to actually get to know us or have a relationship with us?* She nearly snorted aloud at the thought. *It's a sure thing that'll never happen!*

The familiar faint glow of the porch light at the house where she rented a room brought a rush of relief to Mara, and she shoved the vestiges of Jonathan's memory to the back of her mind where it belonged. It had been a long day, and all she wanted was to lock herself in her room and get some much-needed sleep before she had to get up and start all over again.

Francesca awoke late on Saturday morning in her stuffy room, the smell of cigarettes and sweat assailing her but tempered by the realization that she was at last alone. Her final customer had left before daylight, and she had fallen into an exhausted sleep. It was only the mounting heat of her cramped quarters that pulled her back from the only escape she had found in the last few months of her terrifying life.

"Mama," she whispered. "Papa. Where are you? Do you know what's happened to me yet? Are you looking for me?" Hot tears squeezed from her eyes as she buried her face in her dirty pillow. "*Por favor!* Please, Papa, come and find me. Get me out of this terrible place. I want to go home!"

Silence was her only answer, as it always was when she dared to utter such words. Daily, whenever she found herself alone for even a few moments, she instinctively begged her parents to come and rescue her. She knew they couldn't hear her, but she couldn't allow herself to give up crying out to them, for it was the only hope she had. Since the day she had walked the streets of Juarez with her girlfriends, knowing she had been forbidden to do so because of the gang violence but determined to enjoy some freedom with her *muchachas* and make it back home before her parents realized she was gone, she had lived

69

with a depth of regret she had not realized was possible. The *if onlys* had nearly driven her mad, as she endured one horrible day after another, locked up with no way to escape the nightly torture that brought her owners such financial reward. Why hadn't she run away, like her friends, instead of standing frozen in place, too frightened to move until she was snatched up and stuffed into the back of a van, where she was tied up and gagged and not allowed out until they had reached their destination in the US?

Francesca knew she was one of several slaves in the large house where she was held, let out only under strict supervision for short periods of time and that only to show her that she had no freedom even when she was out in public. She thought of the day earlier that week when the man known as El Diablo had taken her on her first outing since grabbing her and spiriting her across the border to what he had informed her was her "new home." He had assaulted her that first night and nearly every night since, in addition to selling her favors by the hour to anyone who would pay. Oh, how she had hoped that leaving that torture chamber of a house would give her a chance to escape, but it had not been so. El Diablo had not let her out of his sight even for a moment. And he had made it quite clear how dearly she would pay if she tried anything.

Besides, she had realized, *where would I go? What would I do? I don't know anyone. I don't even speak the language that well.*

And so she had stayed at his side, returning to the house for yet another night of humiliation and pain. Nothing had changed as a result of leaving the house, and Francesca was truly coming to the point of wondering if it ever would.

The others, she thought. *I've seen others here . . . like me.* ChaCha's face rose up in her mind. An adjoining bathroom sat between their bedrooms, but Francesca had been warned not to speak to her — or to any of the other slaves in the house. *How long have they been here? Have any of them ever escaped?*

The thought that perhaps the only way any had ever truly escaped this place was through death caused a chill to pass over her, and she pulled the blankets over her head, sobbing at the dismal chances that she would ever see her home or family again. She longed for the day when her father would break through the door and rescue her, but how could that ever happen? He had no idea where she was, and even if he found her, El Diablo and the other two men who lived in the house and ruled over the slaves would surely kill him.

I should have tried to get away, she thought. *Even if he'd caught me and killed me right there on the street, I should have run away. Maybe if I'd said something to that waitress . . .* The beautiful young woman's face rose up in Francesca's mind, and she wondered again if the waitress would have at least called the police if she'd known what was going on.

But how could she? I didn't even have a chance to write her a note or say anything or —

She heard his voice at the same time she felt the covers being yanked off her. Terror sent splinters of pain darting up her spine and into her face, exploding behind her eyes. It was a fearful response she had become accustomed to over the months of her captivity.

"Get up," the voice growled, as he grabbed her hair from behind and yanked her head back, forcing her to look up into his contorted face. El Diablo leaned down and hissed his words directly into her face. "So, you think you can hide under the covers and lay around all day? Well, you can't, Frankie. We have company today, someone very special, and he has requested your company. So get up and get in the shower. I want you ready in fifteen minutes."

He shoved her face against his, breathing his foul breath at her. "Do you understand, *mi amor*?"

"My love." More than anything else, Francesca hated that El Diablo sometimes called her *mi amor* — my love. It was bad enough they had changed her name from Francesca to Frankie, but "my love"? It made her want to vomit.

Instead she nodded her head as best she could, though his grip on her hair made it difficult. "*Si*, El Diablo. I understand. And I will be ready."

He continued glaring at her for a moment and then jerked her loose and turned on his heel, heading for the door. "You'd better be," he said. "And you'd better treat this guy right. If I hear any bad reports . . ."

He turned back and glared at her one last time. More than once Francesca had received the results of what El Diablo considered a bad report from one of the customers. As much as she hated what she had to do to prevent such reports from being given to El Diablo, she hated the painful punishments he meted out that much worse. She would cooperate with this so-called special customer and pray that he was pleased. Maybe then she would be left alone to rest for a while.

Chapter 10

Leah had been sure she'd sleep most of the day away on Saturday, after being out with Jonathan until nearly 1:00 that morning and then staying up for a couple hours after that, just talking and enjoying some quality time with her brother. They'd made a pact not to discuss the human-trafficking issue anymore that night, as they'd nearly worn it out and felt the need for something lighter. But always the topic was there, in the back of Leah's mind and, she was certain, in Jonathan's as well. Still, they had honored their ban of the subject and just had an enjoyable time, eating microwave popcorn and drinking sodas until they finally sputtered out and went to bed.

But it was only midmorning when Leah's cell phone pulled her from a sound sleep. By the time she recognized the ring tone and figured out that someone was trying to reach her, she nearly missed the call. Snatching the phone from its resting place on the stand beside her bed, she squinted at the name. Sarah. She grinned. She'd forgotten they had plans to hit the mall today, and, tired or not, she wasn't about to miss it.

"Hey," she said, greeting the girl who had been her best friend since grammar school. "You're up early."

Sarah's familiar laugh broadened Leah's smile. Sarah was the closest thing Leah had to a sister, and though she loved her brother dearly, he wasn't much of a shopping companion.

"It's not that early," Sarah countered. "It's a little after 10:00. I thought you wanted to get to the mall before it got crowded. From the sound of your voice, you aren't even out of bed yet."

"You're right," Leah admitted. "But just give me fifteen minutes, and I'll be ready to go."

Sarah laughed again. "Fifteen minutes? Oh yeah, that'll be the day! It'll take you that long just to wash all that hair of yours."

"Oh, sure, just because you can wash all three inches of yours in ten seconds! OK, give me thirty minutes. Can you pick me up?"

"Absolutely! Mom's Jetta is full of gas and raring to go."

"Perfect. See you in a few!"

Leah clicked off and jumped out of bed. She'd have to hurry, but as long as Jonathan hadn't gotten into their shared bathroom ahead of her, she'd make it. And she imagined it was a relatively safe assumption that her brother was still snoozing since he didn't have to be at work until 4:00.

Grabbing her robe and throwing it over her shoulders, she hurried from her bedroom into the hallway, relieved to see the bathroom door open and the room unoccupied. It was all hers, and it was going to be a great day.

74

Klahan wiped his sweaty palms on his loose pants and waited for someone to open the door. He had never come to the big house without an invitation, but he felt he had no choice. He had stayed awake for hours since leaving Lawan behind in that filthy brothel, agonizing over his chances of getting her out of there alive. He had finally decided that his best chance was to contact the person he had not seen or heard from since his wife died.

Klahan seldom thought of Jaidee anymore, though he had mourned her deeply when she first died. Those first years of being alone had been terrible for Klahan, and he knew his wife's family blamed him for Jaidee's and the baby's death. He was not surprised, therefore, that they had nothing to do with him after that. But now his life had meaning again, a purpose that drove him to the home where Jaidee's brother lived. Would he help him, or was this indeed a foolish pursuit?

The old woman who answered the door scrutinized his ragged clothing and seemed inclined to slam the door in his face until Klahan spoke up. "Please," he said. "I am Klahan. Jaidee was my wife. Please, I must speak with Chai. It is urgent."

Before the woman could shoo him away, Klahan heard a voice from behind her. "So, my long lost brother-in-law has come to pay me a visit at last." The words were encouraging to Klahan, but the snide tone was not. Still, he stood his ground.

"Come in," Chai said, appearing beside the old woman and motioning with his head for her to leave. She did so, quickly, and Klahan stepped inside before Chai had time to change his mind.

Chai, who was several inches taller and a few years older than Klahan, closed the door behind the unexpected visitor. Together they stood, Chai sneering down at Klahan as neither spoke. Klahan hung his head and stared at his feet, marveling as he did so at the rich tile floor that spread as far as his limited gaze could see.

"I must speak to you, Chai," he said. "I know that you and your family prefer not to see me, but my matter is urgent, and I have nowhere else to go."

After yet another brief silence, during which Klahan imagined his former brother-in-law was deciding whether to invite him further into the house or order him back out, Chai finally spoke.

"We will talk here," he said. "I have no wish to sit and converse with you. Tell me why you came and what you want from me."

Klahan swallowed. So he was not to be invited in or ordered out—at least not yet. He would have to be very careful how he presented his request. He knew Chai was an evil man, and a greedy one at that. If he thought there was easy money in Klahan's proposition, he just might agree to help him.

"There is a girl," Klahan said. "A young girl. Very beautiful." He swallowed. "Exceptionally so. She . . ." The words nearly stuck in his throat, but he forced himself to continue. "Her beauty is being wasted in a brothel, her talent thrown away on unworthy men. She is worth so much more, but her owners are too stupid to see it."

"And you are not?"

Klahan recognized the smirk in the man's voice. *Careful,* he warned himself. *He must not suspect what you really want. Let him think that it is all about the money, and that he can outsmart you and get it all for himself.*

"That is why I came to you," he said. "I would like very much to take this girl away from the place where her beauty is wasted, as I know that with the right attentions and setting she could make someone very rich. But I also know I do not have the breeding or the resources to make something like that happen. But you do. You could buy her for what would be a meaningless amount for you and turn it into a major profit. And she is very young—no more than ten or eleven, I think—so she could work for many years."

Chai remained silent, as Klahan kept his eyes averted and tried not to shake or sweat too much. If this attempt did not work out, he would have to resort to the drug trade to try to buy Lawan himself. As humiliating as it was to come to Chai and as dangerous, realizing that the man would want to personally test the merchandise before investing, this was still preferable to getting involved with the ferocious drug lords who nearly ran the entire area.

"I might be persuaded to consider such a business venture," Chai said at last, "though I have two concerns. First, what is in this for you? I know you have not come here strictly for my benefit. And second, why should I believe this one particular girl is any more special than any of the others?"

Klahan had anticipated both questions, though he had hoped the second might be avoided. Obviously that was not the case.

"I will soon be too old to continue working two jobs," Klahan said, his eyes still fixed on the floor. "If I could have a little income from this girl—just a very little, you understand—I would not have to work in the fields any longer. I would be able to supplement my income from my fruit-and-vegetable stand with a small portion of your profits. I'm sure you can understand that I would like to reap a tiny fraction of the money she earns since I am the one who discovered her."

Klahan waited, resisting what he knew was coming regarding Chai's second question. "I might agree to that if what you say about the girl is true. But how can I know that unless I see her myself? I must test her talents, you understand."

He understood only too well, and it was the part of his plan that he despised. But there seemed to be no other way. After all, poor Lawan was already being used by so many men that one more could not make any real difference. Once Chai saw the young girl's beauty and youth, he would surely be impressed. And when he realized through his own experience that inside the lovely and innocent-looking child lived a sensual woman, he would surely agree to Klahan's offer.

Fighting tears of jealousy and rage at the thought of the pompous man who stood before him having his way with his beloved Lawan, Klahan said, "I will tell you how to find her. Then, after you have . . . been with her, I will tell you my plan."

This time Chai laughed aloud. "And what if I decide I want her for myself?" he asked. "What if I decide I don't want to include you at all? What will you do then, Klahan? Have you considered that possibility?"

Klahan had indeed considered it, and he had a plan in place for just such an event. But, of course, he was not about to indicate as much to Chai.

"It is a chance I will have to take," he said, even as he vowed to himself that he would never take such a chance with the girl he loved.

Chai laughed aloud. "Indeed you will," he said. "Indeed you will."

Leah and Sarah hit the mall just in time to smell the freshly baked cinnamon rolls calling them to a late breakfast. Leah's mom had greeted Sarah at the front door and tried to convince the girls to wait while she made them a good breakfast, but they had declined. Now they were ravenous, and they made a beeline for the crowded cinnamon roll kiosk.

"Those things are huge," Sarah exclaimed as they stood in line, waiting to order.

"Who cares?" Leah said. "I'm starved! I just might eat two."

Sarah laughed. "No way. You say that now, but wait till you're halfway through one of those sugary monstrosities. You'll be moaning about being stuffed."

"I doubt it." Leah inched closer, only two customers ahead of her now. "So where do you want to go first — when we finish here, I mean?"

Sarah shrugged. "I don't know. I need some makeup and some shoes for summer. Otherwise, I'm just looking."

"Me too." Leah nodded. She didn't have a lot of extra spending money, even with her babysitting earnings and the few dollars Jonathan had insisted she accept for coming with him the night before. But she was definitely going to need a few things between now and when she left for school in the fall, so now was as good a time as any to start hunting for bargains.

"So what did you end up doing last night?" Sarah asked, digging in her purse for what Leah assumed was money to pay for her "sugary monstrosity."

"I rode along with Jonathan to keep him company while he delivered pizzas. What about you? Did you end up going with your parents to visit your aunt?"

Sarah rolled her eyes. "Yeah. What a drag! I mean, I love my aunt and all, and I'm sorry she's in the hospital, but really, is there anywhere worse to hang out on a Friday night?"

Leah smiled. "Probably not. But hey, family is family."

"I know." Sarah sighed. "And like I said, I love my aunt, but . . . well, you know."

"Is she doing any better?"

"Yeah. They put a pin in her hip, and she'll be starting therapy soon so she can go back home as soon as possible. You know she lives alone, right?"

Leah nodded.

"So that's why she has to go to a rehab for therapy first. Then she'll go home on a walker. They said she's in good health otherwise, so she should heal fast. And get this." Sarah's blue eyes lit up and her face nearly danced with amusement. "They said she's got her youth going for her. Ha! She's in her midforties. Youth! Are you serious?"

Leah grinned and stepped up to the counter. It was their turn to order. Ignoring her friend's comments about her aunt's age, Leah placed her order and Sarah did the same. While they waited, they stood aside to let the next person in line step up.

"So you hung out with Jonathan last night," Sarah said.

Surprised, Leah raised her eyebrows. "Yeah, I did. Why?"

Sarah shrugged, but Leah noticed that the girl's cheeks took on a pinkish hue. "Oh, no reason. Just wondered how he was doing. I haven't seen him much since he came home for the summer—except at our graduation. Does he . . ." She paused, and Leah squinted. What was going on with Sarah? She waited until Sarah finished her question. "Does he have a . . . girlfriend at college?"

So that was it. Sarah, the cute, petite blonde, who had her choice of boyfriends all throughout high school but never seemed overly interested in any of them, apparently now had a crush on Jonathan. Leah smiled and turned away, glad her number had been called for her order. She took the giant cinnamon roll and her cup of coffee and made room for Sarah to pick up hers. Then they turned toward an empty table and headed straight for it.

Sarah sat down and swirled her coffee and picked at her cinnamon roll. "So . . ." she said, "does he? Have a girlfriend, I mean?"

Leah grinned. "Not that I know of. Why? Are you applying for the job?"

Chapter 11

Mara felt so much better after a good night's sleep and a quiet Saturday morning, just lazing in bed with a second cup of coffee and browsing a magazine. But now she was getting restless. It was time to get out and get some exercise before she had to start her afternoon shift. Though the beach was her favorite place to walk, today she decided to try something different. She wasn't much of a shopper and seldom went to the nearby mall, but it would be the perfect place to walk around and pass the time. She might even treat herself to an inexpensive lunch at the food court while she was at it, saving her one free meal of the day at work for later in the evening.

The sun seemed brighter than usual as she set a fast pace from her home to the mall, nearly ten blocks along which she had to wait for a light at nearly every intersection. But she arrived before noon with several hours to spare before she had to report for work.

Mara removed her sunglasses and let her eyes adjust as she stepped inside and glanced around to get her bearings. The food court was straight ahead and already crowded with the Saturday lunch crowd. It appeared she could take her pick of Chinese, seafood, burgers, hot dogs-on-a-stick, pizza, sandwiches, and even sushi. Since she got her fill of seafood at work, she opted for Chinese. Seemed she could never get enough fried rice or sweet and sour pork.

The tables were all filled by the time she got her order, but she spotted one empty corner of a bench not far away. She scurried over to it and plunked down before somebody else beat her to it. Within seconds she was using a plastic fork to shovel in the steamy, delicious food.

"Ever try chopsticks?"

The question came from beside her, a somewhat older man if his age matched up with his voice. Immediately putting her guard up, Mara turned to look at the interloper who had interrupted her lunch.

"Excuse me?" she said.

Just as she'd suspected, the man appeared to be in his late fifties or early sixties, with a receding hairline and a slight paunch. He smiled, obviously awaiting an answer. She didn't want to be rude, but she didn't trust any man, regardless of age. Still, she didn't want to make a scene, so she forced a smile.

"Never learned how to use them," she said, hoping that would end the conversation and she could return to her meal. "Never wanted to."

"You really should, you know," he said. "They're not that hard. I learned how to use them when I was overseas."

Mara nodded. "That's nice." Deliberately turning away from him, she stuffed a large bite of rice in her mouth, willing him to notice that she could no longer talk.

"Be glad to teach you how to use them," he said.

Caught between wanting to slap the man or run for cover, she was spared the decision when a heavyset woman with graying hair approached them. "I got everything I needed," she informed the man. "I'm ready to go if you are."

The man rose to his feet, his brief conversation with Mara obviously forgotten. "Sure," he said, taking a couple of packages from the woman who Mara decided was probably his wife. "Why not? I've had enough of the mall to last me a lifetime or two."

They chuckled and walked away, leaving Mara to wonder if the man had just been trying to be friendly after all. Would she have realized that if she'd had a normal life? She swallowed her rice and stabbed a piece of pork, glancing up as she heard what she imagined was a young woman's voice. As it turned out, it was two young women, talking to one another as they passed by.

"I'm still too full of cinnamon rolls to even think about lunch," the one with short blonde curls said. "I want to go try on shoes at that store down at the other end."

Her companion shrugged, her long red hair bouncing as she walked. "Fine with me," she said. "I can try on shoes all day long, even if I can't really afford to buy them."

The girls laughed and continued on, chattering as they walked. Mara watched them, wondering why the redhead seemed familiar. She hadn't seen the girl's face, but there was something about her hair and her voice.

Mara shook her head. She was just imagining things. After all, her life hadn't afforded her much opportunity to meet other girls her own age unless they too were part of the slave compound. Quite obviously the girls that just walked by had never even heard of such a thing, let alone been involved with it. Human trafficking was no doubt the last thing on their minds. Mara just hoped that she would one day get to the place where it was no longer the first thing on hers.

Rosanna was halfheartedly fighting a rising sense of abandonment, though part of her longed to give in to it and just have a good old-fashioned pity party. Michael had bounded out of bed early for a rare game of golf with his friends, but Rosanna had been all right with that because she still had both of her children at home. As a result she had limited herself to sipping her coffee and avoiding breakfast until at last she'd heard Leah bounding down the stairs just as the doorbell rang.

Rosanna had moved to open it, but Leah beat her to it. When Sarah entered, Rosanna had hugged her in greeting and excitedly offered to make the girls a nice big breakfast. They had declined, opting to dash off to the mall and grab something to eat there.

That left Jonathan. Maybe that was just as well, Rosanna had decided. How few times did the two of them get to spend alone together these days? But by the time Jonathan had showered and come downstairs, he had quickly announced that he was off to play a game of baseball with his buddies before he had to leave for work.

And so Rosanna was alone, sitting in the porch swing and pushing it back and forth with her sandaled foot. The cold glass of lemonade just didn't have the same refreshing zing to it that it did when her family was there to share some with her. Was this what the empty-nest syndrome was like? Rosanna thought it probably was, and she figured she wasn't going to like it much.

She heard the back door open at the same time Michael's voice rang out. "So there you are," he exclaimed, going straight to her side and bending down to plant a kiss on her cheek. "I walked into an empty house and thought I'd been deserted."

Rosanna smiled and patted the seat beside her. "That's exactly what happened," she said as he joined her, setting the swing to rocking. "Leah's gone to the mall with Sarah, and Jonathan managed to scare up a last-minute ball game. I offered to cook for them before they left, but they insisted they'd pick something up along the way."

Michael took her hand and squeezed it. "No wonder you feel deserted," he said. "But now I'm home. Will I do?"

Rosanna laughed. "Just barely," she teased. "So how was your golf game?"

"Not bad for an old man," he answered, grinning. "I shot an eighty-five."

"Is that good?"

Now it was Michael's turn to laugh. "For me it is."

Rosanna nodded, satisfied that her husband had enjoyed himself. "Are you thirsty?" she asked. "I made lemonade."

He leaned across her and snagged her half-full glass from the wrought-iron table beside the swing. "I'll just share yours," he said, taking a big swig.

They sat quietly for a moment, as Rosanna became aware of the chirping birds and the light breeze that ruffled their hair and kept the temperature pleasant. "I'm glad you're home. I'm afraid I was starting to feel sorry for myself."

Michael stretched his arm across her shoulders and pulled her against him. "We can't have that. Sounds to me like I got here just in time. What do you say I go take a quick shower, and then we'll take off for parts unknown?"

Rosanna raised her eyebrows. "You mean, no particular destination?"

"Exactly. We'll just drive until we see somewhere we want to stop and eat or walk . . . or even shop, if that's what you really want to do."

With her head still resting against Michael's chest, Rosanna tilted her head up and smiled. "I really have a lot of nerve, feeling sorry for myself when I have the most amazing husband in the world."

"You can say that again," Michael agreed, bending his neck to plant a soft kiss on her lips. "In fact, you can say that just about anytime you want to. But for now, I'm heading for the shower. Give me fifteen minutes."

Rosanna smiled. "It's a date, Michael Flannery. And thanks for putting the empty-nest thing back in perspective."

He laughed and got up from the swing, setting it to rocking again as he headed into the house, whistling all the way.

Leah was certain she'd tried on every pair of shoes in the entire mall, and still she hadn't found any that fit, looked right, and were affordable. Yet Sarah had managed to buy three pairs! She wondered if she was just too picky. Jonathan insisted she was, but hey, what did big brothers know?

Dragging herself from yet another shoe store, she followed Sarah, who was still as bouncy as when they'd first arrived. Where would she want to go now? Surely she didn't want to look at more shoes! Leah was done with it herself. She refused to try on one more pair. This just wasn't her day for a purchase.

And then she saw her. The girl didn't look to be much older than Leah or Sarah, and yet she somehow gave the appearance of an experienced woman. Her short, sassy dark hair framed her dainty face and wide hazel eyes. A smooth olive complexion just added to her sultry good looks, as she ambled from one store window to another, stopping to peer inside but not entering any of them.

"I know her," Leah said, as much to herself as to her friend.

Sarah stopped walking. "Who do you know? What are you talking about?"

Resisting the urge to point, Leah nodded toward the girl, who walked on the opposite side of the mall but in the same direction. "Her. That girl there in the tight jeans and pink blouse. I've seen her somewhere, I'm sure of it."

Sarah shrugged. "So? What's so unusual about that? We run into all sorts of people we know here at the mall."

"I know, but . . ." Leah hesitated. "That's not what I mean. There's something about her."

"So go talk to her," Sarah suggested. "What's the big deal?"

Leah shook her head, though she wasn't sure why. "For some reason I don't think I should."

As she spoke, the girl's glance swept over Leah and Sarah, going past them and then returning to stop right on them. Her eyes widened, and Leah knew she had been right. They knew each other from somewhere.

Mara!

The name nearly exploded in her mind. Of course! The girl Jonathan had rescued two years earlier, the one who had been held captive for so many years. Jonathan had told her she was back in the area and that she had contacted Barbara Whiting, but Leah had never expected to run into her. Now, there she was. And quite obviously, though they'd only actually spoken once when they met in the courtroom during the trials, the recognition was mutual.

"She cut her hair," Leah said, "but I know it's her. Mara. The one—"

Sarah gasped, interrupting Leah. "The one Jonathan rescued?"

Leah nodded, realizing now that she had no choice but to go over to the girl and greet her. What she would say to her she had no idea, but there was no chance to slip away now. She took a deep breath, smiled, and stepped toward the young woman she hadn't seen for nearly two years and had never expected to see again.

Chapter 12

Mara's heart raced at the sight of the two girls walking toward her. They were the same ones she had seen earlier, and she was now more certain than ever that she knew the red-haired girl that led the way. But where?

She felt her eyes grow wide as recognition dawned. Of course! The pizza guy's sister. Her mind went blank on the girl's name, but Jonathan's rose up sharp and clear.

Jonathan's sister. No wonder she had looked and sounded familiar! Though they'd only spoken briefly once and Mara had fought to block the memories of everything connected to that time, it all came flooding back to her now. Her knees nearly buckled, but she stood her ground, forcing a smile as the girls drew up and stopped right in front of her.

"Mara," the redhead said, stretching out her hand. "How are you? I heard you were back in town."

Her arm felt leaden as she commanded it to respond to the girl's gesture. She could scarcely feel her touch as their hands connected in a brief greeting. Mara prepared herself to repeat the process with the blonde, but it wasn't necessary, as the second girl hung back a bit behind her friend.

Thoughts flitted through her mind with lightning speed, as she tried to make sense of them individually. The one that stood out clearest was the comment that the girl had heard she was back in town. Somehow that didn't strike Mara as a good thing. If one person related to that horrible incident two years earlier had heard she was here, who else might know?

Don't be paranoid, she told herself. *The only ones who would want to hurt you are behind bars where they belong, and they won't be getting out for a very long time. You have nothing to worry about.* But her heart was not comforted.

She realized then that the girls were waiting for her response. She cleared her throat. "I'm fine," she said, wishing she could remember the redhead's name. "And you?"

The girl smiled, and Mara was surprised to realize the smile appeared genuine. "You probably don't remember me," she said. "I'm Leah. Jonathan Flannery's sister. You know, the guy who was delivering pizzas when—"

Mara nodded. "Of course I remember you," she said, relieved to know her name. "And I could never forget your brother. He saved my life. And a lot of other lives too."

Leah nodded. "He did, didn't he? I'm so proud of him."

The blonde cleared her throat, and Leah turned toward her. "Oh, I'm sorry," she said, turning back to Mara. "This is my friend, Sarah Peterson. Sarah, Mara . . . Jimenez, is it?"

Mara nodded. She still hadn't gotten used to hearing her last name. For so many years she was simply Mara. None of the slaves in the compound were permitted to talk about their past, and that included telling others their last name. Even many of their first names had been changed. Mara was no exception. Her name before she was sold to her uncle and smuggled across the border was Maria, but Jefe had changed her name to Mara. When she found out the name meant "bitter," Mara decided it was the right name for her after all.

Sarah stuck out her hand, and Mara took it, though the girl's grasp was limp and halfhearted, unlike Leah's had been. *So,* Mara thought, *now what? What can I possibly have in common with these girls?* The realization that she'd been wrong when she saw them earlier and had concluded that they'd probably never even heard of human trafficking, let alone been involved in it, popped into her mind. OK, so Leah at least was familiar with it, but certainly not in the same way Mara was. It was one thing to be related to someone who had stumbled onto a human-trafficking situation and even helped rescue someone, but that didn't begin to equate to actually being the someone who was trapped in that lifestyle.

The memory of the young girl who had come into the café earlier that week with the man who was no doubt her owner flashed into Mara's mind. Would there ever be a Jonathan in her life, someone to come along at the right time and place to rescue her? Or was she doomed to live and die in the garbage dump that had become her only reality?

"So," Mara said, trying to focus, "you heard I was back in town. How did that happen?"

Leah's cheeks colored a light pink, and she dropped her eyes before raising them again and answering the question.

"Barbara Whiting is a friend of ours from church," she said. "We—my family and I—have been working with her in a human-trafficking rescue ministry for the past couple of years. She told my dad."

"So Jonathan knows."

Leah nodded. "Yes. He was glad to hear you were doing so well."

Mara raised her eyebrows. Did living in a rented room and working as a waitress count as doing well? For someone who had spent the majority of her life as a sex slave, she imagined it did.

"Excuse me," she said, as kindly and firmly as she knew how, "but I'm due at work soon. I really need to get going."

Leah nodded again. "Sure. I understand. It . . . it was nice seeing you again."

Mara smiled. "Say hello to Jonathan for me, will you?"

Before Leah could respond, Mara spun on her heel and walked away as quickly as she could without actually breaking into a run. Why had she said that about Jonathan? Hadn't she spent the last two years trying to forget he even existed? She hated that the very mention of his name caused her heart to race, and she knew the last thing in the world she needed was to see him again. After all, what was the point? A good, decent guy like Jonathan Flannery would never give a second thought to someone like her. Why set herself up for more pain? Hadn't she already had enough to last a lifetime?

Bursting through the glass doors from the mall into the bright Southern California sunlight, she grabbed her shades from her purse and jammed them onto her face. If only she could block out her memories and feelings as easily as she could the sun's glare.

After two years in the brothel, Lawan had more than enough experience to realize she had been reserved for a very special customer. Though she had no idea who it might be, it was nearly midnight and her companion for the night had not yet arrived. She had been given several hours of extra preparation time, soaking luxuriously in a tub and being rubbed down with perfumed oils by Adung, the middle-aged woman who assisted the brothel's owner by watching over the girls. Lawan felt no special kinship to the harsh woman, but at least she was familiar. And at the moment, her ministrations were especially soothing.

Could it be Klahan? she wondered, knowing even as the thought passed through her mind that it was impossible. The gentle man who treated her with kindness was not a wealthy or important customer. Whoever had reserved her for the night must have paid a large sum of money, for this sort of treatment had only happened to her once before, and that had not turned out to be a pleasant experience. The man who had purchased her favors took advantage of her in every way imaginable, leaving her exhausted and bruised when he finally left the next morning. Was it possible he had come back? Lawan suppressed a shudder at the thought.

"Do you . . . do you know who is coming to be with me tonight?" she asked, wondering if Adung would tell her even if she knew.

The woman who was rubbing her back and shoulders with fragrant oils pinched her just enough to hurt but not enough to leave a mark. "What does it matter?" she snorted. "You are his property for the night, and he has paid well for that right. You have no say in the matter, so just do your job, and do it well. Perhaps he will be pleased with you and will return often. The boss man would like that."

Lawan squeezed back tears. The boss man might like the money she brought in for him tonight, but she doubted that she was going to like anything about it. If only Klahan could be with her instead, holding and caressing her, treating her as if she were special but never hurting her in any way. Oh, how she wished she could run away to be with him!

But of course that was impossible. She belonged to the boss man and always would. Like her older sister, Chanthra, Lawan would die in this horrible place, and there was nothing she could do about it.

"It's time," Adung said. "Put on that silk gown hanging on the door and then follow me. You'll be entertaining your customer in the special guest room tonight."

Hot tears stung Lawan's eyes at the memory of the one other night she'd spent in the guest room. So this was to be more of the same. She slipped into the gown and then followed Adung obediently to the room at the end of the hallway. The sweet smell of incense filled her nostrils the minute she opened the door and stepped inside. Before she could turn back to Adung who remained in the hall, the woman had closed the door and locked it from the outside. Lawan knew it would not be opened again until her customer arrived.

Glancing around the room with its muted lighting and soft music, she tried to avoid looking at the large bed with its crimson silk sheets folded back invitingly. How she wished she could close her eyes and make it go away, only to open them again and see the thin pallet that had served as her bed in her parents' home before she was kidnapped.

So long ago, she thought, straining to hold on to the memory. Had it really been only two years? It seemed so much longer—a lifetime ago. The chances that she would ever see that humble shack or her beloved parents again were nonexistent. This was her life now. Her only hope was her eternal home when at last she was released from this tortuous place to go and be with *phra yaeh suu*. Oh, if only it could be now, this very night, before the man came to hurt her!

But it was not to be. Lawan heard the key in the lock and braced herself. It would be a long night, and no doubt a painful one. She took a deep breath and turned to face her tormentor. Surprised, she realized it was not the same man who had spent the night with her in this room before. This man was older,

94

more so than Klahan, though obviously richer. He was also taller than Klahan and appeared to be strong.

Once again Lawan heard the door lock from the outside, and she knew she was trapped. Though it was already slightly past midnight, she imagined the man would stay with her until long after the sun had risen on Sunday morning.

He smiled and reached out to touch her cheek. "You are just as young and lovely as I was told," he said. "I believe we are going to have a very nice night together, dear Lawan."

The frightened girl swallowed and did her best to hide her fear, though she knew for certain that though the man might enjoy the hours that lay ahead, she certainly would not.

The pain in Francesca's right arm had been nearly unbearable. Even El Diablo had been mad when he finally came in response to her screams. He always told the customers they could do what they wanted with the girls, but they were not to cause any serious damage. Now her arm was broken, and El Diablo had banned her attacker from ever returning.

It was the closest the man she despised had ever come to treating her halfway decent. He had even taken her to the doctor who was kept on the payroll for just such emergencies. Now she was back in her room with her arm in a cast. Was it possible the injury might work out for the best and she'd get some time off work? Oh, to have at least a few days free from the awful men who came to her each night, using and abusing her and then leaving without a care! Surely even El Diablo himself would see the need for her to have a break from such activity.

The door to her room burst open then, and she cringed on her bed at the sight of El Diablo looking down at her. "How are you feeling?" he asked, his heavy dark mustache twitching as he spoke.

Her eyes widened at the thought that perhaps he cared for her after all. "A little better since the doctor gave me that shot," she admitted. "It's still sore though."

He smirked. "And it'll be sore for a while, but that's what happens when you try to resist one of the customers. That's what makes them get rough with you."

Francesca opened her mouth in protest, but then closed it again. What was the point? If she argued with him, he'd just get mad and slap her like he always did. It was better to be quiet. So much for thinking he cared about her.

"I brought you some extra pain pills," he said, placing two white tablets and a glass of water on the stand beside her bed. "You'll need them when your first customer gets here tonight."

Francesca gasped. "You mean . . . I have to work tonight, even after what happened?"

El Diablo glared down at her. "And why wouldn't you? It's Saturday, and tonight's our busiest time. Besides, you're not dead, are you? We lost a good customer because of you, and you need to make that up to us." He leaned down and breathed into her face. "So take your medicine and rest up while you can. Your first customer will be here in a few hours."

A sob rose up from Francesca's chest and lodged in her throat. Just when she thought things couldn't get any worse, they did. How much better it would have been if the man who broke her arm had broken her neck instead. For she had come to understand that death was the only escape she could ever hope for.

Chapter 13

Klahan was in agony. As Saturday night passed into Sunday morning, he groaned as he lay on his pallet in the corner of his humble home. He tried to blot out thoughts of what must be going on at this very moment between the disgusting man named Chai and the lovely young girl named Lawan.

"She will be mine one day," Klahan told himself, his teeth clenched as he spoke the words in an attempt to convince himself of their truth. "Tonight is but a necessary evil to make my plan work. What must be, must be. Just one night, and Chai will be convinced to help me get Lawan out of that brothel. And then . . ."

The thought of the remainder of his plan squeezed his heart with fear. One wrong step and he might lose not only Lawan but his very life. But what choice did he have? He had tried and tried to come up with another answer, some way of rescuing or even kidnapping Lawan without Chai's help, but there simply was no other way. He would have to trust that his former brother-in-law would be as taken with Lawan as he was, even though by the time the morning sunlight peeked through the window the horrible Chai would know the girl so much better than he.

"But only for a night," he reminded himself. "I could not bear it if he went to her again. No, after the desecration of this night, I will move quickly. Lawan will soon be mine, and never again will I have to endure the thought of her being with another man—especially Chai."

The thought comforted his heart only slightly, as he squeezed his eyes shut in a futile attempt to darken the images of a beautiful young girl being abused by a man who had no heart or mercy.

"I will make it up to you, Lawan," he whispered. "Once you are mine, I will treat you as you deserve. I will show you what it is to be truly loved and adored. Then you will give yourself to me gladly and willingly. You will see, sweet Lawan." He smiled in spite of his pain, as he thought yet again of how the young child's parents had named her so perfectly—Lawan, beautiful. "Yes, you are beautiful, Lawan. Your name fits as if it were created just for you. And soon I will possess your beauty for myself. No one else will ever touch you again. No one."

98

"Are you going to tell Jonathan about running into Mara?"

Leah stopped in the middle of the crowd, forcing several people to detour in order to avoid walking into her. She turned to Sarah and frowned. "Are you serious? Of course I am. Why wouldn't I?"

Sarah's blue eyes seemed to have lost their usual shine, as she blinked in what Leah recognized as her nervous or even guilty reaction. "Oh, no reason," Sarah answered, shrugging her shoulders as she spoke. "Just curious, that's all."

Leah grinned as she recalled Sarah's question earlier about whether or not Jonathan had found a girlfriend at college. So, maybe her best friend had a crush on Leah's big brother after all.

"You like him, don't you?"

Sarah's eyes grew wide, and her face paled. "I didn't say that."

"You didn't have to. It just took me a while to figure it out, that's all."

Sarah opened her mouth and then closed it again and turned away, resuming their trek to the next shop. Leah hurried to catch up.

"Come on, admit it," she urged. "It's not like I'm going to be mad or anything. I mean, he may be my brother but I also know he's a hunk. Girls have been following him around since he was ten."

Sarah stopped again, and this time her eyes flashed. "Exactly," she said. "So what chance do I have? I've had a thing for Jonathan since we were in junior high, but if you didn't even notice, how could I expect him to?" She pressed her lips together and shook her head before continuing. "I don't have a chance—never did and never will. So let's just forget about it, OK?"

"But, why?" Leah was determined now to dig deeper. "You know, I could drop some hints or—"

Sarah grabbed Leah's arm. "No," she ordered. "Don't you dare say a word—ever! I'd die if you did. I'd never come to your house again." She leaned close and lowered her voice, though the pitch intensified. "I do not want to talk about this. Do you understand?"

Leah felt her own eyes widen, as she stared at Sarah. It was obvious the girl was serious, even if she was being a bit melodramatic.

"Fine," Leah said at last, shrugging as if she were dismissing the topic but knowing full well that she wasn't. "We won't talk about it—for now anyway. But I really don't see what the big deal is."

99

With that she took off for the next store on their list, leaving Sarah to catch up at her own pace. But Leah couldn't wipe the smile off her face as she walked through the door to the shop filled with jewelry and trinkets and loud music. First Mara, and now Sarah. Her Saturday afternoon had just become a whole lot more interesting than she'd ever expected.

The sunlight streamed through the window, awakening Lawan and throwing her into confusion. Where was she? Her room was never this bright, even during the heat of the day. And her mattress certainly wasn't this soft.

She squinted, glancing around to get her bearings. Her heart raced as her memories came into focus. The tall man who had called her by name and continually told her how beautiful and special she was — he was nothing like Klahan, who told her those same things and yet never took advantage of the favors he had paid for. No, the man who had paid extra to have her all to himself had certainly taken advantage of every favor he had paid for, several times over, but at least he had been kind and had not beaten her as she had expected.

Another glance at the opposite side of the bed and around the room assured her that he had already left and had apparently covered her before doing so, allowing her to sleep at last. Lawan was strangely touched by the gesture, as she wondered why the man had asked for her in the first place and paid so much extra just to leave after a few hours. She had expected him to stay for several more hours but was greatly relieved that he had not.

Slowly she rose from the bed and found the silk gown she

had been wearing the night before now lying on the floor. Picking it up and slipping it over her head, she sighed at the softness, knowing she would not be allowed to keep it once Adung came to fetch her and take her back to her room.

It had been a strange night, but at least it had not been as bad as many she had experienced since coming here. "*Kap koon*," she whispered. "Thank you, mister, for not beating me. And thank You, *phra yaeh suu*, for bringing me through another night alive."

She realized then the sunlight was indeed streaming through the large window, something she was not privileged to see in her usual room with its one tiny window placed too high for her to peer through. Slowly, cautiously, she tiptoed to the source of light that beckoned her now, her heart racing at the thought that she could be in a lot of trouble if Adung or the boss man came in and caught her. But the sunshine and the thought of seeing what she had heard were lovely gardens just outside this particular room's window was just too tempting to resist.

Before she could position herself to pull back the sheer drapes and feast her eyes on a sight she had nearly forgotten existed, she heard the key in the lock and scurried back to the bed, jumping under the covers and turning toward the wall, willing herself to breathe deeply and evenly.

When Adung's voice ordered her to get up, she continued her ruse and pretended to wake up from a deep sleep, rolling over and expressing surprise at the fact that her customer had already gone.

"Do not worry about that," Adung said, motioning her to get up and follow her from the room. "You had an easy time last night, so now you can help the day girls with their customers. Come on. The first one will be waiting for you shortly."

Chapter 13

Lawan sighed and followed the woman down the hallway, back to the darkness of the room that had become her home over the past couple of years, the room where her sister Chanthra had died . . . the room where yet another man would soon arrive to have his way with her once again. Would it ever end? Lawan wanted desperately to believe it would, but she could not help but think that perhaps Chanthra had escaped the only way possible. It was an escape that was sounding better to her with each passing day.

Chapter 14

I can't believe we were gone nearly all day," Rosanna observed as she and Michael walked through the door that led from the garage to the cheerful, airy kitchen and flipped on the light. "I feel bad about leaving Leah by herself for so long."

"It's Saturday night," Michael reminded her, closing and locking the door behind him. "And it's not like you didn't call and let her know."

Rosanna smiled as she opened the refrigerator and peered inside. "True. And she said she was fine with staying home alone, especially after spending most of the day at the mall with Sarah. Still . . ." She turned, startled to find him standing so close, nearly breathing down her neck.

He grinned. "Surprise." He bent down to kiss her and then pulled away just enough to gaze into her eyes. "So what are you doing looking in the refrigerator? You can't be hungry after that big dinner we had."

Rosanna laughed. "Not a bit. I just thought you might be thirsty."

Michael shook his head. "Always thinking about everyone else, aren't you? Then again, that's what I love about you."

"Not the only thing, I hope."

"Let's see." Michael lifted his eyes toward the ceiling, as if trying to think of an answer. "How do I love thee?" he asked, looking back down at her. "Let me count the ways."

She giggled. "You're a nut, you know that?" She stood on her toes and kissed his chin. "But a romantic nut, and I like that."

"Hey, you're home!"

Leah's voice interrupted their playful exchange, and Rosanna felt her cheeks flame as she turned toward her daughter, who stood just a few feet away, dressed in her favorite flowery pajamas.

"Just got here," Michael said, releasing his hold on Rosanna and walking over to plant a kiss on the top of Leah's tousled hair. "What have you been doing all evening?"

Leah shrugged and sat down at the old maple dinette set in the breakfast nook. "Reading mostly. And waiting for Jonathan to get home from work. He promised to bring some pizza home."

"That'll be a few hours yet," Rosanna said, still standing in front of the open refrigerator. "Can I fix you a snack to hold you over?"

Leah's eyes lit up. "How about one of my favorite sandwiches?"

Rosanna smiled, her heart warming to the familiar task. Grilled ham and cheese sandwiches had been her daughter's favorite comfort food since she was a little girl. There was nothing she'd enjoy more than fixing one for her right now.

"Coming right up," she said. "Michael, how about you?"

"Are you kidding me?" He laughed and rubbed his stomach before sitting down next to Leah. "I'm still stuffed from all that seafood we had an hour or so ago."

"Me too," Rosanna agreed, rummaging around for all the necessary ingredients. "But I just thought I should ask."

She'd scarcely set the sandwich fixings on the counter and closed the door when Leah dropped the bombshell. "You won't believe who Sarah and I ran into at the mall today."

Rosanna turned from the counter and fixed her eyes on Leah. Something in the girl's voice told her it was more than a casual meeting with an old friend. Michael's attention was riveted on Leah as well.

"Mara," she said simply, and then paused before continuing. "Sarah and I were just walking around the mall when I glanced over and saw her. I was pretty sure it was her, even though her hair was a lot shorter. And when I saw her eyes, I knew for sure."

Rosanna set down the knife that she had been about to use to spread mayonnaise on the bread and instead walked over to join Michael and Leah at the table. "Are you sure?" she asked, even though her daughter had just told her she was.

Leah nodded. "Absolutely. We even went over and talked to her. She looked good. Beautiful as ever. And just like Barbara Whiting said, she's living and working right here in San Diego." After another pause, Leah added, "Sarah asked me if I was going to tell Jonathan about seeing her."

Rosanna raised her eyebrows. "And are you?"

"Sure. Why not?"

Rosanna couldn't think of any reason not to do so, and yet a vague resistance gnawed at her. "Exactly," she said at last. "Why not?" Her eyes met Michael's then, and she knew he was wrestling with the same thoughts and emotions that she was experiencing. The last two years had been relatively peaceful ones for their family, but somehow it seemed as if all that was about to change.

It was Sunday morning in Thailand, and Chai was back home, sitting at his table and waiting for the old woman who cooked his meals to serve him some much-needed breakfast. The long night had exhausted him, but it had exhilarated him as well. For once in Klahan's miserable life, he had been right. The girl was beautiful—exceptionally so. And with the right training and attention, she could bring in a fortune for years to come.

Chai smiled. She would also give him all the pleasure he needed on a personal level. And as for Klahan, he was easily cut out of the deal. The fool had already given him everything he needed to arrange the transaction himself. Why did he need Klahan? He did not; therefore his former brother-in-law was expendable. Chai would go straight to Lawan's owner and buy the girl outright. The girl's boss man would no doubt drive a hard bargain, but money talked, and money was something Chai possessed. Soon he would also possess the girl whose name meant beautiful, and there would not be a thing that the peasant Klahan could do about it.

Smiling as the old woman placed a pot of steaming tea in front of him, he realized how much sweeter this business deal would be simply because it would give him yet another opportunity to outsmart the stupid man who had come to him thinking to turn a profit and get the girl for himself.

She is mine now, Chai thought. *And I cannot wait to see your face, Klahan, when you realize that.*

Chai waited as the old woman poured his tea and then dismissed her with a wave of his hand. His eyes were heavy, but his heart was light. It would be a good day indeed.

Francesca's arm throbbed, despite the additional pain pills she had swallowed. She still couldn't believe El Diablo had stooped

106

so low as to send three customers to her that night, one right after the other. And none had been in the least concerned or careful about her recent injury.

All was quiet now, as she lay in her dark room, hoping the pain in her arm would soon subside but knowing that, even if it did, the pain in her heart would never ease. The memory of her home in Juarez, poor and simple though it was, teased her with images of sunlight dancing on her mother's dark hair as she stood over a tub of hot water and scrubbed the family's clothes. How Francesca regretted the many times she had argued with her mother when the older woman ordered her to help with such backbreaking tasks! And how Francesca now wished that she was back in that familiar setting with her arms plunged into that hot water, scrubbing and rinsing and spending time with the people she loved. Instead she had foolishly put herself in a position where her family had not been around to protect her. Now she was paying a terrible price.

Would this be her life until the day she died? If so, how quickly would that day come? Francesca couldn't imagine that she would survive long in her current situation. But with each passing day and every customer who came to her room to abuse her, she found the prospect of death more appealing. None of the men who came to her, however, were as mean and evil as El Diablo himself. Never before had she realized the depth to which her hatred could sink, or how easily she could kill someone if given the chance. She now knew that, given a chance, she wouldn't hesitate to plunge a knife into her owner's dark heart . . . and then to dance with joy to know that he was burning forever in the flames of hell.

107

Chapter 15

Sunday morning dawned slightly less bright than the usual Southern California summer day, but Jonathan didn't mind. He'd gotten in late the night before, surprised that even Leah hadn't waited up for him—or at least for the pizza he'd brought her. But she'd left him a note saying she'd already eaten and would wait and have the pizza for breakfast.

He yawned and stretched in a room that still held hints of gray, which he decided was no doubt the reason he'd shut off the alarm and gone back to sleep. Most mornings the sunlight blazed through his window and forced his eyes open even before the alarm did its thing. But not today.

Glancing at the now silent alarm, he realized he couldn't wait much longer. Leah was no doubt already done with her shower and downstairs heating leftover pizza in the microwave. And he knew without even checking that both his parents were showered and dressed and ready for church. Jonathan was relatively certain that neither of them had ever walked in late for a service in their entire lives; as a result, he and Leah had learned to make sure they were ready on time as well.

Throwing off the covers, he pulled himself up and grabbed some clean slacks and a shirt from the closet. As he fumbled through a dresser drawer looking for matching socks, his mind snapped to attention at the memory of the P.S. Leah had added to her note the night before: "I have something to tell you about Mara."

His heart accelerated, much as it had when he first read the words. And then he had lain awake for nearly an hour, wondering what Leah's news about Mara might be. Well, there was only one way to find out. Heading for the bathroom, he prepared for a quick shower so he could zip downstairs and snag his sister for some alone talk before leaving for church.

Jonathan frowned as he stepped into the warm water. Why did he think he needed to talk to Leah alone? Or was it just that he wanted to guard his reactions to whatever he might learn about Mara? Most likely that was the reason. Leah would probably read his emotions when she told him her news, but he'd just as soon his parents weren't around to do the same.

He stuck his head under the spray. It was great to come home for the summer and be with his family, but it sure made it tough to have any privacy.

Barbara knew she had to tread lightly when it came to Mara. The girl was doing well—better than most who had come out of such a terrible situation—but Barbara knew she was fragile. And though Mara had been the one to initiate the contact, Barbara also knew she could pull away again at any time.

Still, it was important to re-stress the need for Mara to report to her immediately—or to the police if she preferred, though Barbara doubted that was the case—if she ever again spotted the man and the teenage girl. But was that really the reason she was considering calling Mara that Sunday morning? Why not wait until afternoon, once church was over? In fact, why even call at all? Did she really have anything new to say to

Mara, or was it just an excuse to try to strengthen the tenuous bond between them?

Barbara sighed. She already knew the truth. Despite having worked with numerous trafficking victims, Mara stood out to Barbara. There was something about her that made the older woman want to take her home and mother her, despite the fact that she herself had never married or had children of her own. But more than that, Barbara had such a spiritual burden for the lovely young woman. She couldn't think of Mara without sensing the need to pray for her — not only for her physical protection and emotional healing, but most of all for her salvation. Barbara was nearly certain that God was calling Mara to Himself, and that He expected Barbara to pray to that end.

"All right, Lord," she said, grabbing her purse and heading for the door. "I know what You want me to do. You put Mara on my heart this morning so I'd pray for her, not so I'd call and invite her to church, though that's what I'd like to do. Forgive me for trying to get in the way of what You're doing, Father. But oh, work in that girl's heart, please! She's been through so much, Lord. I can't even begin to imagine the scars she carries. But You can heal her, Father, and I know You want to."

She closed and locked the door behind her and headed for her car, parked in the driveway. The sun was just starting to peek through a thin layer of summer fog. By the time she got out of church in a couple of hours, the day would no doubt be as sunny and bright as she had long since grown accustomed to in this part of the country. She just hoped that California sunshine would melt that little chunk of icy fear that still lodged in her heart when she thought of Mara — and also of the young girl that Mara had seen in the café. Barbara imagined Mara was right in what she suspected about the man and the girl, and it grieved her to think what that frail teenager might be enduring at this very moment.

***

Chai was not one to let an opportunity pass him by, particularly once he had made up his mind about what he wanted. It was Sunday evening, and it had taken him less than twenty-four hours from the first time he laid eyes on Lawan until he sent a message to her boss man, offering to buy her for a handsome amount. Chai was also a savvy businessman, and he knew Lawan's owner would not accept the initial offer, despite its generosity. The man would decline, protesting his affection for the young girl and her value to him at the brothel. But it was all about bargaining, and Chai could play the game better than most. Besides, he had the funds he needed to play as long as it took to win. When the courier returned with a note in response to Chai's offer, he paid the man and closed the door in his face before returning to his favorite chair to study the words folded up in the piece of paper.

Chai nearly laughed aloud at the predictability of the note. The man understood Chai's interest in the exceptionally beautiful young girl, but she was not for sale. Particularly because of her youth, the man could not part with her because she had many good years yet ahead of her. And even if it were not for the money—Chai could no longer hold back a chuckle at that point—the boss man had to decline the offer simply because Lawan was very dear to him.

Chai snorted. Dear, indeed! She was a commodity, nothing more. A lovely one, yes, but an object to be used for the man's profit. And now it was up to Chai to convince the slimy weasel that he could better profit by selling Lawan than by keeping her in his stable of girls.

Another offer then, Chai thought, *while the thought is still fresh in his mind. This time it will be an offer he cannot afford to decline, more money than he could make off Lawan if she lived another ten years — which she never will if she continues where she is. But with me? With the best food and care, the highest rank of clientele? Yes. Then she could easily live another ten years, possibly even longer — and remain beautiful and healthy in the process.*

He smiled. *And in addition to recouping all my investment plus some, I will have the personal services of little Lawan for myself. She will live here with me, and I will share her only with those I feel are worthy. It will be the best life the poor wretch can expect, and certainly better than what she has now.*

Pleased with his own generosity and wise business sense, Chai wrote out his offer and prepared to call the courier once again. This time he was certain that Lawan's owner would gleefully accept.

Chapter 16

Klahan had closed up shop early that Sunday afternoon, determined not to miss anything that went on at his former brother-in-law's home. He hated losing out on even the small amount of money he would earn by keeping his stall open, but the situation with Lawan took precedence over everything else right now. Besides, if everything worked as planned, he would not need the vegetable stand any longer. He and Lawan would have enough money to live comfortably for years to come — compliments of Chai.

It was easy to blend in with his surroundings as he sat quietly behind the bushes near a house across the street from Chai's, a slight breeze cooling the sweat that nearly drenched his body. Klahan wondered how much of that sweat was due to the hot, muggy weather and how much to the knowledge of what might lie ahead. Either way, he was familiar enough with the layout of Chai's home to realize it was highly unlikely that the man would spot him. Besides, the disgusting man was probably busy scheming to get Lawan away from the brothel and to eliminate Klahan's involvement in the entire situation.

Klahan paid closer attention now that the sun was down. It was more likely that Chai would send for the courier again now that it was dark. This time, Klahan knew, the offer would be greater — far beyond Lawan's owner's ability or inclination to refuse. The plan would soon be in place, and if Klahan had predicted even one of Chai's actions incorrectly, Klahan could be dead before the night was over. Then Lawan would truly belong to Chai, and that was not a thought Klahan could endure, even if he were already dead.

He smiled at the thought, even as he strained his eyes for movement on the street. Klahan knew with certainty that Chai would cut him out of all future plans for Lawan; he knew too that if he gave Chai any trouble about it, Chai would not hesitate to kill him. Therefore Klahan would have to act first.

The slight sound of shuffling feet on the evening breeze caught his attention, and he stood to attention and peered closer at the figure moving toward Chai's front door. Was it the courier?

Yes! Klahan's patience had paid off. The man had come and would soon leave to deliver Chai's written offer to the man who owned Lawan. The deal would be sealed before sunrise, and Klahan knew that Chai would trust no one else to pick up the girl and bring her to his home. Chai would personally go for her, and when he did, Klahan would be ready. If his plan worked as he so desperately hoped, Lawan would at last be his before another morning had come and gone.

Chai could scarcely contain his excitement. Lawan's owner had greedily and readily accepted the generous offer, and now he awaited Chai's arrival to make the exchange. Chai would keep him waiting just long enough to make him anxious to complete the transaction quickly—but not so long that Chai and his new possession would not return home before sunrise.

Chai stood in his room and admired himself in the mirror. He had chosen a simple but elegant white silk shirt and dark trousers, affirming his superiority to the lowly brothel owner. Chai wanted little Lawan to be duly impressed with her new master. After all, she would exist to do his bidding from this night forward.

The memory of Klahan, cowering in Chai's entryway as he stood, several inches shorter than Chai, presenting his plan, caused the self-assured Chai to laugh aloud. The small man who had once wooed Chai's sister into an ill-suited marriage that had eventually cost her life would never see one bit of profit from the purchase of Lawan. Chai had not yet decided whether or not he would kill the man he had despised for ruining his sister's life, but Chai was certain of one thing: Klahan cared for Lawan and wanted her for himself. For that, as well as Chai's sister's death, the despicable little man whose name meant "brave" would pay dearly. Perhaps allowing him to suffer by keeping him from what he wanted most might be the best way to exact that suffering.

Chai smiled at his image in the mirror. He was indeed a tall, imposing figure, still strong and handsome, unlike the pathetic Klahan. Little Lawan would soon come to worship the man she would call "Master," and there would be nothing Klahan could do about it.

Lawan could not imagine why she'd had no customers yet that night, while her roommate, Kulap, was already entertaining her second of the evening. Lawan lay on her mattress with her back to the pair, ignoring the sometimes muffled sounds that drifted her way. She had long since become accustomed to the familiar noises and easily tuned them out, as she allowed her mind to focus on more pleasant times—times before she was kidnapped and brought to this place of no escape. Times even after she arrived when the older girl, Chanthra, had helped her through the initial adjustment.

Chanthra, Lawan spoke silently. *You finally escaped, didn't you? You went to be with* phra yaeh suu. *How beautiful it must be there! Are our parents there as well by now?* Lawan imagined they were, as she could not fathom their surviving the loss of all three of their daughters. They had given up Chanthra to what they thought was a home with a well-to-do family, though that had hardly been the case. And then they had given up Mali, their baby, to be adopted by a family in a faraway place called America. Oh, how Lawan prayed Mali had fared better than Chanthra!

Or than me, she thought. *Why did I ever wander from the village? If only I'd stayed near our home, as Maae warned me. How she must have grieved when I never returned! Oh, Maae, I am so very sorry!*

The door opened then, and Lawan rolled onto her back to see the man who had no doubt purchased time with her. Her eyebrows raised in surprise at the sight of Adung standing in the doorway. The woman ignored Kulap and her guest, and they seemed not even to notice that anyone had entered. But Adung came straight to Lawan's bed and stood over her, glaring down.

"You have caught the eye of a fine businessman," she hissed in a loud whisper. "The one from the other night who took you to the private room. He has returned for you."

Lawan raised her eyebrows in surprise but stood immediately to her feet. No doubt Adung wanted her to bathe and prepare for another night with the same man. Lawan swallowed, hoping the man would be as easy with her tonight as he had been previously.

118

Adung grabbed her arm and shoved her toward the door. "Hurry," she said. "We must bathe and dress you quickly. He will be here shortly to pick you up."

Lawan frowned. Pick her up? What did that mean? Did she dare ask?

Before she could decide, Adung, who followed closely behind her as they scurried down the hallway toward the room with the large bathtub, said, "The boss man is quite pleased with the large sum the man has paid for you. You will belong to him now, to do with as he pleases. You will even live at his house, which I understand is quite large and expensive."

Lawan stopped without thinking, nearly causing Adung to trip over her. The woman smacked the back of her head. "Stupid girl," she said. "You nearly tripped me. Now hurry up and get into the tub. We don't have time to prepare you as we did before, but we will put you in a fine dress and send you on your way. It should not be difficult to replace you with another girl before the week is over, so we will lose no money over you. In fact, the boss man tells me we have earned enough from your sale to make up for several girls like you." The woman laughed and shoved her into the bathroom. "Now hurry up," she repeated. "We haven't much time."

Lawan's thoughts were spiraling as she climbed into the already filled tub. The warm water felt luxurious as she sank down into it, but her heart thudded against her ribs in fear. Though the man had treated her better than most who came to this place, she did not know him or have any idea what it meant for someone to buy her "to do with as he pleases." What would he please to do with her? This place she now lived had brought her nothing but pain and heartbreak, but at least it was familiar. It was her last contact with her sister Chanthra, and she had even begun to feel somewhat of a kinship with Kulap. What was to happen to her now?

Hot tears filtered through her closed eyes as she tried to block out her fear and pray. Was it possible that her life might become more tolerable now? The thought that it might become worse was something Lawan simply could not allow herself to consider.

Chapter 17

Klahan was afraid to breathe. He had managed to carry out his plan so far, and that was nothing short of a miracle. He had slipped into Chai's house soon after the pompous man had left to retrieve Lawan. Only the old housekeeper remained, and Klahan knew she was nearly deaf. Once the old woman had gone to bed, which she always did soon after sundown, she did not hear another thing until she awoke in the morning and reinserted her hearing aids.

Little had changed in the ostentatious house since Klahan and his wife had visited here years ago. How Klahan had despised those visits, knowing that Chai looked down upon him and pitied his sister for marrying what he considered a worthless man.

But who has the upper hand now, Chai? He smiled, secure in the knowledge that when the man returned home and came to his room with Lawan, Klahan's presence would not be detected. He was completely hidden behind the heavy damask curtains that covered Chai's extensive and well-stocked closet, but Klahan would hear every sound made within the room's four walls and would therefore know exactly when to make his move.

His heart raced as he heard the front door open. Chai and Lawan had arrived! He closed his eyes, imagining he would hear better as he strained to make out the words Chai was speaking as his voice drew nearer.

"You are home, my little Lawan. This is where you will live from now on, here with me."

There was a pause, but the girl did not respond. Chai soon picked up where he'd left off, the sound of his voice nearly at the bedroom door now. "And this, my own little beauty, is where you will learn to be my personal slave, to do my bidding and to please me in every way. If you learn well, I will treat you well. If not . . ."

His voice trailed off, and Klahan's heart squeezed in anger at the implication of the unspoken words.

The bedroom door opened then, and Chai said, "But let us not discuss anything unpleasant on your first night here, for surely you will never do anything to displease me, will you?"

When again there was no response from Lawan, Klahan swallowed and waited. Chai's voice rose a notch then as he said, "Did you not hear me, Lawan? Though I want you to be silent unless I tell you to speak, I most certainly expect you to answer when I ask you a question. Do you understand?"

A strangled "yes" was the first word Klahan heard from the girl he loved, and it nearly forced him from his hiding place. But he stood still and waited. He must not move until the time was exactly right. He could not afford to make even one mistake.

"Good," Chai said, a smile returning to his voice. "Now answer my previous question. I said, you will never do anything to displease me, will you?"

"No," Lawan whispered.

"No, what?" Chai demanded. "What did I tell you to call me on the way over here? Have you forgotten already? Must I remind you so quickly?"

"No, master," Lawan said, her voice trembling. "I have not forgotten . . . and I will not displease you, master. I will do anything you say."

"And you will love every minute of it," Chai growled. "Is that clear?"

"Yes, master."

"Good. Now, I have paid a lot of money for you, and I intend to get my money's worth, beginning now. Please disrobe and go into the bathroom, over there." He paused, and Klahan imagined Chai pointing. "Take a bath and then come to me here. I will be waiting for you on the bed."

"But, master, I . . . I took a bath before you came for me."

The sound of a slap and then a yelp of pain filled the air, and Klahan nearly exploded from his hiding place. Only his determination to carry out his desperate plan kept his feet still.

123

"Do not ever question me," Chai growled, his words low and menacing. "Now go. Take a bath and prepare for your first night in your new home, for this is how it will be so long as you continue to please me. Though I may share you with others who are willing to pay me well for my generosity, only I will own you and only I will decide what is to be done with you each day or night. Do you understand, sweet Lawan?"

The girl was obviously weeping by then, as her words broke through her sobs. "Yes, master. I understand."

The sound of a thud and another cry of pain, which Klahan could only imagine came from the girl being tossed in the direction of the bathroom and landing against something, nearly elicited a cry from Klahan's lips as well. But again he held himself still. Just a little while longer.

Despite the warm, perfumed water, Lawan could not stop shaking. She had wanted so much to believe that her life would be at least somewhat better now that she would belong to one man rather than the owner of a brothel, but it would not be so. Though her life had definitely changed, nothing was better. Nothing would ever be better, she imagined, until she followed her sister Chanthra and went home to be with *phra yaeh suu*.

"You have been in there long enough," called the man whom Lawan now knew was named Chai but whom she would refer to as master. "Come to me at once."

Shivering more from fear than from the chill of climbing out of the warm tub, she pulled a soft pink towel from the rack and wrapped it around her. The man would surely take it from her soon enough, but at least she could emerge from the bathroom with a shred of dignity.

Leaving wet footprints behind her, Lawan stepped through the door into the bedroom. She gasped at the sight of her new owner, sprawled out in a silk robe on the bed, eyeing her hungrily. Though she had already spent one night with him, she had quickly forgotten how big the man was—and how muscular. He could snap her in two if she displeased him. She tried to hold back the tears, but they spilled over onto her cheeks, even as she moved obediently to his side.

The man's dark eyebrows lifted as he looked into her face. "You are crying, my beautiful one?" He smiled then and reached out to touch her cheek. His hands were smooth, like those of one who had never done hard labor. "Surely it is from joy," he said, caressing her face with one hand while he pulled her close with the other. "Come, sweet Lawan, let us celebrate our new life together. This will be the first of many wonderful nights that we will share. You belong to me now, only to me." His face was close to hers, and she could feel his warm breath as he spoke, his voice making her flesh crawl. "And do not worry. If I decide to allow someone to purchase you for a night, you will still be mine. You are an asset to me and will bring me much wealth, as I will only lend you to very special customers. But ours will be much more than a business arrangement, for I am your master and you are my own sweet pet. No one will take you from me, Lawan, so do not worry. As I told you, you are mine forever—so long as you do not displease me. Do you understand, sweet Lawan?"

Lawan nodded, afraid to speak but knowing that Chai might become angry if she did not answer him. She swallowed and managed to squeak, "Yes, master."

He rewarded her with another smile and kissed her forehead. "Climb up here beside me," he said. "My shoulders are tense. I would like you to rub them before we get started."

With that he turned on his stomach. When Lawan did not move, he spoke again, though without lifting his head. "Now, Lawan. Do not keep me waiting."

The tone in his voice spurred her on, and she climbed onto the bed beside him and began using her tiny hands to rub his huge shoulders. His face was turned to the side and his eyes were closed, as if he were enjoying her ministrations, and so she continued even after her hands grew tired. How long must she continue, she wondered. She imagined until he told her to stop.

And then a hand over her mouth, coming from behind, prevented a scream as she was tossed aside and another body took her place over Chai. The man had a large knife in his hand, and before Lawan could scream, he plunged it with the full force of his body into Chai's back. Lawan's new master's eyes and mouth opened wide, but the smaller man continued to stab him in the neck and head and back. Warm blood squirted everywhere, even onto Lawan, and she cried out in terror. Who was this man, and why was he attacking Chai? Would he kill her next?

The thought energized her, and she sprang to her feet, ready to race out of the room and toward the front door. And then she heard the voice.

"Lawan, wait!"

The familiarity stopped her midstride. Wide-eyed, she turned back to see the gentle man named Klahan, the man whose name meant brave and whom she had imagined she might be in love with, straddling Chai's now lifeless, bloodied body, the knife still raised in his hand. He too was covered with blood, nearly as much as Chai. Klahan stared at her, the fear in his eyes nearly as evident as the terror in her heart.

"Do not run away," he said, his voice hoarse now as tears flooded his eyes. "Please, Lawan. I did this for you. For you! To save you. To get you out of that brothel and also away from Chai. I could not bear for you to be hurt and used any longer."

Lawan wanted to run, but her mind cried out, *Where would you go?* And her heart would not let her move. Had Klahan come to rescue her? Had he killed her master for her? Was she safe with Klahan, as she had often imagined she might be? Or was this a trick so he could also plunge the dripping dagger into her?

As if he could read her thoughts, Klahan dropped the knife and slowly climbed down from the bed. He held out his arms to her. "Come, Lawan. I will take care of you now. No one will ever hurt you again. I promise."

Lawan's heart pounded so loud she wondered if Klahan could hear it. Oh, how she wanted to believe him! But the horror of what she had just seen . . .

"I know," Klahan said, his voice gentle and his eyes still brimming with tears. "I did a terrible thing. But he was a terrible man, and he was going to hurt you, just like all the others. I could not let that happen. I love you, Lawan. I will protect you. Come to me. Please."

Slowly the girl stepped forward. One step, two. Then she was face-to-face with him as he knelt down beside her and took her into his arms. The rusty smell and slippery feel of the blood made her recoil, but his soothing words and tender touch finally won her over, and she relaxed in his arms. Was it possible that her ordeal was finally over? Had she at last found someone who would care for her and treat her with kindness and love, as her parents had once done? If so, she would love and serve Klahan forever—and gladly so, though she closed her eyes to block out the sight of the bloody, lifeless man on the bed behind them.

Would the police come? The thought once again turned her relieved heart to ice, as it raced with the implications. If Klahan was arrested, what would happen to her? Would they throw her in jail too? Return her to the brothel? Turn her out into the street?

Lawan began to cry, sobbing out her concerns to the man who gently stroked her hair. "Do not worry, little one," he whispered. "I have a plan. But we must act quickly. Do exactly as I tell you, all right?"

Lawan pulled back and looked into his eyes. Could she trust him? She swallowed. She had no choice. She would trust him and pray very, very hard.

She nodded. "Yes."

"Good. I want you to put on your clothes and go wait by the front door. Do not go outside until I get there. Just stand very, very still, and do not make a sound. Do you understand?"

Lawan nodded again and dressed quickly. When Klahan stood up and went to open the bedroom door, she hurried out and made her way to the front door where she had so recently entered with Chai.

And then she waited, just as Klahan had instructed. She heard footsteps, a door opening, a brief and muffled cry, and then a door closing and more footsteps. What was going on? And who had cried out? Should she go and check on Klahan? No, he told her to wait, and so she would, no matter what she heard.

The first wisps of smoke were beginning to tease her nose when Klahan hurried out to her. "Come," he said. "We must go quickly, but not this way." He picked her up and rushed to another door that led into a dark alley. "They won't see us leaving from here," he whispered. "Just be quiet. Do not make a sound."

And then they were running through the night, Lawan bouncing on Klahan's shoulder, as he stumbled several times but never fell, his breathing becoming ragged as they continued down darkened streets that Lawan did not recognize, never darting into the light or moving among other people. At last they came to a very small shack, where Klahan opened the door and let them both inside.

"We are home," he said. "For now. We will rest here and then clean up before moving on tomorrow night, when it is dark once again. It is safe here for now, but if your former owner finds out you were not killed in the blaze, he just might come looking for you. We must be far away by then."

Klahan set her down and lit the candle that sat on a small table in the middle of the one-room abode. "Here," he said. "I have buckets of water and clean clothes all ready for us. When we are cleaned up, I will fix you something to eat, and then you can rest. I know you must be very tired."

Lawan's mind swirled from one thought to another. So Klahan had not only killed Chai but the housekeeper too . . . and he had set the house on fire. The realization caused

128

her confidence in the man who had rescued her to falter. The man was a killer. How could she trust him?

But he had done it for her. And now he was going to clean her up and feed her and let her rest. At that moment, she could not imagine anything she would like more. Her mind was made up. She would trust him. She would love and serve him and stay at his side so long as he would have her. For deep down she knew that she had no other choice. And so far, at least, he had not done one thing to hurt her.

Less than an hour later, as the predawn light of Monday morning moved into the Golden Triangle area of Thailand, Lawan slept peacefully, her head on the shoulder of the man whose name meant "brave" and who had rescued her at last.

Jack had been known as Alley Cat for so long he scarcely remembered ever having another name. Besides, he was rather proud of the nickname. It fit him—stealthy, sly, quiet, and yes, sneaky. Some might consider the comparison an insult, but not Jack. He had earned it over many years of hard work.

He told himself this assignment was no different, though it had a personal element to it. Truthfully, though, he would never have taken it if it weren't for his little brother, Tom. Just the thought of him sitting in prison nearly tore Jack's heart out. He'd do anything to help Tom—always had and always would.

Turning a corner and melting into the background as much as possible on this dark Sunday evening, Alley Cat did his best to live up to his name as he prowled the back streets and alleys of Chula Vista where his target had been spotted.

Mara. Strange name, he mused. *Never knew anybody with that name before. I wonder what she did to make this Jefe dude so mad? Must have been really bad.*

He shrugged to himself and paused as a couple of guys burst out of a bar onto the street, laughing and stumbling and obviously more than slightly intoxicated. Alley Cat doubted that either of them was sober enough to drive, though they headed straight for an old pickup truck parked nearby.

Not my problem, he reminded himself. *If they want to wrap themselves around a tree, that's their business. I just need to find this Mara chick.*

He refused to allow his mind to go to the next step and all that he had been ordered to do once he located Mara. Jack personally found the assignment more than a bit distasteful, but what choice did he have? He had to protect Tom, and right now this was his only shot. Besides, this Jefe guy had made sure he knew that if he didn't follow through on what he'd been ordered to do to Mara, Tom would endure the exact torture that had been meant for the girl. However bad Jack might feel about what he'd been told to do to Mara, he wasn't about to let Tom suffer in her place. And it was a given that this Jefe meant business.

Another weird name, he thought. *Mexican for boss—Jefe—but boss of what? He's doing some major time, so it must be something big. No doubt this Mara chick had something to do with it. Probably ratted him out or something, and now he wants revenge.*

He shrugged to himself. He almost never hurt anyone unnecessarily. Sure, he'd had to defend himself a few times, meaning that he'd hurt a couple of people pretty bad. But he'd never been snagged for it. His rap sheet showed nothing but breaking and entering and petty theft charges. He imagined

130

that's why Jefe had been willing to let him take this job. Prison gossip traveled fast, and Alley Cat knew his strength and ability to cause major injury to people who threatened him while still having a relatively clean record made him the perfect candidate for the job. He just hoped he could pull it off without tarnishing his choir boy image.

Jack nearly laughed at the thought but managed to restrain himself. He liked to remain as invisible as possible, and laughing out loud would definitely draw attention. With his lips pressed together, he continued silently down the street, just blocks from the ocean, passing various shops, now closed for the day, and an occasional restaurant or café where the tantalizing smells of pizza, fried fish, and Mexican food drifted out on the night air, making his stomach rumble.

I should've had something to eat before coming out here, he thought. *But hey, business first. Can't let anything get in the way of protecting my little brother. Been looking out for Tommy since we were kids, and just because he caught a bad break and got sent up for a couple of years doesn't mean I'm going to let him suffer any more than necessary now.* If doing what he had to do to this Mara person would offer Tom the protection he needed in prison, then Jack would carry out his orders. And he'd do it well too — not just for his brother's sake but for the sake of his own reputation. Once Alley Cat accepted an assignment, he took pride in his work, whatever it might be.

Chapter 18

It had been an exceptionally busy afternoon and evening at the café, and Mara was more than ready to clock out and head home now that it was finally closing time. One last couple lingered at a booth toward the back, and Mara had gone to check on them more than once, asking if they'd like dessert, clearing away their plates, and even laying the bill down in front of them. But the young lovebirds hardly noticed her. Mara wasn't even sure why they'd bothered to come in since they'd scarcely touched their food. They'd spent the last couple of hours gazing into one another's eyes and speaking in low, hushed tones, occasionally stopping for a light kiss or two.

Mara sighed. Enough already! The open sign on the front door had already been turned over to read closed, and even the cook had gone home. Julio, the busboy, was nearly done with the dishes, and Mara had finished cleaning the counter and filling the salt and pepper shakers at each of the tables. Maybe if she flicked the lights off and on it might catch their attention.

She shrugged. It was worth a try. Flipping the light switch twice, she kept her eyes on the lingering customers. Sure enough, they broke eye contact and turned in her direction, blinking in obvious surprise.

The man with the close-cut blond hair was the first to speak, as he glanced down at his watch and then back at Mara. "Hey, sorry about that. I didn't realize it was so late. We . . . kind of lost track of time."

His date's cheeks flushed and she giggled. They both looked to be in their early twenties, and watching them brought back the memory of another couple who had sat there recently—a young girl who Mara was sure was being held against her will by the middle-aged man she'd been with. What a contrast in behavior between that couple and the one who now clung to one another as they rose from their padded bench and snuggled together on their way to the cash register.

Mara met them there, smiling as she took their money and rang up their purchase. When the man handed her an extra $10 and said it was for keeping her so late, she thanked him and accepted it gladly. It was quite a bit more than her usual tip, and she could certainly use it.

She locked the door behind them and returned to the cash register, once again surprised that the owner would trust her to count the money and then place it in the tiny safe in the kitchen. No one had ever trusted her that way before, and she had no intention of breaking that trust.

At last she was done and could go home. She turned to check on Julio and found that the quiet young man with the ready smile was drying his wet hands on a towel. He hung it up and turned to her. "All done?"

Mara smiled and nodded. "All done," she said. "At last. Let's get out of here."

They headed for the door, and Julio unlocked and opened it for her, waiting for her to step through ahead of him. "Need a ride?" he asked.

The offer was tempting, but she shook her head. She really didn't want to get close to her co-workers—or anyone, for

134

that matter—beyond what was necessary to maintain a good working relationship.

"Thanks," she said, "but it's only a few blocks, and the walk will do me good. The fresh air makes me sleep better."

Julio nodded and turned toward the parking lot beside the café, while Mara headed in the opposite direction. She hadn't taken more than a couple of steps when she spotted a shadowy figure less than half a block away, moving silently in her direction. Though she tried to tell herself she was overreacting, the chill that shot up her spine convinced her otherwise.

Spinning on her heel, she called out, "Julio, wait!"

The young man who was just unlocking his car stopped and looked in her direction.

"Is that offer for a ride still open?"

"Sure. Come on."

Heart racing, Mara hurried to the parking lot and nearly catapulted herself through the passenger door into the front seat. Hurriedly pulling the door shut and locking it, she glanced back toward the spot where she'd seen the figure moving toward her. He was gone. Though she looked up and down the street in each direction, she couldn't see him anywhere.

Did I imagine that I saw him? No, I'm sure of it. And if I've learned anything in all the horrible years I spent with my tio, it's to trust my instincts and run while there's time. Better safe than sorry, as they say.

Jack was not a happy man. He had spotted the couple walk out of the café and then head in opposite directions. His plan had been to check out any females of the right size and age who

135

might be walking alone in the area, as it was doubtful that this Mara chick had a car. But before he could get close enough, she had turned and nearly run away from him. Why? Had she seen him? And so what if she had? It wasn't unheard of for people to be on the streets at that hour, though he could see where it might spook a girl by herself to see somebody like him headed her way at night. Still, her reaction raised red flags. Though the girl named Mara wouldn't know him, she might suspect that Jefe was out for revenge. If so, she'd be especially cautious, maybe even paranoid, which could fit the description of the chick who just ran from him.

Was the guy driving the car her boyfriend or husband? Jack doubted it. If he were, they wouldn't have parted at the front door and each started off alone. And Jack wouldn't have overheard her asking if the offer for a ride was still open. No, that was more of a question for someone you knew casually. What made the most sense was that the two of them worked at that café and had just closed up for the night and were heading home. If his car had been close enough, he would have followed them. Since he'd parked his car several blocks away so he could prowl around, he'd just have to make it a point to return here the next night and watch for the girl to come out again at closing time. This time he'd make sure she didn't spot him before he got close enough to see her face. If she wasn't Mara, no loss. But if she was, then he'd be well on the way to securing his little brother's safety during his time behind bars.

"We must remain inside all day," Klahan said to Lawan as he fixed her a light breakfast. "Do not go to the door or make any noise. We do not want to draw any attention to ourselves this day. I do not believe that your former owner will hear of the fire and Chai's death before we are gone from here, but we must not take any chances." He placed a cup of tea in front of her at the tiny table in the middle of the room where she sat, her large eyes watching his every move. Recognizing the trust he saw there, he reached out and caressed her cheek.

"You are indeed beautiful, sweet Lawan. And now you belong to me. I will not allow anyone to hurt you ever again."

Tears pooled in the girl's dark eyes, and she nodded. "*Kop koon*," she said. "Thank you for rescuing me." She dropped her eyes then. When she looked back up, the tears had spilled over onto her silky cheeks. "The one called Chai—he is dead. But what was the sound I heard as I waited by the door? There was a noise, a cry."

Klahan pulled up the only other chair in the house and sat down beside the girl he loved so dearly. "I did only what I had to do," he said. "I could not take a chance that the old housekeeper would awaken and call for help before we escaped. You understand, do you not?"

He waited, surprised at how very important it was to him for the girl to think well of him. Klahan took one of her little hands and held it between both of his, watching her response.

At last she nodded. "I understand. You did it to protect me."

Klahan's heart soared. She understood! And he was nearly certain that she loved him, even as he loved her. Once they were safely away from this place, he would at last take from her what was rightfully his—but gently and with tenderness and respect. He would teach her what it was like to truly be loved, for he knew she had never experienced such a thing at the brothel and certainly would not have known it with Chai.

He lifted her hand to his lips and kissed it. "We will leave tonight," he said, "as soon as it is dark. We will go far from here where no one will look for us. We will be safe and very happy."

The girl's brows drew together. "But how will we live? I have no money. We must eat."

Klahan kissed her hand again and smiled. "I have already thought of that, my dear child. There was no need to allow Chai's money and jewels to be destroyed with him in the fire. I knew where he kept them, and now they are mine. They will provide everything we need. You must not worry, sweet Lawan. Klahan will take care of everything."

Chapter 19

You're my sister too." Anna's statement was shy but firm, and Leah's heart melted at the words. She loved the almost five-year-old with the wide almond eyes and ready smile as if she really were her little sister, but what did Anna mean by "too"? True, from what Kyle and Nyesha had learned from the adoption agency, Anna — formerly Mali — did have two sisters, though one had apparently been adopted by a wealthy Thai family and lost touch with her birth family. Leah was certain Anna had been too young when she left Thailand to remember her sisters, or her parents for that matter, but the statement caught her attention.

"Yes," she said, kneeling down beside the little girl who sat on her bedroom floor, playing with her baby doll. "I'm your sister too."

Anna smiled, appearing satisfied by Leah's response, and went back to cooing and rocking her "baby."

It was Monday morning, and Nyesha had asked Leah over the weekend if she would come and stay with Anna today. As always, Leah was delighted to accept. She had arrived just moments earlier and knew that Nyesha had not yet left.

"I'll be right back," she told Anna, rising from her kneeling position. "I need to talk to your mommy before she leaves."

Anna nodded, humming to her doll, and Leah slipped out the door and headed for the kitchen where she'd last seen

Nyesha. She was still there, cleaning up a few dishes from breakfast, her back turned to Leah but her hips swaying gently to the song she hummed to herself.

Leah smiled, remembering how Anna hummed to her doll. Seemed the little Thai girl was taking on more of her adoptive mama's traits and mannerisms all the time.

She cleared her throat. "Nyesha?"

The humming stopped as Nyesha shut off the water and turned around, wiping her hands on a dish towel. Leah loved that about her. Some people would have responded without abandoning their task, but Nyesha gave people her priority.

"I was just wondering about something," Leah said.

Nyesha smiled. "Want to sit down and talk? I've got a few minutes yet before I have to leave."

Leah nodded. "If you don't have time to finish cleaning up, I'll do it."

"Now that's an offer I won't pass up." Nyesha laughed as the two of them took seats across from one another at the table.

Leah found herself wondering how many times she'd sat in this very spot, talking with this lady she so admired. The thought relaxed and reassured her that she could ask her friend anything.

"Anna said something a few minutes ago," she began. "She said I was her sister . . . too." She frowned. "That made me wonder if she might remember her family in Thailand. Do you think it's possible?"

"Probably not," Nyesha answered without hesitation, "though the thought has crossed my mind on occasion too—especially lately. She's been asking us a few questions about our family." She laughed, her dark eyes twinkling. "Just yesterday she wanted to know if she got her skin color from her Thai family or from Kyle and me blending our colors together."

Leah grinned. It sounded exactly like something the curious little girl would ask. And why not? At not quite five years old, the concept of adoption and natural-born children was probably still a bit confusing to her.

Nyesha's smile faded slightly, and her words took on a more serious tone. "In fact, she's been asking about what she calls her 'Thai family' quite a bit lately. We've never kept anything from her and have told her what we thought she could understand about her past life and how she came to live with us, but it's made us realize that our knowledge is a little sketchy. Kyle and I are considering contacting the agency to see if we can find out anything else about her family — maybe even some updates on the parents and remaining sister. Who knows? They might even have other children by now."

Leah hadn't considered that possibility, but it was an intriguing one. How would Anna feel as she grew older and her curiosity about her birth family grew? How would Leah feel if she were in the same situation? No doubt she'd want to know as much about them as possible, not to mention about their country and culture.

"Do you think her parents were Christians?" Leah asked, the thought suddenly becoming important to her.

Nyesha nodded. "Yes, the agency assured us they were. In fact, that had a lot to do with our getting Anna. The birth parents wanted her raised in a Christian home."

"I can see why," Leah agreed. "I'd feel the same way."

"Leah? Are you coming back to play with me?"

Anna's small voice interrupted the conversation, and Leah immediately wondered how much the girl had overheard. She smiled at the young child. "Yes, I am." She rose from her seat. "Right now, in fact. Let's go!"

She caught a flash of Nyesha's smile as Leah and Anna joined hands and headed down the hallway. They hadn't even made it through the door of Anna's bedroom before Leah once again heard the sound of Nyesha's humming.

Leah sighed as she took a seat on the floor beside the dark-haired little girl. She was glad she'd talked to Nyesha about Anna's comment. It would be interesting to see if the agency had any further information for them about the child's birth family, so very far away in Thailand. But for now, Leah would just enjoy every minute with her adorable little charge.

Francesca woke up feeling as if she were rolling on an undulating sea. She had endured her usual long and grueling work night, finally falling into an exhausted sleep after her last customer left just before dawn. Now, a few hours later, she jumped from bed and raced to the small bathroom she shared with the girl in the next room. The bathroom was in between, with a door on each side. Francesca caught a glimpse of the girl who went by the name of ChaCha sprawled across her bed, oblivious to the sun's rays shining through her window.

Francesca scarcely made it to the toilet and raised the lid before she fell to her knees and lost everything she'd eaten the night before—and then some, she imagined. The same thing had happened the morning before, and she'd attributed it to the pain meds she was taking for her arm. Now she wasn't so sure.

"Not a good sign," she heard from behind her.

She didn't lift her head. Apparently ChaCha had awakened and come to check on her. "Pain meds," she managed to mumble, hoping the girl would accept her explanation and go away.

"Maybe," came the reply. "And maybe it's something else."

Francesca was only fourteen and had been a virgin when she was kidnapped three months earlier, but she knew enough to understand what ChaCha was implying. Oh, how she prayed the girl was wrong! But she'd already considered the possibility herself.

"What are you going to do if you're pregnant?"

A stab of fear left Francesca lightheaded and once again clinging to the porcelain bowl. If only ChaCha hadn't said the words! But there they were, hanging in the air between them. What would she do? Francesca had no idea. She imagined the bigger question was what would El Diablo do?

She shrugged her shoulders and shook her head, still not turning to look back at the girl who had forced the issue Francesca did not want to confront. She had so hoped she could ignore it and it would go away, but the morning nausea wasn't the only sign that something was going on inside her body.

A baby, she thought. *I'm too young to have a baby. And what would happen to it here at this place?* She squeezed her eyes shut. Some things were just too awful to imagine. There was a time she would have hoped such a development would mean that El Diablo would let her go, but now that she knew he wouldn't even give her a night off for a broken bone, she realized that being pregnant wouldn't change a thing in his eyes—except possibly the need to get rid of the baby so it wouldn't interrupt her productivity.

Hot tears pricked the back of her eyelids. ChaCha was saying something, but she couldn't concentrate. All she could think of was that things just continued to get worse. If she really was pregnant, her already unbearable life had just become more complicated.

143

Darkness had once again fallen over the Golden Triangle, and Lawan sensed Klahan's tension as they prepared to leave. She trusted him because she had no other choice and she wanted desperately to believe he truly loved her, but her heart yearned to run as far and as fast as she could, back toward the little village where she had once lived with her parents. But how could she? She had been blindfolded and trussed like an animal when she was brought to the brothel. She would not have any idea which direction to go or even how far it might be.

Lawan blinked away tears as she watched Klahan pack a few belongings and supplies—including what he called his "treasure" that he had taken from Chai—into one large sack and one smaller one. She imagined she would carry the little one, and she appreciated his consideration in giving her a smaller load. Klahan was indeed a kind and gentle man, and she told herself over and over again that she was blessed to have been rescued by one such as he. Still, she did not really want to belong to anyone, not even one as good and brave as Klahan. What she wanted more than anything was to go home and be a little girl again, loved and cared for by her parents. But it was too late. That life was over, and she knew she must accept that she would never again see her family here on this earth.

Not even Chanthra, she thought, remembering the short time she and her older sister had spent together in the brothel. Oh, how she missed her older sister, but how glad she was that Chanthra no longer suffered! Lawan reminded herself to be grateful that her life would not end in the same painful, miserable way. At least Klahan was giving her a chance to live the rest of her life somewhere other than in a brothel where she was nothing more than a means of profit for her owners. The reminder helped her look with more grateful eyes at the man who busied himself in the dimly lit room.

At last he turned to her. "We are ready," he said, a loaded sack in each hand. "Come, we must go now so we can get as far away from here as possible before morning light."

Lawan rose from the mattress where she had slept the night before and went to Klahan's side, reaching out for the smaller bag. He hesitated and then released it to her, his hand touching hers in the process. "I will watch over you," he said, their eyes meeting and holding until Lawan dropped her gaze. She believed him. She had to. That he had killed two people the previous night was a fact she could not allow herself to contemplate.

Chapter 20

The San Diego sunshine was nearly at high noon by the time Mara rolled out of bed. She had the day off, and she was taking full advantage of it, luxuriating in a few extra hours sleep and planning to do nothing more than sit out on the porch in the afternoon and absorb a few rays.

It promised to be exceptionally warm today, so she snagged some shorts and a sleeveless blouse on her way to the shower. With such a perfect day in the offing, why did she feel so uneasy?

She turned on the water and frowned as she waited for it to warm up. Could it be that she was still bothered by running into those two girls at the mall on Saturday? True, they were a reminder of her past life, which in itself was enough to ruin her day. But seeing them stirred up more than memories of her horrible life with Tio; it also stirred up feelings about Leah's brother, Jonathan, and that was almost more disturbing than the nightmare that was her life until Jonathan rescued her.

That must be it, she told herself, stepping into the shower and closing her eyes as the warm spray hit her face and flowed down her body. *I'm just grateful to him for what he did for me, for helping me escape from my uncle. Surely that's all it is.*

She lathered shampoo into her hair as another image floated into her mind, this time of the young couple who had stayed so late at the café the night before. Their presence had bothered her more than she'd wanted to admit, as she had watched them being totally lost in one another's company.

I'll never experience a relationship like that, she told herself, *and I don't want to. Life is better alone. The last thing I need is some guy confusing things.*

But the image of the loving couple sitting in the café's back booth blurred into the memory of the young girl sitting there just a few days earlier, obviously entrapped by the man who held her in his clutches. How she despised that man, and she didn't even know him! Would someone come along to rescue that girl as Jonathan had done for her — before it was too late?

The memory of Jasmine, who had not been rescued but had been beaten to death by one of Jefe's henchman, brought a flood of tears to her eyes. Mara had grown to care for the girl more than she cared to admit.

We lived in a violent place then, she reminded herself. *It could as easily have been me.*

The sense of danger that she'd experienced the night before when she spotted the man heading toward her in the shadows as she left work washed over her again, and she realized what it was that had been bothering her since she woke up. It wasn't memories of the past so much as it was fear of the future. She had foolishly allowed herself to believe that the worst was behind her, and life could only get better now that she was an American citizen with a job and the freedom to pursue anything she wished. But who was she kidding? The man she'd seen last night no doubt had nothing to do with her, but he was a reminder that Jefe could reach out and grab her, even from behind bars.

She released her grip on her emotions then and allowed her tears to flow freely down her cheeks, mingling with the warm water from the shower. Would she ever be safe and able to lead a normal life? She had desperately tried to believe she could, but at this moment the possibility seemed highly unlikely.

❧

Lawan's legs ached, and the sack seemed to grow heavier with each step. But she could not complain. Klahan's sack was much larger and heavier than hers, and he continued on without a word. They had crept down streets and alleys, staying in the shadows as much as possible, and were now on the outskirts of the lights and bustle of activity that seemed to make Klahan so nervous. Perhaps he would allow them to rest a while now that they were on the outskirts of town.

Klahan looked down at her then and slowed his pace. "Are you tired, little one?"

She could scarcely see his features in the night's darkness, but she heard the concern in his voice. "Yes," she admitted. "Very much."

Before she could say another word, he took her bag from her and placed it in the same hand where he carried the larger sack. Then he reached down and lifted her with the other arm, holding her close against his chest.

"We will stop soon," he promised. "I will watch for a safe place."

Though she knew she should protest his willingness to carry not only both sacks but her as well, her eyes were just too tired and her body too weary to say a word. Instead she placed her thin arms around his neck and laid her head on his shoulder. If she could just close her eyes for a few moments.

She awoke as Klahan placed her gently on the ground and sat down beside her. "This is a quiet place," he said. We are hidden among the bamboo trees, far enough from the road that no one will see us. Go back to sleep, Lawan. I will rest as well, but only for a short time. We have a long way to go before we will be safe."

Lawan nodded. *Safe.* It was a word that seemed almost foreign to her. How long had it been since she had felt safe? More than two years, since she'd been kidnapped when she strayed too far from her parents' home. She had paid dearly for her foolishness. Had her debt finally been paid? Was she at last going to have a somewhat pleasant life, one not filled with pain and humiliation?

Her eyes drifted closed once again, as the hopeful thought warmed her and she reached out to take her benefactor's hand in her own. He might be a killer, but he had been kind to her. Perhaps that was the best she could hope for in this life.

Mara had followed through on her plans for the day, spending the early afternoon on the front porch of the boarding house where she lived, flipping through magazines and dozing intermittently. She had managed to block out the negative feelings she'd wrestled with earlier in the day, convincing herself that the incident with the faceless man in the dark the night before had just unnerved her and caused her emotions to go on high alert. A few hours of rest and relaxation and she'd be as good as new and ready to return to work the next day.

"Mara?"

The somewhat familiar voice slowly penetrated Mara's semisleep, as she pulled herself back from the sunshine-induced lull in her consciousness. Slowly opening her eyes, she lifted her head and focused on the middle-aged woman with the just-starting-to-gray curls standing in front of her. Mara pulled herself from her slouch to a straight-up sitting position and frowned.

"I'm sorry," she said. "I can't see you very well in the glare from the sun."

The woman chuckled and moved to take a seat next to Mara, where her features were clearer. Ah, of course. It was Barbara Whiting.

"Sorry I interrupted your nap."

"Oh, I wasn't really sleeping," Mara said. "Just dozing a little."

Barbara laughed again. "I know how easy that is to do in the warm afternoon sunshine." She paused before continuing. "I stopped by the café and found out you were off today, so I thought I'd take a chance and drop by. I hope you don't mind."

Mara shrugged, feeling more awake and alert now. "Not at all. After all, I'm the one who called you to reconnect."

"And I'm glad you did — not just because of the young girl you told me about but also because it's good to know how you're doing. I often thought of you during these last couple of years and wondered how things had turned out for you."

Mara felt her cheeks flame, though she wasn't sure why. She imagined it was because any reference to her past life brought a lingering sense of shame, despite the fact that she told herself daily that none of it had been her fault.

"I'm doing all right," she said. "Working and all."

Barbara nodded. "Yes. And your boss had nothing but good things to say about you. You've made quite a good impression there."

My boss. Jefe used to be my boss, and he never had anything good to say about me. It's hard to believe that anyone else ever could either.

"Anyway," Barbara continued, "I was just out and about today and thought I'd see if I could catch up with you and find out if you've seen that girl again—or the guy she was with. I know you said you'd call me if you had, but . . . well, I'm just so anxious to try to help locate them. If you're right about the type of relationship they have—and I'm sure you are—we need to find her as soon as possible. But then, I'm not telling you anything you don't already know, am I?"

Mara shook her head. "No. And it bothers me too. I think of her at night when I'm lying in my own bed, free from my uncle and that awful place where I spent so many years." She looked into the woman's eyes, willing her to understand. But how could she? She'd never been someone's slave before. "I saw terrible things there," she said, her voice barely above a whisper. "People died—girls younger than me."

Barbara's blue eyes filled with tears, and she reached out to lay a hand on Mara's arm. "I can only imagine. It must have been horrible."

Tears now stung Mara's eyes as well, and she nodded. "I can never begin to describe how awful it really was. And that's why I want to find that girl and get her out of there before . . ."

"Before it's too late."

Mara nodded again.

"Forgive me for thinking you might have seen her again and not called to let me know. I realize now that you're even more anxious to see her rescued than I am." She sighed. "I pray for that girl, and so many like her, every day. Only God can truly rescue them."

Mara thought the woman might be right, but she wasn't ready to admit that out loud. God was just too far away to give Him much credit or express any real trust in Him. But deep down she suspected that He could be the only real chance any of them had.

Chapter 21

Jonathan still had a couple of hours before he had to be at work, and he'd spent most of the morning and early afternoon at the beach, as he often did when he had a little spare time and felt like being alone. He'd walked several miles barefoot on the wet, packed sand, thinking and praying but not really coming to any major decisions or earth-shattering revelations. Now it was time to head home and get ready for his shift.

Cruising through the familiar neighborhood that bordered his favorite beach area, he took his time, tapping out his favorite songs on the steering wheel in absence of a real radio — which he hoped to someday be able to afford. He nearly laughed out loud. Like that would happen any time soon! At least not until he graduated from Bible college, and who knew what would happen then? Maybe he wouldn't even have a car to drive, let alone one with a radio, wherever he ended up.

He turned a corner and slowed as he caught sight of a couple of women sitting on a porch. The one facing in his direction looked like Barbara Whiting from church. The closer he came, the more certain he was that it was indeed the lady from the human-trafficking ministry. But who was the younger woman who sat across from her?

His eyes widened as he drew up even with them, and he hit the brakes. The girl's hair was shorter, but he'd know that face anywhere. Mara!

He caught his breath, telling himself he should stop staring and drive away, but he knew he wouldn't. Instead he steered to the corner and shut off the engine, his heart pounding in his ears as he climbed out of the car.

As he crossed the street and approached the large house, the two women looked up. Barbara smiled in recognition, while Mara's eyes widened in what Jonathan imagined was shock. He forced a smile and did his best to act natural.

"Hey," he said, mounting the first step and then stopping as he directed his words to Barbara, though his eyes kept drifting to Mara. "I thought I saw you when I turned the corner. And then, when I got closer . . ." He turned his gaze completely to Mara then as he climbed the last two steps and stood on the porch. "I couldn't believe it when I saw you sitting here too. How are you, Mara?"

154

The girl's hazel eyes were still opened wide, and she seemed unable to speak. Jonathan watched as her cheeks flushed, and at last her mouth moved. "I'm fine," she said, her voice trembling slightly. "I . . . I'm surprised to see you."

"I was just heading home to change before work," he said, unable to tear his eyes from hers. He'd forgotten how absolutely beautiful she was. "So how are you, anyway?" It was his turn to blush then. "Sorry. I already asked you that, didn't I?"

Mercifully, Barbara interrupted them then. "Mara is doing very well," she said, forcing Jonathan's attentions away from the girl and onto the older woman as she spoke. "She's a US citizen now, living here and working nearby. Isn't that wonderful?"

"It sure is," Jonathan agreed, shifting his attention back to Mara, whose eyes had finally returned to normal. "I don't work far from here either." *Brilliant conversationalist, Jonathan,* he chided himself. She obviously already knew he was delivering pizzas when they first met a couple of years ago. He'd better clarify things. "I'm really only filling in at my old job for the summer while I'm home from college."

She hesitated before responding. "I saw your sister the other day, at the mall with her friend."

Jonathan nodded. "She told me."

The pauses were growing longer, and Jonathan wondered if he should excuse himself and head for home, but he just wasn't ready to stop staring at the girl in front of him.

Barbara cleared her throat. "Well, I need to get going," she said, standing to her feet. "It was good to see you again, Mara—you too, Jonathan."

Jonathan turned and found himself standing almost toe to toe with the woman. "I should go too," he mumbled, hoping Mara would invite him to stay but knowing she wouldn't. "I need to get ready for work."

Mara stood up, drawing Jonathan's attention once again. "I've got things to do inside myself," she said, her eyes fixed just slightly below his. "Good to see you both."

Jonathan searched his mind for something to say that would halt her departure, but he came up blank. Instead he turned to follow Barbara down the steps. "Hope I see you around," he called over his shoulder, ignoring the urge to look back to see if she was watching.

By the time he reached his car he realized the visit hadn't been a complete wipeout. He might not have done anything to impress Mara or to further their relationship, but at least he'd found out where she lived.

Wait a minute, he thought, standing with his hand on the door handle. *Who says I want to further a relationship with her? Come to think of it, I don't think we even have one to start with. And why do I care where she lives?*

He shook his head and climbed inside, finally daring to glance back in the direction he'd come. The porch was empty.

❦

Alley Cat was getting irritated. He'd been so sure he'd stumbled onto something the night before, but as he lurked in the shadows where he could keep an eye on the café where he'd seen the girl, he was beginning to think it was a waste of time.

He'd been hanging around for several hours now, figuring that if she worked there she would come in for the lunch crowd. When she didn't show, he took a quick break and then hurried back. She hadn't appeared for the dinner crowd either, so chances were slim that she would turn up at all—unless she'd slipped in during the few minutes he was away.

Nah. Not much chance of that. But just in case, he decided to go inside for a cup of coffee and scope out the place. Even if she wasn't there, he might be able to get some information from one of the other workers. He might as well eliminate the girl and move on to another spot as soon as possible. He'd wasted enough time as it was.

The dinner crowd was thinning out now that the sun had set and darkness hung over the city. Most people who wanted a really late dinner went somewhere fancier than Mariner's, but Jack thought it was just the sort of place he liked. Good, simple food, not too expensive, with a come-as-you-are atmosphere. Yep, right up his alley.

Alley Cat smiled at his own clever play on words and ordered a cup of coffee from the chubby waitress that offered him a menu. He shook his head and waved the menu away as he waited for his java. When she returned with the half-full glass carafe, he smiled as she poured.

"Thanks," he said, still smiling. "I appreciate it." Before she could turn away he added, "You aren't the same one who was working last night, are you?"

The woman, who looked to be in her midthirties and bored, answered without returning his smile. "No. I only work part-time, on the days when Mara's not here. If you came here to eat yesterday, she's probably the one who waited on you." She scowled. "Can't imagine how you'd mistake me for her, though. She's young and skinny and good-looking. She'll be back tomorrow."

Mara. Jack's heart thumped against his ribs, and his mouth went dry. He'd hit pay dirt.

He nodded. "Yeah, Mara. That was her name. Thanks."

The woman grunted and headed back to the kitchen with her coffee. So, he'd been in the right place at the right time last night after all. But how had she known he was looking for her? Why had she turned and hurried away just when he was nearly close enough to see her face?

Maybe someone tipped her off, he thought. *Or maybe she's just skittish and knows Jefe's out for revenge. Either way, I've got my prey in my sights. And this time she won't get away.*

Warm rays of sunlight and the call of mynahs drew Lawan from a deep sleep. Blinking in an effort to get her bearings, she looked up at the stands of bamboo around her, the morning sun just piercing the breaks between the trees. Still confused, she sat up, wondering why she was on the ground and not on her familiar mattress at the brothel. Where was her roommate, Kulap?

And then she remembered. Chai had come for her—bought her from the boss man and taken her to his home. And then . . . Klahan. Memories and images flooded her mind then, and she nearly cried out. Klahan! Where was he? Had he left her there in the jungle to die?

"I am right here, Lawan," came the soothing words behind her.

Still sitting, she turned and raised her head, as relief washed over her at the sight of the man who had rescued her. The sudden realization that she was not alone after all brought a flood of tears to her eyes, immediately spilling over onto her cheeks as she sobbed. "I thought you left me," she cried. "I was scared."

Pain crossed the man's face as he knelt down beside her. "I would never leave you," he crooned, reaching out to caress her face with a rough hand. "I was only a short distance away, waiting for you to wake up. As soon as we have eaten some of the food I brought with us, we will continue on our journey. We are not far from our destination, though I had hoped to arrive before dawn." He paused, his eyes showing a hint of tears. "But you needed your rest. I could not bear to think that you were suffering. You have already suffered so much, dear child."

Lawan gulped back her tears. Klahan was right. He was also the kindest man she had encountered since she last saw her *phor*, her beloved father. Without thinking, she turned her face just enough to kiss the palm of Klahan's hand. When he sighed and gently pulled her into his arms, she did not resist. She knew he would not hurt her in any way, and knowing that made everything else bearable.

Chapter 22

Francesca dreaded her outing with El Diablo. When he'd come to wake her that Tuesday morning to tell her he was driving her to the doctor to have her arm checked, she'd scarcely been able to conceal her morning nausea as she lay in bed, waiting for him to leave. Once he was gone she'd rushed to the bathroom and once again hugged the toilet bowl in misery, scarcely hearing ChaCha's sarcastic comments as the girl came to check on her. But it was obvious now, at least to Francesca, that she was indeed pregnant. ChaCha had figured it out too. How long would it be until El Diablo or someone else noticed? Perhaps even the doctor would stumble onto it today, though she wasn't going for that reason. But if he did, what would happen then?

Francesca thought of her parents and how they had taught her right from wrong, including the fact that abortion was not a matter of convenience but the taking of a tiny, innocent life. And yet, what would Francesca have to say about it if that's what El Diablo decided to do? After all, she had no say over anything else she was forced to do these days, regardless of how wrong she knew it was. Her life was no longer under her own control, and she wondered if it ever would be again.

Dragging herself from the floor, she ignored ChaCha's running chatter and turned on the shower. She needed to get cleaned up and dressed before El Diablo returned for her, and he had said it wouldn't be long.

She'd scarcely been out of the shower and dressed for more than a couple of minutes when her door burst open and El Diablo stood there, demanding that they leave right away. "I've got things to do, Frankie," he growled, "and they don't include waiting on you."

With her wet hair hanging down her back, she scurried after the man she despised but who held her life in his hands. Before she knew it she was being examined by the doctor who was obviously on El Diablo's payroll and never reported anything to anyone. He simply did what he was told and asked no questions in the process. Francesca breathed a sigh of relief when they walked out of his office toward the black Lexus with the darkened windows; at least it seemed her secret was safe for a while longer.

After a couple of stops, during which El Diablo kept her close at his side, they pulled into a small parking lot next to the café where they'd eaten the week before. Francesca couldn't help but wonder if El Diablo had returned there because he liked the food, or if he hoped to see the waitress with the beautiful hazel eyes. Francesca knew the woman was older than El Diablo's usual teen and preteen girls, but she also knew he had been more than slightly interested in her.

As they walked through the front door of Mariner's, El Diablo's arm around Francesca's shoulder as he guided her each step of the way, she dared to glance up to look for the waitress. Because it was midmorning, too late for the breakfast bunch and too early for the lunch crowd, the place was nearly empty. But sure enough, the familiar waitress stood behind the counter, already aware of their presence as she followed them with her eyes. Francesca looked away, feeling her cheeks heat with shame. Did the woman know what she was, what she was forced to do? Part of her cried out for that to be the case, hoping that she just might try to help her. But another part of her knew better. Anyone who recognized what Francesca did every night would not want anything to do with her. And why should they? Could there be anything worse than what she was forced to endure to please all those awful men and to make money for El Diablo? Certainly there was not.

The very back booth where the two of them had sat at their last visit was the only one taken in the entire place, so they slid into the one just before it. Her eyes still downcast, Francesca waited. What would happen when the waitress came to their table? Francesca hoped El Diablo wouldn't make a scene, but she knew better. Her owner was used to getting what he wanted — one way or the other.

161

Mara's hands trembled, and her breath came in short gasps. They were back, and the first thing she'd noticed was that the girl had a cast on her arm. After days of watching for these two, hoping they'd return or she'd see them somewhere else and could report them, they were actually here. What should she do now? Their sudden appearance didn't warrant a 911 call, but she certainly needed to contact Barbara Whiting so she could alert her contact at police headquarters. But first she'd better at least take them menus and water so they wouldn't get suspicious. Could she do it without her hands trembling or her expression giving her away? She took a deep breath. There was only one way to find out.

Tucking the menus under her arm, she carried a glass of ice water in each hand as she approached their booth. So far, so good. She managed to set the waters down without spilling them and place the menus in front of them just as the man lifted his head and locked his gaze onto hers. A smile—more like a sneer, Mara thought—spread across his face, which could only be described as evil. Mara wondered if he might have been a nice-looking man if his eyes weren't so dark and hard, but it was impossible to tell. Years of violence overwhelmed anything that might once have been kind or even normal in his appearance. If she'd had even a moment's doubt that this man was holding the young girl against her will, that doubt was gone now.

"Well, if it isn't the little spitfire that didn't want to hear what I had to say the last time I was here." He winked and raked his eyes over her figure before returning them to her face. "Hope you had a chance to reconsider because the offer is still open." He leaned closer as he spoke. "I could make you a lot more money than you'll ever see working in this dump."

Mara's heart iced over, and she regained control. She knew how to handle creeps like this, and it wasn't by having a conversation with them. "I'll be back to take your order in a few minutes," she said, pleased with herself that her words came out steady and even. "Meanwhile, can I get you something to drink?"

The man hesitated, his eyes narrowing as he studied her. "Coffee," he said at last. "Black."

When he didn't ask for anything for the girl, Mara glanced in her direction, but her head was bowed as she studied the menu in great detail. Mara wasn't fooled, though. She knew the girl would eat whatever her owner ordered for her.

Turning on her heel, she forced herself to walk at a normal pace toward the kitchen. Once on the other side of the swinging doors, she snatched her cell phone from her pocket, found Barbara's number, and punched send.

Klahan was relieved, though tentatively so. They had made it to his destination, a small village far enough from where they had come that he did not expect to recognize anyone — or have them recognize him. And with the money and jewels he had stolen from Chai, he and Lawan should be able to live comfortably for quite some time. He wanted to be able to care for the girl so she would never again have to be at the mercy of lecherous men who would use her for their perverted pleasure or for financial gain, as Klahan knew Chai would certainly have done.

Not like me, he mused. *I love Lawan and will treat her well. She will give me much pleasure for many years and will even care for me when I am old. She is the perfect companion for my life, better even than the wife who died too soon and left me with no children.* He nodded to himself. Yes, if he used his newfound wealth wisely, he might not have to return to work at all. And perhaps he would even marry Lawan when she was a little older, particularly if she gave him the children he'd never had. He would like a family, after all.

The transaction for the modest house, where he and Lawan would live was complete, and he would take her there now. He glanced down at her, walking beside him, carrying her small sack of belongings while the larger sack was slung over his shoulder. The late afternoon sun shone on her dark hair, causing his heart to constrict. She was a good girl, despite her shameful past. And that made him a good man, did it not? For after all, he had rescued her from that shame. As a result, Lawan would always be grateful and treat him well, and that was really all he wanted from life.

163

The girl had stopped, with her eyes opened wide, when they arrived at the small two-room building that would be their home. Klahan smiled as he watched her. No doubt she had never lived in such a fine place, though it was humble compared to others in the village. Still, it would be enough for the two of them, and Klahan would have to manage his resources wisely.

Lawan lifted her head and stared at him, her eyes still wide. "We will live here?" she asked, nearly in a whisper.

Klahan nodded. "Yes, my little Lawan, we will live here—together. And we will be very happy. I will take care of you, and no one will ever hurt you again."

The girl's dark eyes flooded with tears, and she dropped her bag on the ground. Then she threw her arms around Klahan's legs and wept.

Chapter 23

Mara's racing heart sank when her call went to Barbara's voice mail. It hadn't even occurred to her that the woman wouldn't answer. What should she do now? She had the detective's card somewhere, didn't she—the one who had spoken with her and Barbara at the police station?

Stuffing her phone back into her pocket, she went to the back of the kitchen where the employees hung their jackets and purses while they were working. Frantically she dug through her purse and wallet . . . no card. What had she done with it?

Then she remembered. It was in her room. She could see it now, stuck into the frame of the mirror over her dresser. What had she been thinking when she put it there? Why hadn't she kept it in her purse where she'd have access to it all the time?

Probably because I knew I'd rather call Barbara than a cop, she thought. *As nice as the guy was, I knew he only paid attention to me because Barbara was his friend. But I should have realized I might need to reach him when Barbara wasn't around.*

"Mara? It's starting to pick up out there."

The cook's voice caught her attention. Reluctantly she hung her purse back on the peg and turned around, nodding to Stephen, the middle-aged man who stood over the grill, his face flushed and his eyes anxious.

"You OK?" he asked. "We got a few more customers in the last minute or so."

Mara nodded. "I'm fine," she croaked. "I'll take care of them right now."

Her heart racing once again, she pushed herself back out the swinging doors and into the dining area, where a group of four women waited to be seated. A single customer had plunked himself down at the counter and was already reading the menu. She didn't even let herself glance back at the couple who had initiated her panic; she already knew they were waiting for her to return.

Plastering a smile on her face, she welcomed the foursome and escorted them to a spot at the opposite end of the café from the man and the young girl. The two people who had been seated at the very back booth were making their way to the register. Mara would collect their money, bring water to the man at the counter, and then go take the order from the man and young girl. Her phone was set on vibrate, waiting for her inside her apron pocket. If only Barbara would get the message and call back before it was too late.

Francesca choked down her burger and fries, wishing for something to drink beside water but knowing better than to ask. El Diablo ordered the food, and she ate whatever came her way, keeping her eyes low and her mouth shut except to take another bite.

Still, she couldn't help but notice that the waitress seemed nervous—not that she could blame her. El Diablo was such a creep, and his comments to the poor lady probably had her cringing inside. Francesca just wished she could take a chance and slip her a note or something—anything that might prompt her to call for help. But it was impossible. El Diablo would make sure she never had a chance.

She dipped a french fry into the ketchup and wondered why, if the woman was so obviously uncomfortable around El Diablo, she was so slow in waiting on them. Francesca could tell the lady was getting orders to the other customers quicker, bringing them their bills, asking if they wanted dessert, and getting them cleared out while she seemed to ignore their table. Why not just get them in and out as quickly as possible? It was almost as if she were stalling, trying to keep them there longer.

Francesca nearly shook her head. No. She must be imagining things. The woman just didn't want to come near El Diablo. And why should she? The man was mean and disgusting, and his remarks to the waitress probably scared her off. No doubt that was why she avoided their table and why it took longer for them to get through and get out of there. But Francesca also knew that El Diablo was not a patient man, so she wasn't surprised when he cursed under his breath and hollered "hey" in the waitress's direction.

"Can we get some service over here?" he demanded. "I'd like my bill so we can get out of this dump."

Francesca jerked her head up in time to see the other customers turn their way just as the waitress stopped her walk toward the kitchen. She turned around slowly and said, "I'll be right with you." Francesca dropped her head again. This was not going to be pretty.

When the woman returned and plopped the bill down in front of El Diablo, he snorted. "About time," he said. "What's up with you anyway?" His voice took on a sarcastic tone then as he nearly whispered, "Do I make you nervous, sweetheart? Because I should, you know."

Francesca peered upward and saw the woman's face, a mixture of fear and hatred, glaring down at him. "You don't make me nervous one bit," she hissed. "I've seen a lot worse than you in my lifetime, so get over yourself." Her eyes darted to Francesca then, and the compassion the young girl saw there nearly caused her to cry out for help, but she pressed her lips together and watched the woman walk away.

"Let's go," El Diablo said, grabbing her good arm. "Now."

She dropped the fry she still held clutched in her fingers and allowed him to jerk her from her seat. She hurried to keep up with him as he stormed to the counter, laid down a $20 bill with his ticket, and left without waiting for the change. Francesca knew he was not only angry but humiliated, and that was not a good thing for her. Tears flooded her eyes at the thought of how El Diablo would take out his bad mood on her, and there was nothing she could do about it.

Mara felt sick inside. Why had she let her emotions get the best of her? She should have tried to carry on a conversation with the disgusting man and maybe keep them there a little longer. Now they were gone, heading for the parking lot and —

Wait a minute. The parking lot! Maybe I can get the license plate number.

She set down the coffee pot and rushed for the door, pulling out her order pad and pen. It might be too late, but she had to try.

Sure enough, by the time she was out on the sidewalk, the sleek dark car was pulling away but not before she saw the personalized plate: LDBLO. Frowning, she jotted down the letters, though she couldn't imagine what they meant. She wished she knew more about cars so she could tell Barbara the make and model when she called, but at least she knew it was black and new and fancy. And she had the plate information. Barbara would be pleased . . . if she ever called back.

Mara sighed, stuffed the pad and pen into her apron pocket, and headed back inside the café. She'd done all she could, and now she had to get back to work. The lunch crowd would arrive in force any time now, and the creep with the young girl in tow would just have to wait.

Chapter 24

Klahan had just gotten Lawan started with heating tea and making them a simple meal to celebrate their new home when he heard a knock on the door. His heart jumped at the sound. He knew no one in the village except the man who had rented him the little house.

His mouth dry, he reassured Lawan with a pat on her head before stepping softly to the door and lifting the latch. The last of the evening light was nearly gone when he pulled the door open and saw the outline of a woman standing there. He squinted for a better look and realized she was tall, middle-aged . . . and American. Now he was more curious than ever as to why she had knocked on his door.

"Excuse me," she said, bowing her head slightly. "I am sorry to bother you, but may I talk with you for a moment?" When he did not respond right away, she added, "Alone? It is important."

Klahan's heart lurched. What could be so important that she would come to the door of someone she did not know and ask to speak with him alone? Klahan could imagine no scenario that would be a good one.

Glancing behind him at Lawan, he saw in the room's dim candlelight that she was obediently going about her assigned chores and apparently paying him no mind. Reassured, he slipped out the front door and closed it behind him. Then he waited, wondering if he should speak or just wait for her to do so. He opted for the latter.

"My name is Joan Stockton," she began, her voice low. "My husband, Mort, and I help oversee the orphanage not far from here. We have many workers who help us, of course, but ultimately we are responsible for the care and protection of several hundred children." She lowered her voice another notch, leaning a bit closer as she spoke. Klahan's eyes had adjusted to the semidarkness, and he could almost feel the intensity in the woman's scrutiny. He noticed for the first time that she wore her hair long and pulled back in a clip at the nape of her neck. Though he couldn't be sure in the absence of daylight, he thought she might have brown hair with flecks of gray.

172 "I recognized the girl," she said, sending a spark of fire up Klahan's spine. "When the two of you were walking through town, I saw her and knew she was one of the girls we have been watching for ever since her parents first came to us a couple of years ago. They believed she had been kidnapped and sold into slavery, and I imagined they were right—though I never thought we would actually see her."

The woman paused, as if waiting for Klahan to respond, but he could think of nothing to say. Why had he been so foolish to bring her here, of all places? Why had he not remembered there was an orphanage nearby? He could have taken her to any one of a dozen villages. Why had he picked this one?

The woman named Joan Stockton cleared her throat. "The reason I am so certain of who she is that I heard a rumor about her just this morning, and I recognized the name. And then, a few hours later, I saw her walking through town with you. At least, I am fairly certain it is the same girl. Lawan is her name, and though the one picture her parents had of her was taken a few years ago, she really has not changed much. And if she is indeed the same child, she is in a lot of trouble." This time she leaned so close that Klahan felt the warmth of her breath as she spoke. "Lawan is wanted for murder. The authorities say she stabbed a man and his housekeeper to death and set their house on fire." She paused again and raised her eyebrows. "Do you know anything about this?"

Klahan thought he would faint. He had to get away, had to deny her words, though he doubted she would believe him. But what choice did he have? He must get away from the American woman with the dark, intense eyes. He and Lawan would run away again during the night. But would they be safe in another village if Lawan was truly wanted for Chai's murder? Would they be safe anywhere?

"Her name is not Lawan," Klahan muttered, backing away from the woman and reaching behind him to fumble with the door latch. "Her name is not Lawan!"

Turning away, he pushed open the door and nearly fell inside, startling the young girl who stood in the candlelight, gazing at him in surprise. Oh, if only her eyes were not so trusting! Why had he promised to protect her and care for her, no matter what happened? How could he ever protect her now? It seemed he had rescued her from a terrible fate, only to doom her to yet a worse one.

173

It had been one of the busiest afternoons Mara could remember since she started working at Mariner's. She'd scarcely had a chance to sit down long enough to rub her sore feet or nurse a cup of coffee, but she'd be off soon. She could wait, though her stomach was grumbling about not being fed since her light breakfast early this morning.

Glad I'm getting off early today, she thought as she balanced a stack of three full plates and hurried through the crowded café. *I didn't like getting up early to come in for the breakfast shift this morning, but I won't miss serving dinner tonight—especially if this is any sign of how busy it's going to be.*

She placed the meals in front of the anxious customers, one of them a young boy whose blue eyes opened wide at the sight of his hot dog. "Yum!" he exclaimed, sliding the plate closer to him and leaning over to sniff the all-American offering.

The man who appeared to be his father chuckled and reached across the table to ruffle the boy's hair. Then he smiled up at Mara. "Thanks," he said.

Mara returned the smile, moving her eyes from the man to the woman sitting next to the child. "Can I get you anything else?"

The boy looked up at her, his eyes dancing with excitement. "Ketchup," he said. "I love ketchup!"

His enthusiasm was contagious, and Mara laughed aloud. "So do I," she said. "Hold on. I'll be right back. And how about a refill on your milk?"

The boy nodded, and Mara turned to complete her task. By the time she had brought a bottle of ketchup and a fresh glass of milk to the table, another customer had entered the café, and she turned toward the door. Before she could open her mouth in greeting, she realized she was looking into the concerned blue eyes of Barbara Whiting. As if on cue, all her good feelings melted away, and she remembered the customers who had come in earlier that day and precipitated her call to the older woman with the worried look on her face.

Resisting the urge to rush toward Barbara and pour out her reaction to her run-in with the slimy man and the teenaged girl, she quietly ushered her to the counter where they could at least talk briefly.

"Did you get my message?" Mara asked, her voice soft but urgent. "I did," Barbara said, settling down on the padded stool. "I'm sorry I didn't answer when you called. I was in meetings most of the day, and when I tried to call you back, you didn't answer. I left a message on your voice mail."

Mara raised her eyebrows in surprise. She'd been so busy she must have missed her vibrating phone in all the noise of the crowded café, and she'd never thought to stop and check messages.

"So can you talk?" Barbara asked. "This probably isn't the best time or place, is it?"

Mara looked around. She didn't see much hope for a lull in the crowd, but her replacement was due in less than fifteen minutes. "How about a quick cup of coffee while I finish my shift?" she asked. "I'm off by 4:00."

Barbara glanced at her watch. "Sure, that'll work."

Mara turned over a cup, filled it with steaming brew, then returned to her job, counting the minutes and sighing with relief when the next shift arrived. Within minutes she was hanging up her apron and grabbing her purse.

"I'm starved," she said to Barbara. "Have you eaten? I haven't had a chance all day."

Barbara laughed. "You work at a restaurant and haven't had a thing to eat. Well then, let's go find somewhere else to eat and talk at the same time. I know just the place."

In a matter of minutes the two women were seated at a cozy Mexican restaurant a few blocks away, dipping chips in salsa and talking about Mara's second encounter with the couple from the café.

"She had her arm in a cast," she told Barbara. "That creep—or one of her so-called customers—must have gotten rough with her."

Barbara's eyes reflected her compassion as she shook her head. "I don't imagine that's unusual, is it?"

"Happens all the time," Mara said. "I can't tell you how bad I wanted to do something to help her, but I didn't have that cop's number with me. I left his card at home."

"That's all right," Barbara said, reaching across the table to lay her hand on Mara's arm. "It's not your fault. You did what you could. And as soon as I got the message, I called Detective Burns and let him know. He wants to talk with you about it first thing in the morning. I'll go with you." She dropped her eyes briefly before looking back up. "Of course, I don't know if they can do anything since they're already gone."

176

Mara appreciated Barbara's understanding. Though Mara knew she'd done what she could, she still felt she'd let the girl down by not having the detective's number handy while the man and his captive were still in the café.

"Wait a minute," she said, sitting up straight and reaching for her purse. "Just after they left I went outside and watched them drive out of the parking lot. I don't know much about cars, so I don't know what kind it was, but he was driving a dark car with tinted windows—new and fancy, you know? And something else."

Barbara raised her eyebrows and waited.

"I got the license plate number."

The smile on Barbara's face lit up the room and warmed Mara's heart even more than the salsa in the bowl in front of them. Maybe now they could do something about finding this slimeball and rescuing the poor girl with the broken arm. *And who knows how many others,* Mara thought. She wanted to high-five the woman sitting across from her, but she just smiled and dipped another chip into the salsa.

Jack wasn't taking any chances tonight. He arrived at Mariner's Café with the early dinner crowd, seating himself at the back of the establishment where he could see everyone who came in or went out. He'd have a nice leisurely meal of clam chowder and calamari while he waited for the waitress named Mara to appear. He hadn't seen her yet, but he'd only been in his booth for a few minutes. She'd have to show soon, since the waitress from the day before had assured him she was working today, so he'd just sit tight and wait. Alley cats were good at that.

The place was bustling tonight, a lot busier than yesterday. If he didn't know better, he'd think it was a weekend. Then he remembered. There was some sort of sandcastle building contest going on this week — just started today, as a matter of fact. He'd heard that people came in from all over for the big event. No wonder all the businesses near the beach were busier than usual.

An older waitress with her graying hair pulled up in a bun on top of her head brought him a bowl of chowder, and he dove right in. The food here wasn't bad, and not too pricey either. He ate with one eye trained on the door, occasionally glancing back toward the kitchen to make sure she didn't come in that way.

By the time his calamari arrived, he was getting restless. Where was she? If she was working tonight, she should be here by now, helping to wait on all these customers.

His waitress had turned away when he cleared his throat and said, "Excuse me."

She pivoted and smiled. "Can I get you something else?"

He shook his head. "No, I'm fine, thanks. But I was just wondering. Don't you have another waitress that works here—Maria, Mara, something like that?"

The lady nodded. "Sure. Mara." She smiled again. "All the men ask for her. She's a beautiful girl."

Jack felt his patience wearing thin. "So where is she? I mean, isn't she working tonight?"

"No, not tonight. She actually traded shifts with me today because I had to do something this morning." She glanced at her watch. "She got off a couple hours ago—at 4:00."

Alley Cat swallowed a growl. He wanted to pounce at her and rip her throat out, but he sat still and smiled. "Thanks," he said. "Maybe I'll catch her next time."

The woman laughed. "I'm sure you will," she said, turning away and heading for the kitchen.

"You can count on it," he whispered to himself. "No way is she getting away from me again."

Chapter 25

Klahan could not sleep. He had lain awake all night, twisting and turning, while Lawan slept peacefully beside him. The thought that his actions, meant to set the girl free, had instead put her in the position of being arrested for murder, nearly drove him mad. She was just a child! How could anyone possibly think she had done such a thing?

But, of course, the circumstances leant themselves to that obvious conclusion. Chai had last been seen alive when he retrieved Lawan from the brothel. Within a matter of hours, both he and his housekeeper were dead and his house burned to the ground. Who would have a greater motive than Lawan to carry out such a crime?

I will explain to her what she must say when she is arrested, Klahan reasoned. *Surely she can explain that she was only defending herself. They will go easy on her.*

But he knew that was not so. Despite the fact that Lawan had been kidnapped and forced into sexual slavery, her past would work against her. And if Klahan used the assets he had taken from Chai to defend her, then he too might soon be on trial for murder.

Was there no answer, no way to clear Lawan's name, or at least to hide her from the authorities? Klahan had been so certain that he had the perfect plan and that he and Lawan could at last live together in peace and happiness. Now he realized it could never be.

Hot tears nipped at his eyes as he imagined the look on Lawan's face when she realized what was happening to her. He had delivered her from a terrible life and promised to protect her. Now he could see no option but to abandon her to a worse fate.

The tears dripped into his ears as he lay staring at a ceiling he could not see, listening to the steady breathing beside him. He loved Lawan, did he not? Had he not proved it by risking everything to deliver her from the hands of her owner at the brothel and then Chai? Right now she believed in that love, and trusted him because of it. But what would she think of him when she was convicted of murder? For surely she would be. She had no means of defending herself, and the authorities would certainly not care enough to pursue the truth beyond what now seemed a simple resolution to the case.

Klahan felt a twinge of guilt at the thought that only he and Lawan knew the truth about what happened, and Lawan would be too frightened to speak of Klahan's involvement. At least, he certainly hoped that was so. But what if it was not? What if she told them, and they believed her?

It was a possibility Klahan had not considered until now, but it was one that made the situation even more complicated than it already was. As much as he loved Lawan, what was he to do with her now that she held his life in her hands? She had trusted him, and he had failed her, though she did not yet know that. When she found out, would he still be able to trust her?

Mara was relieved to finally be back in her own room, safe and warm under the covers as she considered the many events of the last couple of days. The unexpected visit from Jonathan had nearly knocked her off her chair the day before. She had already been skittish since the evening she'd spotted the guy walking toward her in the shadows outside Mariner's. Though she'd had no real reason to fear the stranger, she was still grateful that Julio had offered her a ride home.

But Jonathan . . .

She sighed.

Seeing the handsome guy who had been her rescuer had stirred up more emotions than she wanted to deal with in a lifetime. She'd tried for two years to convince herself that the feelings she had for him were just a natural reaction to his hero status; after all, who wouldn't feel something for the person who finally enabled you to escape from hell on earth? And though she didn't doubt that had something to do with it, she also knew there was more—a lot more. There was even a part of her that imagined he felt the same, but there was no way that could be true. No one knew better than Jonathan the type of life she had endured before he arrived on the scene. What normal, decent guy would ever want anything to do with someone like that?

She shook off the thoughts. Enough about Jonathan! Her mind returned to the pair in the café. The memory of the frail girl with the cast on her arm and the terrified look on her face continued to tear at Mara's heart. But at least she and Barbara now had another appointment to go to the police station in the morning. Barbara had assured Mara that thanks to her quick thinking in writing down the license plate, it was only a matter of time until the driver of that vehicle was located. Mara just hoped it wouldn't be too late for the girl.

Making the teenager's rescue the focus of her thoughts, Mara finally drifted off to sleep.

"How long has it been since we've had a sleepover?" Sarah asked, stretching her pajama-clad legs as she sprawled across Leah's bed.

"Too long," Leah answered, sitting on the bench in front of her dresser and watching herself in the mirror as she brushed her long, thick curls. The overhead light cast a gold tint to her red hair, and for a brief moment she wondered what she would look like if she'd been born a blonde. Looking behind her own reflection at the petite blonde who had been her best friend since grammar school, Leah smiled. Better to leave the blonde hair to her pixielike companion. It fit her bubbly personality. Red hair was better suited to someone named Leah Flannery. "We started doing this when we were in grammar school, but I can't remember when we last did it. Why did we stop?"

Sarah shrugged and hugged a raggedy stuffed animal that Leah remembered once resembled a bear and had been Sarah's constant nighttime companion for many years. Watching Leah brush her hair, Sarah said, "I don't know. We used to have sleepovers all the time, but we were pretty young and immature then."

Leah swallowed a grin, the irony of Sarah's comment being made while hugging a stuffed animal speaking volumes.

Sarah's face took on a pensive look then, and she paused a moment before continuing. "I'm going to miss you when you go away to college."

Leah couldn't see well enough to be certain there were tears in Sarah's blue eyes, but she could hear them in her friend's voice. "I know," she said, putting down the brush and turning to face the bed. "I wish you were coming with me."

Sarah nodded. "Me too. But I just don't know what I want to do with my life yet, so community college makes the most sense for now."

"We'll stay in touch," Leah promised, wanting to reassure her friend. "And I'll be home for every major break—just like Jonathan."

Sarah nodded again. "I guess so. But it won't be the same."

Leah stood up and went to sit on the edge of the bed. "That's true," she admitted. "It was tough for me to get used to Jonathan not being here when he first went away to college."

Sarah looked up, and this time there was no question that there were tears in her eyes. "It was tough for me too," she whispered. "When Jonathan left, I mean."

Leah breathed a silent prayer for wisdom before answering. "I always assumed you thought of Jonathan as a big brother," she said. "But it's more than that, isn't it?"

"Yes." Sarah took a shaky breath. "It has been for a long time. But he never even noticed me. And it's just a matter of time until he meets some college girl and . . ."

Leah covered her friend's hand with her own. "I've thought the same thing ever since he left for his first semester, but nothing yet." She tried to smile some encouragement, but she imagined it wasn't working. "Who knows what might happen or what God has in mind?" She squeezed Sarah's hand. "We'll just have to pray about it, won't we?"

Sarah hesitated before nodding her agreement. Leah knew Sarah's commitment to the Lord was just a notch above nominal, but she also knew that prayer was the only way to resolve what could turn into a complicated issue. She supposed it was up to her to take the lead, so she closed her eyes and began to pray, trusting Sarah to follow along—and trusting God to work it all out according to His perfect plan.

Chapter 26

Klahan was scarcely holding back tears when Lawan stirred just before daylight. The thought that he would lose her very soon caused him to reach out and draw her close. He loved the way she looked, the way she smelled and felt—everything about her. Now he would have to give her up, and it was all his fault. Why had he not foreseen this development? It was a logical conclusion, after all.

Was it possible he could keep Lawan to himself for a few more days? Surely the woman from the orphanage did not plan to report them to the authorities, or she would not have come to warn him of Lawan's predicament. Klahan would keep the girl hidden for a while longer—until he could no longer do so without implicating himself in the crime and ending up behind bars with her.

Yes, that is what he would do—what he must do. He would hide her out for a few days and then, before the police could close in on them, he would find a way to turn her in without his name being involved in any way. Perhaps the woman from the orphanage would help him in some way—for the girl's sake, if not for his own.

"Klahan?"

The muffled voice interrupted his thoughts and stabbed his heart with regret. She was so young and helpless. She would never survive a lengthy prison sentence. And yet, she had survived two years in a brothel. Perhaps she was stronger than he imagined.

The girl laid her palm on his cheek. "Are you all right, Klahan?"

He blinked back tears, her tenderness nearly breaking him. "I am fine," he whispered, hoping to disguise the hoarseness of his voice. "I am sorry if I woke you."

"Why are you awake so early?" she asked. "Have you had trouble sleeping all night?"

Klahan nodded in the predawn darkness, though he knew she could not see him. Still, he imagined she sensed his movements. "I have much on my mind," he said, clearing his throat and managing to reinsert a steady tone to his words.

For a moment he thought she might have fallen back to sleep until she said, "Are you thinking of the two people you killed?"

Klahan swallowed. This was not something he wished to discuss with her — or with anyone, for that matter.

"Whatever I did, I did for you, Lawan. Now go back to sleep. We do not need to rise yet."

"I think your conscience is keeping you awake," she said. "My maae used to tell me that *phra yaeh suu* sometimes speaks to us that way — through our conscience. Do you believe that, Klahan?"

Anger swirled with confusion in Klahan's mind at the mention of *phra yaeh suu*. He too had once had a mother who spoke to him of this Lord Jesus Christ, but he had long ago rejected Him. Why must this young girl torture him by bringing up that name once again?

"I do not wish to speak of this," he said, his voice loud and firm now. "I am very tired. We must sleep now, and we will talk again in the morning, though not of this *phra yaeh suu* or of what I had to do to rescue you. Be quiet now and sleep, Lawan, please."

The man lay very still until he heard the girl's breathing return to its even cadence. Then he too closed his eyes and drifted off into a world of nightmares and demons that clawed at his soul.

Nyesha had called Leah on Tuesday night to ask if she could watch Anna on Wednesday. The girl had readily agreed, saying her friend Sarah was sleeping over but that they'd be up early and she could come to the Johnsons' home bright and early.

Now it was morning, and Nyesha snuggled close to her husband on the bench seat at the restaurant. She never cared much for the sitting-across-the-table arrangement when they went out. They did enough of that at home. If this was to be one of their rare romantic days alone together — thanks to Leah who was already at their home, fixing oatmeal for Anna — then she was going to start it off right.

187

She looked up at Kyle, his head bent over the menu and his short blond hair glistening under the lights. The sight of him with his reading glasses perched on his nose brought a grin to her face, and she laid a hand on his arm.

"So, Professor, what are you going to have?"

He looked up, appearing surprised at the interruption. She loved the way he gave his full concentration to whatever he was doing. His attention was never a half-hearted attempt at placating someone or meeting an obligation. Kyle jumped into whatever he was doing with both feet — and all his heart. That's what made him such a good husband and father.

"Sorry, honey," he mumbled. "Did you say something? I was examining the menu."

Nyesha nodded. "Exactly!" She leaned closer and used her most sultry voice. "I said, Professor, what are you having?"

Kyle's light eyebrows raised, and his cheeks colored. "If I dare say anything but you, I'm in trouble, right? And why did you call me professor?"

Nyesha's laugh exploded from her chest, and several heads turned briefly in their direction. "Sorry," she said, lowering her voice again. "I called you professor because you look so cute in those glasses. And because you were studying that menu like you were cramming for a chemistry exam." She stretched to plant a kiss on his cheek. "And no, you're not in trouble, no matter what you decide to have for breakfast. I'm having a California omelet myself."

He smiled. "What a surprise. You always have a California omelet."

"Not true," she said, shaking her head. "I've been known to have a ham and cheese omelet or even a Denver omelet on occasion."

Kyle rolled his eyes. "How adventurous of you!" He glanced back at the menu and then slapped it closed. "Well, no run-of-the-mill breakfast for me. Since I just got permission to order whatever I want, I'm having the crab scramble—with extra onions and cheese."

Nyesha wrinkled her nose. "Disgusting," she said. "That'll teach me to give you carte blanche when it comes to ordering your own food."

By the time the waitress had taken their orders, Nyesha was nearly finished with her second cup of tea, while Kyle had scarcely touched his orange juice. "What's on your mind?" she asked, once again laying her hand on his arm to get his attention. The hard feel of sinew and muscle beneath her touch stirred her heart as she waited for his answer.

He shrugged as he looked down at her. "Anna," he said. "I was thinking about what you told me, how she's seemed more interested in her birth family lately. We expected that when she was older, but now, at not quite five? Isn't that a little young?"

"I would have thought so," Nyesha admitted. "But with Anna . . . I don't know. She's special somehow." She smiled. "Oh, I know. All parents think that about their children, but I really do believe it's true about our daughter. Most people think she couldn't possibly remember anything about Thailand or her original family, but I sometimes wonder, don't you?"

Kyle nodded. "I do. And I think maybe we should contact the agency to see if there are any updates on her family that we should know about."

189

Their eyes locked, dark brown and deep blue, and they made the decision as one. "I agree," Nyesha said. "I've been thinking about it anyway. If nothing comes of it, fine. But at least we'll have tried. We owe it to Anna to have as much information for her as possible, if not for now, then for later, when she's old enough to understand and starts asking some really serious questions." She grinned. "I mean, it's not like she won't notice that she doesn't look like either one of us."

Kyle laughed. "That's for sure. Meanwhile, we'll just keep calling ourselves the rainbow family and let her figure it out from there."

The waitress arrived then, balancing a meal in each hand as the Johnsons turned toward the tantalizing aroma. It was time for the two of them to get on with their day, knowing that Anna was safe at home with a caregiver who loved her nearly as much as they did.

Jefe was disgusted. How inept was this Alley Cat person, to have had Mara in his sights and yet missed her? The man now knew where she worked; how was it possible that he had not yet captured her and gotten started on his assignment?

He sat in the midmorning sun and watched the various activities in the yard. It was the most dangerous location in the entire prison, where gangs congregated and fights broke out over a careless word or a flippant gesture. Jefe didn't care; he wasn't in the least concerned for his own safety. He was well connected in the criminal world that existed behind bars, a leader who called the shots in this world as well as the one where he had once walked free. Though he would much prefer to be outside the prison walls, he would make the best of it on the inside, where drugs were plentiful and anything could be bought for a price.

Including Mara's torture and death, he thought, grinning to himself as he watched two muscle-bound, tattooed inmates compete with one another by cranking out one-armed push-ups. Others gathered around to watch them and place bets on who would win, betting treats from the canteen on their favorite. In the distance he could see Jack's younger brother, Tom, sitting on the ground, pressed up against the chain-link fence in an attempt to remain as invisible as possible.

The guy's a sitting duck, Jefe told himself, smirking at the thought. *He's counting on his big brother, Jack, coming through on his assignment with Mara even more than I am. And he's probably right. Old Alley Cat will do his job — sooner or later. But for Tom's sake, he'd better make it sooner. Without some serious protection, that guy isn't going to last a month.*

Chapter 27

Klahan watched another day come to an end in the Golden Triangle. He had been restless throughout the daylight hours but insisted he and Lawan stay inside. She had cooked two simple meals for him but had said little, though Klahan caught her sneaking looks at him from the corner of her eye. As hard as Klahan tried to pretend that nothing had changed, that everything was all right, he knew she sensed otherwise.

With the day drawing to a close, he did his best to calm himself so he would not spend another sleepless night, fretting over what he must do. If only he could find a way to postpone it a bit longer, but sooner or later Lawan would step outside the safety of these four walls and someone would recognize her. If Klahan had not turned her in before that happened, he too could be arrested. As much as he loved the beautiful child, he was not willing to pay such a horrible price.

"Come and lay beside me," he called to her, as she completed her chores in the tiny cooking area. "Please," he added, a stab of guilt forcing the final word.

Eyes wide and full lips pressed shut, the obedient girl did as he asked. As he drew her into his arms, his heart raced at the warmth of her closeness. How he longed to consummate their relationship at least once before he turned her over to the authorities, but could he bring himself to do it?

"You are sad," Lawan whispered. "Why, Klahan?"

The stab in his heart cut deeper. If only the woman from the orphanage had not seen them, then at least he could have continued in ignorance for a time, enjoying the pleasures he had waited for so long. He sighed. What good was it to wish things different? Wishing did not change things. His life with Lawan was not to be. And if he did not deal with things quickly and in the right manner, he could find himself in very serious trouble. As he saw it, he had only two choices. He could turn in Lawan and then use his newly acquired financial resources to get as far away as possible in case she told them of his involvement in Chai's death, or he could do what was necessary to make sure Lawan could never tell anyone.

Once again the light touch of her hand on his cheek stirred up more emotions than he could discern. Why must she be so tender and loving? It had not been such a difficult thing to kill the evil Chai or even to do away with his old housekeeper. But this young, sweet child whose very beauty tugged at Klahan's heart? That would be another thing entirely.

"*Phra yaeh suu* will help you if you will just ask Him," Lawan crooned, continuing to stroke his cheek. "He has helped me many times—even when I was forced to live in that awful place with the boss man and Adung." He heard a catch in her voice before she continued. "Even when Chanthra died. And He will help you too because He loves you very much." She raised up on one elbow and stretched to kiss Klahan's forehead. "And I love you too, Klahan."

The explosion of pain drove him to his feet. "I do not want to hear about *phra yaeh suu*," he screamed, stumbling toward the door. "Leave me alone! Why do you torture me?" He yanked open the door and stepped out into the humid evening air, and then raced away from the house as if demons pursued him. Tears nearly blinded his sight, but he ran on, stumbling and falling but picking himself up and continuing on. He told himself over and over that it was the girl's fault. She was the one who had caused this entire mess by bewitching him and forcing him to do things he did not want to do, just so he could be with her. But his heart replied with every pounding beat that it was not so, and he loathed himself for the truth of it.

Mara and Barbara left the police station just as the Southern California sunshine was reaching its zenith.

"What do you think?" Mara asked, her stomach rumbling with noonday hunger but too nervous even to consider eating. "Are they going to find them now?"

"I believe they're going to try," Barbara answered as they descended the stairs to the sidewalk. She stopped at the bottom step and turned to Mara. "And yes, I believe they'll be successful — sooner or later — because you were quick enough to think to get that license plate. If the guy is still in the area, they'll run across him sooner or later. And I don't see any reason to think he isn't still around. He no doubt has his stable of girls in some house nearby, so he's not going anywhere."

"Sooner or later?" Mara frowned, squinting at the sun and wishing she'd thought to grab her sunglasses before leaving her room this morning. "Does that mean you think they won't seriously go looking for them?"

"They'll watch for him," Barbara answered, "but no, I don't think it'll be a priority." She sighed. "I wish I could tell you differently, but I know how these things work, and there are just too many other things at the top of the list." She laid her hand on Mara's arm. "But that doesn't mean they won't find him. The guy obviously cruises around town in that car, and thankfully he's just vain enough to have a personalized license plate—though for the life of me I can't imagine what LDBLO means. But who cares? It'll make spotting him a lot easier."

Mara nodded. "Good. Maybe they'll even come back to Mariner's, though I doubt it. He didn't like my reaction the last time he was there, so they'll probably find a new spot to eat out."

"True," Barbara agreed. "But the neighborhood where you work is going to be patrolled a bit heavier now, since that's likely where he'll return, even if it is to a different restaurant. Chances are he lives in the area, so that helps a lot." She patted Mara's arm. "Be encouraged. You did your part, and the police are going to find him."

"And the girl," Mara added.

Barbara's lips pressed together and she nodded. "And the girl. Yes."

It was noon before Francesca managed to drag herself through the shower and apply a dab of makeup. El Diablo didn't like it when his girls weren't ready for clients at any hour after lunchtime on, though most didn't come until later in the day or early evening. Francesca hoped the latter would be the case today. Not only was her stomach still feeling queasy, but she was sleepy much of the time lately. ChaCha had told her that was part of being pregnant.

"How do you know that?" Francesca had asked her.

The bleached blonde, with the drawn-on eyebrows who was only a couple years older than Francesca, had laughed in response. "Are you kidding me? I'm speaking from experience, muchacha." She leaned forward and held up three fingers in front of Francesca's face. "Three times," she said. "I've been pregnant three times already."

Francesca had felt her eyes grow wide. "But what happened? To the babies, I mean?"

ChaCha laughed again. "Babies? Get a clue, Frankie. You don't really think I stayed pregnant long enough to have babies, do you?" She shook her head. "No way. As soon as El Diablo found out, he took me for what he called a 'procedure.' They sucked out the little blob inside me before it ever had time to turn into a baby."

Even now, heat exploded in Francesca's chest at the memory of ChaCha's words. No way were those words true! Already Francesca knew that her "tiny blob," as ChaCha called it, was a baby. She also knew that El Diablo would kill the little one as soon as he found out.

195

How could she keep it from him? She could try to hide the morning sickness, but sooner or later her stomach would start to grow, and then what would she do? ChaCha had also told her that she tried to hide it the first time, and El Diablo warned her that if she ever did that again he would beat it out of her and she wouldn't need the procedure. From then on ChaCha had told him the minute she suspected.

I can't tell him, she thought, flopping down on her bed and staring up the ceiling. *I have to keep it a secret as long as I can. Maybe, somehow, I can get away from here before he knows.*

She had begged ChaCha not to tell, and the girl had reluctantly promised. Could she trust her? Francesca doubted it, but what choice did she have? She squeezed her eyes shut and tried to pray, but the God of her parents seemed so very far away.

Chapter 28

Klahan ran into the night, pushing himself until he thought his lungs would explode. He was beyond the lights of the village when he stumbled yet again, and this time he made no effort to rise.

Phra yaeh suu. Phra yaeh suu. The name echoed in his mind, even after he covered his ears with his hands. "Leave me alone!" he cried. But the name continued to call to him.

At last he buried his face in the dirt and wept, remembering how his own maae had taught him of *phra yaeh suu,* even as Lawan claimed her mother had done. So how was it possible that the little girl who had suffered so much still clung to her mother's teachings, when he had so long ago rejected them?

The memory of the girl's feathery touch on his cheek stabbed his already broken heart. How could he betray her?

The depth of his own depravity and selfishness washed over him in waves, as he convulsed on the ground, wishing he could die but terrified at the realization that if he did, he would surely go to a place of torment much worse than where he was at that moment.

"Is there any hope for me?" he whispered. To himself . . . or to God? He was not sure. "Or is it too late?"

I have loved you with an everlasting love.

The words seemed to drift on the wind, and yet he knew there was no wind on that sultry night.

"How is it possible?" Klahan dared to ask. "How can You still love me after all I have done?"

I have already paid the price for your sin. All you must do is receive My forgiveness. Do you wish to receive it, My son?

Tears exploded anew from Klahan's eyes. "Yes," Klahan sobbed. "Oh yes, Lord! Please, please forgive me."

A sense of peace burst forth from Klahan's heart and seemed to flow out into his limbs, as he felt himself wrapped in a blanket of warmth. For the first time in his life, he truly felt safe, and the joy that followed was more than he would ever be able to express in words.

Surely dawn would break soon, Lawan thought, and with it would come the return of Klahan. She had lain awake most of the night, praying for the man who was her rescuer and protector, even as she wondered what had happened in the past couple of days to change him so. Something was wrong, but she had no choice but to wait until he was ready to tell her about it.

Her eyes were heavy, and she was just beginning to drift off when she heard the door open. Klahan had returned. Should she rise to greet him or wait for him to lie down beside her?

Before she could decide, she sensed his presence as he lowered himself to the sleeping mat they shared. He wrapped his arms around her and pulled her close, the wetness on his cheeks alerting Lawan to the fact that he was still quite emotional. She wished she knew what to say to help him, but because she was not clear on what he was experiencing, she simply lay still and waited.

"Dear Lawan," he whispered, his chin resting on her head. "You have been through so much. How could I even think of subjecting you to more?"

Lawan was confused, but she patted his cheek in an effort to comfort him.

Klahan's voice broke. "You trusted me," he said, "and I planned to betray you." He kissed the top of her head. "From the first time I saw you at the brothel, I wanted you for myself. I could not bear to think of all those other men, using you, hurting you."

His voice drifted off for a moment, and then he continued. "I told myself it would be different with me. I would not touch you until you belonged only to me. But then I would have used you, even as the others."

Lawan wanted to protest that he could never be like the others, but she remained silent and listened.

"Certainly I would never have hurt you," Klahan said, "but I would have used you just the same. I wanted you for my own pleasure, my own needs. I never gave a thought to what you might want or what was best for you. And then, when the woman from the orphanage came and said she recognized you, I . . . I was willing to sacrifice you for my own safety."

He pulled her tighter, nearly crushing her against his chest. "Oh, Lawan, can you ever forgive me?"

Forgive Klahan, the man who had risked everything to rescue her? Why would she need to forgive him?

His voice leveled out then, as he said, "I have already asked *phra yaeh suu* for forgiveness, and He has given it." He choked back a sob then. "I am forgiven, Lawan. Forgiven by God Himself! Now I ask it from you as well. Please."

Lawan's eyes filled with tears as she realized what this man had just told her. "Oh yes," she cried. "Of course I forgive you! And I rejoice with you, dear Klahan. But . . ." She took a deep, shaky breath, blinking back more tears. "But I do not understand what you mean when you say you were going to sacrifice me. I am confused."

"Shh," Klahan crooned. "Of course you are confused, little one. But do not worry. I have taken care of everything. Just as I promised, this time I have truly protected you. You will be all right." He paused. "And so will I."

Leah had been surprised to see Sarah show up at the Wednesday evening service. She usually came only on Sunday mornings, when her parents insisted. Though Leah wanted to believe her best friend was there because of a deepening relationship with Christ, she couldn't help but wonder if it had more to do with the fact that Sarah hoped to see Jonathan there, since he seldom missed a service when he was home from college.

Now that the service was over and much of the congregation was milling about, chatting and visiting, she wasn't surprised when Sarah insinuated herself between Leah and Jonathan as they stood talking to one of the youth leaders. Sarah hadn't shown much interest in the youth group since they were in middle school, but suddenly she seemed fascinated with the discussion.

"Well, I need to get going," Jonathan said, interrupting the flow of conversation. "I promised my boss I'd come in and pull a couple of late hours tonight." His dark brown eyes landed on Leah. "Need a ride home, Sis?"

Leah shook her head. "Nah, I think I'll hang around awhile and head home later with Mom and Dad."

Before Jonathan could turn away, Sarah's cheeks flamed as she said, "I'd like a ride."

Leah raised her eyebrows. Where had that come from? Leah knew her friend had arrived at the service with her parents, so why wouldn't she go home with them as well?

"Mom and Dad are staying after for some kind of meeting," she added quickly, obviously doing her best to appear nonchalant but not fooling Leah one bit. "I'm kind of tired, and I'd really like to get home as soon as possible. Would you mind, Jonathan?"

Leah's big brother flashed a smile. "Of course I wouldn't mind. It's not like it's out of my way or anything. Sure. Come on—if you don't mind riding in the heap I call a car."

Sarah's laugh was nervous, but she didn't miss a beat as she followed Jonathan toward the door. Leah realized then that her eyebrows were still raised. She lowered them at the same instant she closed her mouth. Sarah's long secret crush on Jonathan appeared ready to sneak out into the open. Leah only hoped her friend's heart wouldn't be broken in the process. Jonathan had always treated Sarah like a little sister, and Leah couldn't imagine that he would ever feel any differently toward the petite blonde.

Then again, she reminded herself, *stranger things have happened around here lately.*

Chapter 29

Mara hadn't felt well all afternoon. She told herself it was just lack of sleep and worry about the girl she'd seen in the café with the guy who was obviously her owner. She'd told herself repeatedly to leave it alone, that she'd done all she could and it was up to the cops now. But the image of that young, terrified girl with the cast on her arm had torn at her heart for hours. Either she'd made herself sick over it, or she really was coming down with something.

"You OK?" Julio asked as he brushed past her with a tray full of dirty dishes, headed for the sink.

Mara looked up, reminding herself that she was at work and needed to behave professionally. "I'm fine," she said. "Just a little lightheaded. Maybe I need to eat something."

"How about a nice hot bowl of soup?" the cook called out from behind her.

She turned to look at the kind, middle-aged man who spent so many hours over the hot grill each week. Usually a bowl of soup would sound perfect, but at the moment the very mention of it made her stomach churn.

"I don't think so," she said. "Thanks anyway, Stephen. I guess I'm not hungry after all."

The man's forehead drew together. "Are you feeling all right? You really don't look so good."

Mara let her shoulders slump. Who was she kidding? She felt terrible. But what could she do? The dinner crowd would arrive in a few hours; there was no way she could take off, though the lure of her bed was nearly overpowering.

"Listen," Stephen said, stepping close to her. "Maggie called earlier, asking for extra hours. She really needs the money. Why don't I call and ask her to come in and finish your shift for you. Julio can take his break and drive you home. It'll do you good."

Mara opened her mouth to protest, and then shut it and nodded. "Thanks," she said. "If you can get Maggie to come in and cover for me, I'll gladly go home. I'm sure I'll be good as new tomorrow."

In moments she was seated on the passenger side of Julio's old car, her head leaning back and her eyes closed. Going home and catching some sleep was sounding better to her all the time.

Anna had fallen asleep in the car on the way home from church, and Kyle had carried her inside, transferring her to her bed without waking her. Now Kyle and Nyesha looked forward to finishing off their special day together with a few more minutes of alone time before heading for bed.

Sitting with their feet up in the reclining loveseat, Nyesha's head rested on Kyle's shoulder. The family room was dimly lit by flickering candles and filled with soft jazz coming from the sound system he had installed a couple of years earlier. Kyle imagined life couldn't get much better than it was at that very moment. In addition to the nice breakfast they'd had to start off their day, the two of them had spent time browsing some antique shops near the beach and then taking a picnic lunch out onto the sand and watching the surfers and sunbathers take advantage of the gorgeous Southern California weather.

Now they were home after a challenging midweek church service, their daughter was asleep, and the house was quiet. Kyle found himself wishing he'd taken off two days instead of one, but he knew he really needed to get back to work. He was grateful to have a job at the advertising agency that enabled him to support their little family while Nyesha stayed home with Anna.

"Do you have any idea how blessed we are?" he murmured.

Nyesha sighed. "I sure do. It's a good thing I'm not a superstitious person, or I'd think things were just too good and we were headed for trouble. But I know better. Our lives are in God's hands, and that's true whatever comes."

"Amen to that, beautiful lady." Kyle smiled into the semidarkness and then paused. "You know, I was thinking a while ago about what we discussed regarding Anna and her birth family. I hate to admit this, but selfishly I'd rather not pursue it. I mean, I guess I like to think of her as ours, period. But I know she'll get more and more curious about her early life as she gets older, and I suppose we really should see if we can find out anything more recent."

"I know what you mean," Nyesha answered without moving. "I've thought the same thing. After all, we're her mom and dad now. This is her home. But Thailand is where her roots are, and we owe it to her to have as much information for her as possible—when she's ready for it."

"Exactly. And who knows when that will be?"

Nyesha chuckled. "Knowing that little girl, it won't be long. Sometimes she seems so young and vulnerable; other times she's like a grown-up in a small body."

Kyle smiled and kissed the top of his wife's head. "That's Anna, all right—both sides of her. So are you going to follow up then?"

She raised her head and gazed into his face, the warmth in her dark eyes stirring his emotions. The only thing more beautiful than Nyesha's physical appearance was the heart God had placed inside her. "I'll get started first thing in the morning," she said and then grinned, her eyes twinkling even in the muted light. "But first let's finish off a perfect day before we start thinking about tomorrow."

Alley Cat was back at Mariner's long before the dinner crowd arrived. He wasn't about to miss that girl again. This time he'd go inside, settle down at a back booth, and not move until he'd made sure she was working. Then he'd wait outside until she got off. If that kid didn't give her a ride home like he had the night Mara had seen Jack in the shadows and run away from him, then this time he'd have her. It would be the start of a painful relationship—on her part anyway—but it would also be the start of his brother's protection in prison. And that was the only thing in this entire world that really mattered to Jack.

The sand sculpture contest was still going on in town, so even between meals the shops and eateries near the water were busy. Mariner's was no exception. Jack managed to snag an empty booth toward the back and sat facing the door and the kitchen. Sooner or later the girl named Mara would make her entrance—and then her fate was sealed.

Meanwhile, his stomach grumbled. The chubby waitress he'd seen once before had brought him a menu and a glass of ice water when he first came in, so he studied the menu while peering over it occasionally, each time he heard someone come in. So far, no Mara.

After a few moments the waitress returned, bringing the coffee he'd requested and asking if he was ready to order. He tossed the menu on the table and said, "A burger with the works — extra onions. And fries. Throw in a salad too, will you? I'm hungry."

She smiled. "Sure thing. Be right back with the salad."

Jack considered asking about Mara, but he didn't want to get a reputation as a guy with a "thing" for her — some sort of stalker — particularly once Mara turned up missing. The last thing he needed was to see his face in a drawing on a "person of interest" poster around town.

Nearly an hour passed by the time he finished eating, and still no sign of the girl. He ordered a slice of peach pie, though he couldn't imagine stuffing it down his already full stomach. He'd give it another thirty minutes, and then he'd leave. If she hadn't come by then, she wasn't going to show.

He'd picked at his pie for nearly twenty minutes when he heard the waitress talking to someone who had just come in and sat down at the booth behind him.

"I didn't know you were going to be working tonight," a young woman said.

The waitress responded, sounding a bit weary, "I wasn't scheduled to, but I asked for extra hours. When Mara got sick, they called me in and I jumped at it. I'm a single mom with two kids to support," she said. "And now that they're teenagers, I need all the money I can get."

The young woman and her male companion laughed, as their conversation continued. But Jack was no longer listening. He had snatched up the bill the waitress had left earlier and was already heading for the cash register. He couldn't believe he'd missed her again. What was he going to have to do to catch up with this chick?

Chapter 30

Jonathan was surprised when he got home from work and found Leah waiting up for him. "I thought you'd be in bed by now. Didn't you get up early to go to the Johnsons' place to babysit?"

Leah's long red curls glowed golden beside the lamp where she sat on the family room couch. She was wrapped in a blue robe, though her feet were bare. She smiled up at him. "Did you really think I could sleep without finding out how things went with you and Sarah?"

Jonathan frowned. Sarah? What did she have to do with anything? All he'd done was drop her off at home on his way to work.

"I don't get it. What's up with Sarah?"

Leah raised her eyebrows, her smile still in place. "Are you kidding me? You haven't figured it out yet?"

Jonathan shook his head. She wasn't making any sense. "Figured what out?"

Leah's cheeks colored slightly and her smile faded. "Maybe I shouldn't have mentioned it, but Sarah was so obvious in her efforts to get a ride with you that I figured she must have said something."

"Something about what? Leah, could you just spit it out, please? I don't have a clue what you're talking about."

Leah hesitated, and then seemed to make a decision to plunge ahead. "Sarah has a crush on you. She's had it for a long time but just recently decided to tell me about it."

Jonathan dropped onto the couch beside his sister. "Are you crazy? Leah, you're not making any sense. Sarah's part of the family—practically another little sister. How could she have a crush on me?"

Leah shrugged. "I have no idea how, but I know she does. She told me. I should have seen it, but like you, I never even thought of it. But now, looking back, I can see the signs." She sighed. "I just hope she doesn't kill me for telling you. You won't say anything, will you?"

"Are you serious? No way would I say anything about this. I mean, it's weird." He paused, picturing the cute blonde that had hung around their house for as long as he could remember. "Sarah? Really?"

Leah grinned. "Really. And yes, it's weird. But I'm wondering how you'll feel once you get used to the idea."

Jonathan's eyebrows shot up, and he shot up out of the couch almost as quickly. "I'm not getting used to it," he insisted, determined to make his point. "She's a friend, a sister-type friend, and that's it. Got it?"

Leah looked surprised. "Hey, don't get mad at me, Bro. I'm just telling you what I know."

"Yeah, well, forget about it," Jonathan said, turning away and heading toward the kitchen. "I'm going to go get a snack. You can join me if you want, but only if you promise not to talk about Sarah. That subject is closed."

Joan was nervous. She had told no one but her husband about the visit she'd had from the man named Klahan, and they'd agreed to keep it quiet as he had requested. But if he didn't follow through on his promise within twenty-four hours, they also agreed they would have no choice but to alert the authorities. They had to do whatever they could to help Lawan, and after hearing Klahan's confession, it was obvious the girl was innocent.

The orphanage was just beginning to come awake after a long night's slumber. Tousled heads lifted from sleeping mats, as wide eyes gazed about at the large dormitory-like rooms where a total of nearly five hundred children were housed.

Joan smiled at the thought. She and Mort had not been able to have children of their own, but God had answered the cry of their heart and given them an abundance of little ones. She only wished their charges hadn't had to endure such suffering before coming to them.

At least they made it here, she reminded herself. *How many of them never do? How many of them end up in a place like Lawan was for the last couple of years, kidnapped from their homes, sold into slavery — and not living long enough to escape. Though Klahan's motives were wrong and the lengths he went to in order to get Lawan for himself absolutely horrifying, I can't help but appreciate the fact that he at least got her out of that terrible brothel. How I wish I could empty out those disgusting places and bring all those bruised, battered children here where they would be safe!*

The increasing chatter of children around her blended with the chortles and calls of mynahs and roller birds from the jungle outside, drawing Joan back from her reverie. No time to daydream. There were hungry mouths to feed and oh, so many chores to do! She would remain busy all day, even as she waited and prayed that Klahan would do as he promised.

211

Lawan moved slowly about the cooking area, careful not to awaken Klahan, who had only recently fallen asleep. She knew he was exhausted, though he had not told her where he had been or what he had done while he was gone. But she knew for certain that he would be hungry when he finally woke up, and she wanted to have his food prepared. Besides, she too was hungry after a long and nearly sleepless night.

She stopped and looked at the man who lay curled up on the mat. She had grown to love him almost as a father, though she had only recently dreamed of being his wife, only because she wanted so desperately for him to love and care for her. Somehow, now, she knew that he would do so, though not in the way either of them had imagined.

Klahan stirred, but he did not groan or cry out in his sleep as he had so many times before. He seemed at peace, and Lawan knew that was because he had come to know *phra yaeh suu*—as she did, as Chanthra had, as their parents had.

Why do I think of my parents as being dead? The thought came unbidden into her mind. Was it because she had not seen them in two years and held out little hope that she ever would, at least not until she followed Chanthra to heaven? Were her *maae* and *phor* already there too waiting for her along with their oldest daughter? And what of her baby sister, Mali, the one who had been adopted by a family so very far away, in a place called America? Would Lawan ever see little Mali again?

She would be nearly five years old, Lawan mused, stirring the rice that bubbled on the burner. *Would I even recognize her if I did see her?*

She shook her head. There was no sense wondering about things she could not change or control. Right now she must focus on the food she was preparing for herself and the man who had rescued her—the man whose name meant brave. For a reason she could not understand, her heart ached at the thought.

Chapter 31

Thursday morning dawned bright and sunny, the sharp light piercing Jonathan's eyelids and pulling him from a deep sleep.

He blinked and squinted at the source of the offending light. Why hadn't he remembered to close the blinds before falling into bed last night? And then he remembered. Sarah. Leah's stunning news had disturbed him more than he wanted to admit, and he'd had a tough time falling asleep at all.

Glancing at the illuminated clock by his bed, he realized it was nearly 9:00, later than he'd expected. Still, he could have used a few more hours of sleep. Besides, he had the evening off and no real plans, so why get up any earlier than necessary?

Sarah's pixielike face popped into his mind, and he frowned. He'd always thought she was cute, but cute like a pesky little sister. How could she even think of him as anything but a big brother? Maybe Leah was wrong. It just didn't make sense.

He sighed and threw back the covers, pulling himself to a sitting position on the side of his bed. Might as well shower and go downstairs for breakfast. His mom was always hovering around when he was home, hoping for a chance to fix him some of her special pancakes or omelets. Jonathan grinned. Today he just might take her up on it. Then he'd see what he could do to get another ballgame going, or maybe just head over to the batting cages to burn off a little energy. If nothing else, it would help distract him from thoughts of Sarah.

He frowned. Why did Leah's announcement about Sarah bother him so much? Why couldn't he just ignore it? And why, each time he allowed himself to think of her for even a moment, did he suddenly find his mind drifting from Sarah to Mara?

Mara. The memory of her sitting on the porch with Barbara Whiting tugged at his heart. What he'd really like to do today is drive over to the place where Mara was staying and ask her to go for a ride with him. But, of course, he couldn't do that, could he?

Jonathan shook his head and stood up. All this daydreaming about Sarah and Mara must mean it had been way too long since he'd gone out on anything even close to a real date. But if he was ever going to make that happen, he was definitely going to have to find someone besides his kid sister's best friend or a mysterious girl who had spent the majority of her life as a slave.

Snatching his jeans and a relatively clean T-shirt from the back of the chair that sat in front of his computer, he headed for the bathroom. Maybe, if he stood under the hot water long enough, he'd be able to clear his head and think straight again.

*

❦

Where are we going? Lawan wondered. She was unfamiliar with the area, having passed through it for the first time when Klahan brought her to their new home only a couple of days earlier. It had been dark then, and it was dark now. The ever-present drone of daytime insects had been replaced with the clicks and cricks of the nocturnal ones. Even the sounds of the limited nightlife of the village had faded away as they continued their trek into the jungle. To keep from stumbling and to help dismiss her fear of night creatures, Lawan held tightly to Klahan's hand, sensing that he had a clear destination in mind but unable to imagine where it might be.

She reviewed the day in silence. When Klahan had finally awakened, he had gratefully eaten the simple meal she had prepared. From that point on he had been especially quiet, and Lawan was certain he had heavy thoughts on his mind. And yet, more than once when their eyes had met, he had smiled at her with sad eyes, even though his words were positive and encouraging. She had been especially happy when he spoke of *phra yaeh suu* and assured her that he shared her faith. But when she had tried to pursue the topic and have a conversation with him, he had again grown pensive, so much so that she had nearly felt his pain.

As night fell, he had packed their meager possessions back into the two sacks they had been carrying when they so recently struck out on their journey, taken her hand, and walked out into the growing darkness. Since then Klahan had not said a word. Lawan, trained to follow the lead of all male authorities, remained silent as well.

Her legs were growing weary and her eyelids heavy when she noticed faint lights in the not-too-far distance. Was it another town or village? A farmhouse? Her heart leapt to think it might be bandits or slave traders, sitting around a fire. Surely Klahan would not betray her and turn her over to men like the ones he had helped her escape!

Less than fifty yards from the lights, Klahan stopped, exerting pressure on Lawan's hand until she did the same.

"Joan Stockton," he called, a name that sounded strange to Lawan, particularly as Klahan struggled to pronounce it. "I have come back, as I promised. And I have brought the girl with me."

Lawan felt her eyes widen, and her heart began to race. Had she been wrong about Klahan after all? Had he brought her to slave traders to sell her for a profit?

Hushed voices spoke words Lawan could not fully hear nor distinguish. Still she and Klahan did not move. Her head felt light as she waited, wondering at the fate that awaited her. Then, without warning, a man and woman appeared out of the darkness, stopping just a few feet in front of them.

Lawan squinted, trying to make out their features. It was too dark to be certain, but she thought they were foreigners. When the woman spoke, her accent heavy, she was certain of it.

"You have brought Lawan?" the woman asked.

Klahan's grip on her hand did not waver. "Yes," he said, his voice quavering only slightly. "As I promised."

The woman's tone softened when she spoke again. "And the rest of the promise?"

Klahan's hand grew damp, and Lawan thought she felt him tremble before he answered. "I will keep the rest of the promise as well," he said. "As soon as I know Lawan is safe."

"She will be safe with us," the man said, his voice deep, his accent less pronounced. "So long as we know you have done what you promised, then we will take her under our protection."

A pause hung heavy in the night air, until Klahan released her hand and dropped to his knee beside her. "These are good people," he said. "They will take care of you and protect you, as I wished to do." Lawan heard him swallow a sob before he continued. "I have done many bad things in my life, but now I know *phra yaeh suu* has forgiven me, and I must do what is right."

He stood to his feet and turned as if to go, but Lawan threw her arms around his waist. "Do not leave me, Klahan," she begged, hot tears filling her eyes and streaming down her face. "Please, Klahan! Take me with you!"

Klahan turned back and placed his hands on Lawan's shoulders. "Sweet, lovely Lawan," he whispered. "I cannot take you where I am going. I must pay for my crimes, and you must stay here where you will be safe. It cannot be any other way."

Klahan lifted his head and fixed his eyes on the couple who stood just behind them. "Take her inside," he said, his voice breaking. "Please. I must go now."

Lawan felt strong hands grasp her waist and lift her from the ground. Kicking her feet and flailing her arms, she screamed, "No! No, Klahan! Do not leave me. Do not let them take me!"

But Klahan was already moving quickly, wordlessly into the darkness, leaving Lawan in the clutches of a man she did not know. What would happen to her now? The possibilities crashed down upon her, and she stopped fighting, collapsing in tears and resignation. So her life in captivity had not ended after all, and Klahan had not rescued her as she had believed. Would her new owner be as terrible as the one she had before? Only time would tell, and Lawan knew from experience that there was nothing she could do about it.

219

❧

The sun was especially hot today and nearing its noon pinnacle, but Jefe didn't care. He had a privileged seat in one of the few shady spots in the yard, and he wasn't about to give it up to anyone.

Not that anyone would challenge me, he thought, smirking. *I'm Jefe and I run things wherever I am—even in here.*

He glanced at the uniformed correctional officers patrolling the yard, with others positioned on surrounding walls and in turrets, high above the inmates, eyes trained to catch the first hint of a problem. Jefe had to hand it to them — they caught most instances before they turned deadly. But there were always a few that couldn't be stopped in time.

Is that what had happened with Tom? Jefe imagined so. He hadn't been there, but bad news traveled fast in prison. Apparently Alley Cat's brother had been in the wrong place at the wrong time, or looked at someone he shouldn't have, or said something that sounded disrespectful. It could have been any one of a dozen things, but whatever it was, he'd been found earlier that morning with a shank protruding from his bleeding stomach. Jefe had heard that he wasn't dead but close to it — not that he cared one way or the other. Tom was just one more worthless bum, doing time because he was too stupid not to get caught. But Jefe cared a lot about how this latest turn of events would impact his business deal with Jack. That was really all that mattered to Jefe these days, so for that reason he hoped the dumb kid pulled through. Prison officials might not notify Jack as quickly over a stabbing as they would if Tom died. If that happened before Jack got hold of Mara, Jefe would have to start over in his plan to exact revenge from the girl who had betrayed him.

Life could sure get complicated at times, he thought. Making Mara pay should have been an easy assignment. What was taking Alley Cat so long? All Jefe wanted was to hear that he had her. Then Jack and Mara would be out of touch for a few days until it was over, meaning the prison officials wouldn't be able to get hold of him during that time.

Jefe smiled. That's all he needed — just another day or two, maybe even a few hours. Alley Cat would send word that he had caught his prey, and Jefe would relax and enjoy himself as he imagined her suffering. Time enough after the assignment was completed to tell Jack about the untimely incident with his brother.

Chapter 32

The morning mist dispersed in layers, revealing thick bamboo forests surrounding what appeared to be a compound with several large buildings. Lawan sat on a sleeping mat near an open window in the midst of that compound, blinking back tears at the sound of elephants trumpeting their greeting to the new dawn. She decided she must be somewhere near an elephant camp, where *mahouts* cut sugarcane to earn a day's wages. Beyond that, she had no idea where she was or why.

The rising sun warmed the room quickly, as girls of various ages raised their tousled heads from thin pillows and glanced around, their gaze eventually coming to rest on the newcomer. Lawan squirmed under the scrutiny of so many pairs of wide, dark eyes. Was she truly in another brothel, and were all these girls slaves who belonged to the man and woman who had placed her on this bed the night before?

Though they had been kind to her and treated her gently, assuring her in their foreign-sounding tongues that she was safe and she did not need to be afraid, she wondered if such a thing could ever be true. Klahan had made such a promise, and now he had abandoned her. What was to become of her now?

"Who are you?"

The question came from a girl of about four or five on the mat next to Lawan's. Should she answer?

Lawan scanned the spacious room again. Nearly thirty or more girls sat or lay on mats, staring at her in anticipation of her answer. None looked scared or abused, and none was naked. Lawan found a glimmer of hope in those facts.

"I am Lawan," she said at last.

The child who had asked her name giggled at the response. "I like your name," she said, smiling as she rose from her mat and stepped to stand in front of Lawan. "I am BanChuen."

Zinnia flower, Lawan thought. *It fits her.* Hesitating as the thought crossed her mind that BanChuen was about the same age as her own sister Mali would be now, if she was still alive. Lawan's heart constricted at the realization that she would probably never know if Mali or any of her family still lived. Chanthra's fate was the only one she knew for certain.

Tears sprang into Lawan's eyes, and she felt helpless to stop them. As they spilled over onto her cheeks, BanChuen's face crumpled as well, and she threw her arms around Lawan's neck. "Do not cry, Lawan. We love you, and we will take care of you."

Other voices moved close, surrounding Lawan with comforting words, as Lawan wept the heart-wrenching tears born of hard, painful experiences. At that moment she wanted nothing more than to be a little child again.

224

❧

Mara had been undecided all day about returning to work. She felt somewhat better than she had the day before, but found herself wishing it were her day off and she could take it easy until Friday. As busy as they'd been all week, the sand sculpting contest would wind up this weekend, and Mariner's would be packed the whole time. It would be nice to rest up before the onslaught, but she'd just about decided she'd have to pull herself together and go in anyway when her boss called and told her to go ahead and take the evening off. As much as she hated to lose a night's pay—not to mention the tips—she had smiled when she hung up the phone.

Now, with the evening sky turning varied shades of lavender, she watched from the front porch as the last rays of sunlight blinked the end of Thursday across the San Diego landscape. She rested her head against the back of the old rocker that had quickly become her favorite perch and tried to remember Mexican sunsets when she was a child. Why did that seem centuries ago, as if she'd lived it in another lifetime?

Probably because I did, she told herself. *I was young then . . . and innocent. My parents didn't treat me very well, but it was all I knew—that and my so-called tio who always visited me and told me how much he loved me.*

She snorted, reminding herself how grateful she was that the lecherous old pervert was finally behind bars where he belonged—and where he could no longer hurt her. There was no doubt in her mind that if she hadn't been rescued when she was, sooner or later her dear *tio* would have killed her.

But I was rescued, wasn't I, Tio? And now you are the one who suffers—as it should be! May you suffer a thousand times over for every time you hurt me or the others!

The thought of Jasmine, murdered by one of Jefe's hired thugs, brought fresh tears to Mara's eyes. After all the years she had tried to train herself not to cry, it always surprised her when certain memories overrode her training and turned her into an emotional wreck.

Crying doesn't do any good for anyone, she reminded herself, angrily swiping at her tears. *Jasmine is dead, and she's*

225

not the only one Jefe murdered over the years. There's nothing I
can do about it, so what's the point?

The image of the girl sitting in the booth at Mariner's beside
her owner gelled in Mara's mind, threatening to release a new
wave of tears, but she steeled herself, refusing to give in. *I can't
bring Jasmine back by crying*, she thought, gritting her teeth,
*and I can't help the other girl that way either. I just hope the
cops find that creep and get her away from him before it's too
late, if it isn't already. The poor girl. She probably trusted men
once too like I did. But never again. Never again!*

Jonathan was pleased that the day had turned out so well after
all. Though he'd been unable to raise a ballgame on such short
notice, he'd worked off some stress at the batting cages and then
spent the afternoon at the beach, leaving just before sunset to
head home. But as happened so often, his old VW Bug seemed
to have a mind of its own, and the next thing he knew he was
driving down the street where Mara lived, his eyes darting back
and forth from the road to the house as he drew close. For some
reason he wasn't surprised to see her sitting on the porch.

Suddenly nervous, he considered driving by without
stopping, but he knew she would have heard the Beetle's
approach and spotted him by now. He might as well stop and
say something brilliant like, "I just happened to be in the
neighborhood."

Right.

Jonathan sighed and pulled to the curb, shut off the engine,
and opened the door, determined to appear more confident
than he felt. He pasted a smile on his face and prayed it didn't

look too wooden, then made his way from the street to the porch and up the steps.

The dim porch lamp cast just enough light that he couldn't mistake the shock that marred her otherwise perfect face. But wait. It was more than shock that detracted from her usual beauty. Her skin was splotchy and her eyes puffy. Had she been crying?

All the greetings he'd rehearsed from the time he parked the car until this moment disappeared, and he stood before her without one word to offer. He swallowed, knowing he owed it to her to say something but clueless as to what that should be. Instead he sank down in a beat-up redwood chair beside her and cleared his throat.

"I'm sorry," he said at last, watching for a reaction. "I should have called first."

She blinked and shrugged, the perfect picture of nonchalance. "No need," she said, her voice slightly thicker than usual, confirming his suspicions that she'd been crying. "So what do you want? Why'd you come?"

He swallowed, wishing he had an answer that made some sense. What could he say? He came because she was always on his mind? Because his car steered him in this direction? Because he couldn't stop thinking about her? Because he was looking for Barbara Whiting and thought she might be here again? Because he thought she was absolutely beautiful and couldn't erase her face from his memory?

He wrestled with speaking what was on his heart or blurting out some ridiculous excuse that she wouldn't believe anyway. Finally he decided on something in between.

"I've been thinking about you," he said, noticing that her eyes narrowed at his words. "I wondered how you were doing with your job and all."

It sounded so lame that he knew she'd never buy it, but at least he'd broken the silence.

She raised her dark, perfectly shaped eyebrows. "Really? You've been thinking about me?"

He nodded, his mouth suddenly as dry as his palms were damp. What in the world was wrong with him? You'd think he'd never talked to a girl before. Then again, with all the girls he'd known in his life, he'd never met one who affected him as Mara did.

He took a deep breath. "So . . . are you doing all right? I mean, is there anything new or exciting going on in your life?"

Mara frowned. "What do you mean by that?"

Jonathan's heart skipped a beat. Had he said something wrong, something to offend her?

"I'm sorry," he said. "I didn't mean to . . ." He stopped. This conversation was going downhill fast.

"I just wanted to see you," he said. His heart was racing by now, but he left the words hanging in the air between them, and waited.

Mara stood to her feet. "Well, you saw me," she said, turning and reaching for the door. "It's getting late. Good night, Jonathan."

Chapter 33

Mara lay on her bed in the darkness, disgusted with herself. Why had she been so rude to the one person who had been willing to risk his life to rescue her? But despite the question, she already knew the answer. It was because he was also the one man who threatened the protective wall she had built around her heart, the one man who made her feel vulnerable—and that was something she could not tolerate.

The sound of an occasional passing car or a barking dog were the only interruptions to her silent reverie. Even as she'd walked into the house and climbed the stairs to her room, she'd listened for a knock on the door, hoping he would try to convince her to come back outside and talk with him. For truly that was what her heart wanted. But instead she had heard the sound of his old beater car starting up and heading down the street, taking him away from her and her tainted world, back to his where human slavery was just a cause.

She sighed, reminding herself that she would shed no more tears over the situation. She was who she was—a young woman with a horrible past and a tentative future. The only way she could make that future work was to bury the past, and being around Jonathan was not going to make that happen.

Mara knew she would always owe Jonathan for what he had done, and she was ashamed that she had treated him so shabbily. But there were only two possible explanations for the way Jonathan was acting toward her. First, he was no different than all the other men who'd passed through her life, using her for their own pleasure. Jonathan might have a nicer approach than most, but the end result would be the same. Or second, he really cared and wanted to have a relationship with her. That scenario was much less likely, but even if it were true, it would never work. She and Jonathan were complete opposites. He came from a good, loving family. He was a college student — a Bible college student, at that! — and he had a great future ahead of him. She, on the other hand . . .

No sense even going there. The next time she saw Jonathan she would apologize for her behavior and use the excuse that she had been tired and not feeling well. But that would be it. She was not going to set herself up to be hurt ever again. Enough was enough.

230

❧

Lawan had been surprised to realize she was hungry when she sat down to eat her morning meal with the other children. She now realized there were several hundred of them, living in the buildings on the compound. The two people who had taken her from Klahan the night before, whose strange names she had learned were Joan and Mort, seemed kind, as did the other adults, but she could not make herself relax around them. Surely they wanted something from her, and she must be prepared when they revealed what it was.

She was nearly finished with her food when Joan came up and sat down beside her on the long backless bench. "How are you, Lawan?" she asked, her voice soft and her dark gray eyes gentle. Did she dare trust her? Lawan could not decide.

She nodded. "I am fine," she replied.

"You slept well?"

Lawan nodded again, knowing it was a lie. She dropped her eyes, ashamed but unable to admit that she had not slept at all. She had stared into the almost complete darkness, listening to the unfamiliar sounds of children breathing around her and wondering where Klahan had gone. If only she knew that, perhaps she could make sense of the rest.

"Klahan," she said, still not daring to look up. "He will come back?"

The woman named Joan laid a hand on her arm, and Lawan shivered at the uncomfortable sensation. "I am afraid not," Joan said. "Do you understand where Klahan went?"

Lawan shook her head, her eyes fixed on the nearly empty rice bowl in front of her.

Joan paused and then leaned close to speak in hushed tones. "You know what Klahan did to Chai and his housekeeper."

Lawan swallowed as tears sprang to her eyes. She nodded. She knew but preferred not to think of it.

"When I saw you and Klahan come into town, I recognized you," Joan whispered. "You were being sought for the murders."

Lawan jerked her head upward at the words, feeling her eyes grow wide. The woman's Thai was not good; perhaps Lawan had misunderstood.

"I told Klahan about it," she explained, locking eyes with Lawan, dispelling the girl's doubts. "He came to me later and confessed that it was he who had committed the crimes. He asked if I would take care of you here at the orphanage if he turned himself in." She paused. "Do you understand what I am saying, Lawan?"

Lawan understood, though she had trouble believing it. The man called Klahan, who had promised to love and protect her, had given up his freedom for her. How was that possible? Though he had done a terrible thing by killing two people, maybe he had lived up to his name after all.

Yes, she decided. The man whose name meant brave had done a courageous thing. Not only had he kept his promise to take care of her by bringing her here to this place, but he had turned himself in so she would no longer be accused of the crimes he had committed.

She could not hold the tears back any longer. As they flowed down her cheeks, Joan gathered Lawan into her arms and held her close, humming a song to her about *phra yaeh suu*. For the first time since she had been taken away from her parents, Lawan dared to believe that she just might be safe at last.

The morning light had scarcely penetrated Francesca's window when she awoke to a churning stomach that sent her racing for the bathroom. Once again pressed against the toilet as she coughed and heaved until tears streamed down her face, she wondered how much longer she could keep her secret from El Diablo. So far ChaCha was the only one who had guessed, but sooner or later she would no longer be able to hide the changes in her body. Then what would happen to her and to her baby?

Breathing deeply, she tried to regain her strength before pulling herself up and heading for the shower. She had to make herself presentable before anyone saw her in this condition. She only hoped she would get some rest today before her first customers arrived in the afternoon. Lately it seemed that all she wanted to do was sleep, but El Diablo allowed her little time for that.

At last she lifted her head and pushed herself to her knees. Before she could stand to her feet, she realized she was no longer alone. "Will you help me, ChaCha?" she murmured. "This morning sickness is getting worse instead of better. I don't know how I'm going to keep El Diablo from finding out."

An arm reached under her waist and yanked her up before turning her around and plunking her down on her feet. "Don't worry, Frankie," he growled, glaring at her as he leaned in just inches from her face. "El Diablo already knows. And I should beat it out of you, just to show you that I can." He sneered. "But I don't want to lose any income by messing up that pretty face of yours, so we'll just go visit Doc this morning and let him take care of the problem."

He grabbed her throat and placed his face nose-to-nose with hers. "Don't think that means you'll get any time off, you hear me? I'll teach you to keep things from me. You'll be right back here working by the time the sun goes down tonight. You got it?"

233

When she didn't respond, he tightened his grip until she felt her eyes would pop out of her head. The room was going dark, and just before she thought she would pass out, she managed to nod. He released his grip and threw her to the floor.

"Get dressed," he said. "You have fifteen minutes, and then I'm coming back for you."

Weeping, Francesca watched him turn and storm from the room, slamming the door behind him. The horror of what was about to happen to her and her baby was so overwhelming that she couldn't move until she felt ChaCha kneel down beside her.

"You'd better get going," she warned. "If he comes back and you're not ready . . ."

Francesca swallowed and forced herself to get up, leaning on ChaCha as she did so. How much worse could it be if El

Chapter 33

Diablo did return and she wasn't ready? She shivered at the thought. She just wasn't brave enough to find out. With her friend's help, she would somehow get dressed and make it through this day.

Chapter 34

Mara had been awake since before dawn, having done nothing more than doze throughout the night. Her rumpled sheets were proof of that, she thought, as she pulled herself from bed and headed for the tiny bathroom connected to her room. She couldn't afford to miss more work tonight; she'd have to go in, with or without sleep. But at least she had plenty of time before she had to report for the evening shift. A shower and an early morning walk might clear her head, and then she could come back and get some sleep before leaving for work.

The morning sunshine was trying to make its appearance, fighting to break through the marine layer, as she descended the porch steps, zipping her windbreaker as she walked. Should she stop for something to eat, some coffee maybe? No, definitely not coffee. Then she'd never catch any sleep. Maybe just a muffin and juice at one of the early-morning eateries along the way.

The cries of seagulls mingled with passing motorists as Mara set a brisk pace toward the beach. There was always at least one breakfast joint open by now, particularly down at the water's edge where early risers liked to go to jog or just sit and watch the waves. No doubt wet-suited surfers would already be there, balancing themselves on their boards in death-defying ways that never ceased to amaze Mara. After all the danger and pain she'd endured in her lifetime, she couldn't imagine taking such risks on purpose.

By the time she'd snagged a poppy seed muffin and a plastic bottle of orange juice, even the foot traffic was starting to pick up. She consumed her breakfast slowly, watching the crazy surfers zigzag on top of the waves and then shoot beneath them, coming out on the other side just when she thought they were lost forever. By the time she was through, her eyelids were growing heavy from the increasing sunshine, which seemed to have won the battle with the fog. It was time to go home and try to catch some sleep.

Leaving the crashing waves behind, Mara moved toward the block that would take her home. She was ready to turn the corner when a flash of movement and a muffled cry caught her attention. Turning to the right, she felt her eyes widen at the two people who stood on the sidewalk in front of a private medical clinic less than a block away. The man's back was to Mara, but the young woman's face was turned slightly toward her, enough so that Mara's breath caught in her throat.

The couple from the café! She was sure of it. The girl even had a cast on her arm. The man was speaking in low tones, and the girl seemed to be crying, begging. Before Mara could make out a word they said, the girl broke free and leaned over a bush in front of the clinic, where she quickly vomited into the greenery.

Mara's heart raced as she stepped back far enough that she hoped the couple wouldn't see her but where she could still watch their movements. The man looked none too happy about what the girl had just done, but when she was finished, he grabbed her by the noncasted arm and steered her inside the clinic. Mara was certain the girl was still weeping.

What kind of clinic is that? Mara tried to remember if she'd ever seen any sort of sign out front that would identify that type of patients that were seen there, but she couldn't. She knew only that it was a medical facility of some sort. But the girl's vomiting raised a flag that Mara couldn't ignore.

I've seen it before, she thought. *I've experienced it. She's pregnant, and he's taking her there for an abortion.*

The realization made her want to scream, to run into that clinic and rescue the girl, though she knew that was impossible. She dug in her jacket pocket. Where was her phone?

She sighed, picturing it sitting on the charger by her bed, right where she'd left it. That ruled out calling Barbara or the police, though she could race home and call from there. Would she be able to reach Barbara in time? If not, would the police respond to her call and do something? Probably. But would it be soon enough?

She had to try. It might be the only chance the girl had, and it would certainly be the last chance for her baby. Taking a deep breath, Mara streaked toward home, praying she wouldn't be too late, praying that Barbara would answer, praying that if there really was a God, He was listening.

Francesca felt as if her heart would break apart into a million pieces and dissolve into tears. She wanted to be anywhere but there in that cold, sterile office, stripped down to a paper gown with her feet in the stirrups. The same doctor who had set her broken arm had given her a shot and told her she would hardly feel a thing. Then he'd added, "You'll be as good as new in a couple of days."

Those were the words that had restarted her tears, as she realized that not only was the doctor about to kill her baby, but El Diablo would never give her a couple of days to heal. He had already assured her she would be back at work before the night was over. How was that possible? How could even someone as evil as her boss expect such a thing from her?

Soft instrumental music played somewhere in the background, no doubt piped in to help her relax, but Francesca knew there was no way that would happen. If she didn't know that El Diablo was sitting in the waiting room, right outside the door, she'd jump off that cold steel table and run out into the street in her flimsy paper gown, screaming for help. But she'd never make it. And he'd already assured her that if she tried anything, he'd kill not only her but her family as well. He claimed to know the exact street and even the house where they lived, so she didn't doubt for a moment that he would do exactly as he'd said.

Tears dripped from her eyes and down her cheeks as she waited for the doctor to return. How much did El Diablo and others like him pay this man, who claimed to be a healer, to murder babies and patch up girls who had been beaten by their so-called customers? The doctor was a middle-aged man, one who looked as if he might have a daughter her age. Would it do any good to try to appeal to him as a father?

The door opened then, and the doctor came in. But he wasn't alone. El Diablo accompanied him, his face hard as he glared at her. Quite obviously he wasn't going to take any chances, and her slim thread of hope that she might be able to convince the doctor to help her unraveled in front of her eyes.

No hope left, she thought. *I am so sorry, little one. I wish I could save you, but I cannot. Only God can do so. Please, Señor, if You can hear my silent begging, save my baby!*

The doctor lined up his instruments on the tray beside the table where Francesca lay, trembling from terror more than the cold table beneath her. She squeezed her eyes shut. It would be over soon. She prayed that her child would not suffer much.

Mara forced herself to stay in her room, pacing as she waited for Barbara to arrive. The older woman had answered her phone on the second ring, bringing a sense of relief to Mara that mingled with her ongoing feeling of urgency. She'd scarcely blurted out what she saw than Barbara hung up to call the police. In moments Mara's phone rang, and she now knew the police were on their way to the clinic, while Barbara made her way to Mara's place. All she could do now was wait.

She veered off her back-and-forth path and stepped to the window, pulling back the white lace curtain and peering outside. It wasn't that she thought she could see the clinic from where she stood, but at least if she saw Barbara pull up, she'd know she didn't have to wait alone.

Why didn't she hear police sirens?

The thought popped into her mind, causing her heart to race once again. Would the police come with their sirens on? If they did, wouldn't that alert that creep and give him a chance to escape? If he did, would he take the girl with him?

The possibilities swirled through her mind, as she imagined the terrified girl in the clutches of an unscrupulous doctor and her owner, who cared nothing for her except that she continue to make money for him. But then another possibility popped into her mind. What if the clinic was some other sort of facility? What if the man hadn't brought the girl there for an abortion after all?

239

She shook her head. It didn't matter. Whatever the reason, the police were looking for this guy, so if they got to him in time, they'd pick him up. Then that poor girl just might have a chance.

Mara pushed herself away from the window and plopped down on her bed. Any thought that she might get some sleep before she went in for her shift that evening was gone. All she wanted now was to know the girl was safe.

She shut her eyes. She had prayed earlier, while she was running back to her room to get her phone to call Barbara. Should she try praying again? Did she even believe it would do any good?

Before she could answer her own questions, she heard the sound of footsteps hurrying up the stairs, and then a quick rap on the door.

"Mara? It's me, Barbara."

Mara jumped up and scurried toward the door. At least now she'd have company while she waited to see if the girl and her baby would make it.

Chapter 35

Francesca was feeling a bit drowsy from the effects of the shot the doctor had given her, but she could still hear intermittent conversation between the doctor and El Diablo. Had the doctor started the procedure yet? She didn't think so. Was it going to hurt? She was sure it would, but not nearly as much as it would hurt her baby.

"Can you hurry it up?"

El Diablo's voice penetrated her thoughts, and immediately she tensed. It was time, and there was no way to escape this. She squeezed her eyes even tighter, wishing they would at least put her to sleep. But she knew El Diablo didn't want her to have any more medication than absolutely necessary.

Other voices, more distant and indistinguishable, floated into her self-imposed darkness. It sounded like several people. Must be out in the waiting room. She hadn't seen anyone when they came in except a woman whom Francesca had assumed was a receptionist. That might account for the woman's voice, but she heard men too and they seemed to be coming closer.

The door burst open then, and Francesca's eyes flew open at the same time. What was going on?

Two men in suits flashed badges at the doctor and El Diablo, and her heart nearly stopped. What was going on? Were the men policemen? Had they come to rescue her? Whoever they were and whatever they were doing, she could tell El Diablo and the doctor were none too happy about it.

"Can I sit up?" she asked, wondering how she'd gotten the nerve to speak. But somehow she knew this might be the only chance she'd ever have to escape the horrible life she'd been living for the past few months.

The older of the two men who had come into the room turned toward her. Once again he flashed a badge and told her he was with the police. "Of course you can sit up," he said, helping her to a sitting position and subtly pulling her gown down over her legs. "What's your name?" His dark eyes cut from her to El Diablo and back. "Is this your father?"

Francesca felt her eyes widen as her owner turned and glared at her. She could read the threat in his look, and she wondered if she should take the chance and tell the truth, or confirm the lie and not risk El Diablo's wrath.

"Tell them, Frankie," he said. "Tell them you're my daughter."

No. She would never forgive herself if she didn't at least try to get away from him, once and for all.

"My name is Francesca," she said, her voice shaky but clear. She returned El Diablo's glare. "Not Frankie. And I am not his daughter."

She turned away from the man who had tortured her for so many months, took a deep breath, and fixed her eyes on the man in the suit, whose eyes showed the compassion she needed to plunge ahead. "He kidnapped me. And he . . ." She dropped her eyes once, and then raised them again. "He made me do terrible things. Now he's forcing me to kill my baby."

El Diablo uttered a curse word, as Francesca felt herself go limp. Tears began to pour from her eyes. Was it possible her nightmare was over? Would she finally get to go home to her family? It was almost too much to hope for, but it was the first

time she'd felt hopeful in a very long time, and she wasn't about
to let go of it.

❧

Barbara flipped her phone shut and looked up at Mara. The
girl's dark eyes shimmered with tears.

"Is she OK?" Mara asked, her chin trembling. "Did they
rescue her?"

Barbara nodded, fighting her own tears. This situation had
impacted her deeply, but she could only imagine what it was
doing to Mara. The memories that must be haunting her at this
very moment had to be hideous, but at least the two women,
separated by years and experiences, could celebrate together.
Mara had been right from the beginning that the man was
holding the girl captive, forcing her to work as a sex slave.
When Mara spotted them this morning, he had been taking
the terrified girl for a forced abortion. Barbara couldn't help
but believe that God had used Mara to intervene and rescue
the girl and her baby, but she wasn't so sure Mara would agree
with that assessment.

Sitting on the edge of the bed, just inches from Mara,
Barbara reached out and covered the younger woman's hand
with her own. "Thank God," she said, "they got there in time.
And it was just what you thought."

Tears spilled over onto Mara's cheeks. "They saved the
baby too?"

When Barbara nodded, Mara collapsed into her arms and
wept on her shoulder. Barbara was soon crying with her, as she
imagined how personal this news must have been for Mara.
As many years as she'd been involved with ministries that

rescued trafficking victims, she knew she could never really understand the depth of the victims' horror or pain. But she knew Someone who could, and she would continue to pray that He would gently touch and heal this precious young woman who no doubt sobbed not only in relief for the girl who had been rescued but also at the memory of her own many losses.

Jonathan had slept in, and it was nearly noon on Friday when he finally emerged from the shower and headed down the stairs to get something to eat. He could still feel the sting of Mara's rejection the evening before; he'd spent many hours tossing and turning in bed, thinking about it.

Forget about her, he told himself, hitting the bottom of the stairs and turning toward the kitchen. *She's not interested. And that's a good thing. She might be beautiful, but she's also seriously broken. Who wouldn't be, in her situation?* He shook his head as he pulled open the refrigerator door and spotted a bottle of orange juice. *Besides, who needs it? I've got to head back to college in a few weeks. I sure don't have time for romance, and if I do, I'll find someone at school, somebody I have something in common with.*

He poured a glass of juice and grabbed a couple slices of leftover pizza. Should he heat them up? Nah. Cold was fine.

He plunked down at the table and chomped down on cold pepperoni and cheese just as the back door opened and Leah popped in, followed closely by her petite blonde shadow. The minute Jonathan spotted Sarah, he remembered Leah's words about her best friend having a crush on him. He felt his cheeks warm at the thought and dropped his eyes, but

244

not before he saw the hopeful look in her blue eyes. He also noticed a smattering of freckles across the bridge of her nose and wondered why he hadn't paid attention to them before. She actually was kind of cute.

"Hi," she said, dropping into the chair across from him while Leah snagged a couple of glasses and filled them with iced tea. "How have you been?"

Jonathan looked up. Her eyes were brighter than he remembered. He grinned. "Fine. You?"

Her smile widened. "Good. Just hanging out with Leah today." She paused, watching him as he took another bite. "That pizza left over from work?"

He nodded. "Yeah. A couple of days old, but still good."

"Totally. I love leftover pizza. You eat it cold, don't you?"

He nodded again.

"Me too."

This time the pause was about to get awkward when Leah sat down between them. "You working today?"

Jonathan felt his shoulders relax. "Yeah. In a few hours." He swallowed and then frowned. "So where's Mom? She's usually down here trying to talk me into a five-course meal or something."

Leah laughed. "I know what you mean. She does that to me too. But right now she's gone to meet Dad for lunch." She rolled her eyes. "One of their dates or something."

Jonathan chuckled. He liked that his parents still made a big deal of going out on dates together, even if they were getting kind of old for that sort of thing.

"So what about you two? What are you up to today?"

Leah shrugged. "Just hanging out, enjoying the sun. But I'm going over to the Johnsons' place later to babysit Anna. Maybe you can drop me off on your way to work."

"I don't have anything to do tonight," Sarah said, snagging Jonathan's attention as he swiveled his head in her direction. He saw a tinge of color in her cheeks and realized she was hinting at something. "Maybe I could ride with you when you drop Leah off, and then I could go on your deliveries with you, like Leah did the other night."

The words hung in the air, and Jonathan was glad he didn't have a bite of pizza stuck in his throat at the time or he'd probably choke. When no one said anything to break the silence, he finally took a deep breath and spoke the only words that came to mind. "Sure, why not?"

When he dared a peek at Leah, her eyes were wide. With surprise or excitement? He wasn't sure, and he told himself it didn't really matter. After all, Sarah was like another sister to him, and she was just going to keep him company for a few hours. It wasn't like they were going out on a date or anything. And besides, she'd cornered him. What else could he do?

He sighed, pushing out images of Mara's hazel eyes. Maybe it would do him good to spend some time with someone who at least enjoyed his company. And it was obvious that someone certainly wasn't Mara.

Chapter 36

Brass-bowled torches perched atop bamboo poles, set at six-foot intervals around the compound. They flickered through the long, eerie Thailand night, interrupted by occasional jungle noises that Joan had long since learned to ignore. She loved it here—loved the people in general, the children at the orphanage in particular. Her husband felt the same way, she knew. Though they'd originally come here for a one-year assignment, they had now been in country for nearly seven years, with only two brief furloughs to the States. But they had no children of their own back home, no real close family ties, so why not stay where there hearts now yearned to be, planted here in the Golden Triangle where they devoted themselves to these homeless children, many of them rescued from brothels.

Lawan's sweet face swam into view. She truly was a beautiful child, though Joan could only imagine the tortures she had endured over the last couple of years. She hoped to reunite the girl with her family, but she would not mention the possibility to the child until she knew for certain that it could be done. If she had learned anything over the years of her service in this foreign land, it was that nothing was permanent. Situations changed, circumstances shifted, people died. It happened more often than not, and there was no sense getting the girl's hopes up only to dash them again. Better to let her grow accustomed to her new home and make friends with the other children. No doubt Lawan had forgotten how to be a child, so this was the perfect place for her now.

Of course, Joan knew the girl missed Klahan. Though he had been in her life such a short time, he was the closest thing to a knight in shining armor that the child had known in a very long time.

Since she was stolen from her parents and her village, Joan thought. *Is there any chance her family is still alive, still in the same place after two years? And if not, then what? She must certainly forget Klahan. He will never get out of prison . . . even if his life is spared. But thank God he did the right thing and gave Lawan a chance at regaining her freedom. Perhaps he did care for her after all . . . in his own strange way.*

Yes, she told herself, it was definitely best to wait for now and let the girl heal—at least a little—while Joan did her best to try to find the child's family. The contact with them had been so vague, and so very long ago. But at least she had a starting place. That was more than she had with most of the children who came to them there.

She sighed and lay down on the sleeping mat, next to the spot where her husband lay snoring. Morning would come soon enough. The children had been asleep for hours. It was time she tried to do the same.

Sarah could scarcely keep the grin off her face and the excitement out of her voice. As a result, she'd kept her mouth firmly shut since they left Jonathan and Leah's place. She had huddled, unmoving, in the back of Jonathan's dilapidated blue

Bug on the way to drop off Leah, who sat up front with her brother. But when Leah climbed out of the car, she had held the front passenger seat forward so Sarah could unfold herself from the cramped back quarters and make the move to the seat beside Jonathan. It was a spot she had long dreamed of occupying, and now her dream had become a reality.

Did he have any idea how she felt? She had sworn Leah to secrecy, but she knew the brother and sister team were close and shared many of their secrets.

As he tapped the accelerator and picked up speed, leaving Leah behind, Sarah dared a glance in his direction. His eyes were straight ahead, and she noticed his jaw twitch. Nerves? Possibly. Irritation at having been stuck with her for the evening? She certainly hoped not.

"So," she ventured, eager to break the silence, "where do we go first?"

Jonathan glanced at her before returning his eyes to the road. His eyebrows were raised, and she realized how dumb her question had sounded.

"We'll go to the pizza place first," he said, as if explaining an elementary fact to a small child. "I have to check in, get my delivery orders, pick up the pizzas and load them into the car, and then we can go." He shot her another quick glance. "I'm sorry, but you'll have to wait in the car while I go inside."

She nodded, hating that her face flamed at the slightest embarrassment. "I understand. No problem. I'm the one who invited myself along, after all."

Jonathan didn't argue the fact or even soften it with an "I'm glad you came" comment. Sarah sighed. This could turn out to be a long and awkward night, though she continued to cling to the hope that it would instead be an evening when Jonathan would realize that Sarah was more than just his little sister's best friend. More than anything, Sarah wanted him to see her as an attractive young woman, one worthy of his romantic interest. An unlikely expectation, she realized, but certainly not an impossible one.

She remained quiet until they pulled into the parking lot and Jonathan excused himself to go into Slice of Italy Pizza. The aroma of baking dough and tomato sauce, not to mention the cheese, made Sarah's mouth water. She should have eaten something before leaving Leah's, but she had been too excited to feel hungry. Now she wondered if her growling stomach would accompany them throughout the evening and keep her blushing every few minutes. Great impression that would be!

Sarah closed her eyes and leaned her head back against the seat, as the sun shining through the open window warmed her and made her eyelids heavy. When she heard the car door, she opened her eyes, surprised to see Jonathan returning so quickly. He loaded a large leather pouch filled with several pizzas into the back seat, and then climbed in beside her.

"That didn't take long," she said.

He smiled, looking more relaxed than before he'd gone into work. "I was gone thirty minutes," he said. "I was afraid you'd be bored."

Once again she felt the flush climb up her neck and into her face. So she'd fallen asleep! Did he realize that? Probably, though she told herself it didn't matter. Somehow, though, she knew it did, at least to her.

She took a deep breath. "So now what?"

Still grinning, he started the car. "Now we head for the first stop. And when we get all our deliveries made, we'll find a nice spot to stop and eat the extra pizza I brought with me." He turned toward her, and their eyes locked. "I don't know about you," he said, "but I'm starved."

Sarah's heart raced and her mouth went dry. She wanted to answer him, but the best she could do was nod, as he turned back to look out the windshield and steer them from the parking lot out into the street. The slight hope she'd clung to about her time with Jonathan was still alive and growing.

Alley Cat was worried. Time was passing by, and still he hadn't managed to intercept Mara. In the meantime, Tom's safety hung in the balance. Jack knew what it was like in prison; he'd spent many years behind bars and knew what was required to survive there. Tom didn't have it. He wouldn't last six months if Jack didn't hurry up and do the job he'd been assigned by Jefe in exchange for Tom's protection.

That was the other thing that bothered him. Tom was allowed a collect phone call every week, and he always called Jack's landline every Friday afternoon. The sun was starting to go down now, and still no call from his brother. Jack couldn't wait by the phone much longer; he needed to get down to Mariner's and watch for Mara. But why hadn't Tom called? Something was wrong, and he didn't like it.

Unfortunately, he could see only two choices. Either he left his room and headed for the café to grab the girl, or he waited in his room in case Tom called. He could also start trying to call the prison and see if he could track down some information, but the way messages got passed back and forth there, it could take days before he found out anything. He'd do better to try to utilize his underground connections and see if he could find out something that way. Maybe he could even get to Jefe and learn something from him.

Jefe. More than once Jack had asked himself if he could trust the obnoxious creep, and more than once he'd come to the conclusion that he could not. But what else could he do? He had to try to protect his little brother any way he could, and right now Jefe was the only game in town.

Sighing, he shook his head and made his decision. It was getting late. The dinner shift at Mariner's would start soon. He'd just have to take a chance that he'd hear from Tom later. For now he had a job to do, and he couldn't do it until he snatched the elusive Mara. Tonight he'd make sure she didn't get away again.

Chapter 37

So much had happened so quickly that Francesca's head felt as if it were spinning. First she'd been whisked out of the clinic to the police station, where a Spanish-speaking female detective had taken her under her wing, making communicating so much easier for the shaken girl. When a social services representative arrived to join them, the detective had gently interviewed Francesca, and she had at last poured out her unbelievable story of terror and suffering. By the time she was finished, she had nearly collapsed from exhaustion.

Since then she had been taken to a temporary shelter where she was able to take a shower and then fall into bed, imagining she would immediately go to sleep. Instead she had tossed and turned, drifting between dreams and thoughts, crying intermittently, even as the sun faded outside her window and darkness settled in.

My parents are coming, she thought, the nearly unbelievable words echoing in her mind. *They're bringing my parents here. I'll see them soon!*

The shame of having them learn of what she'd endured the past few months tempered her joy at the thought of seeing them again, but surely they would understand that everything she had done had been forced upon her. But the baby . . . What would they think about that? What would they want her to do? She was certainly too young to be a mother, and sadly, she didn't even know who the father was. But one thing she knew for certain. Her parents would never want her to have an abortion. The little one who grew inside her was safe now.

And so was she. The tears started fresh as the realization washed over her. Every horrible memory would certainly fade . . . eventually. Wouldn't it? Oh, how she hoped so! She just wanted to return to her home in Juarez and live in peace with her family once again. If only the others could do the same.

The thought brought a stab of guilt, as she realized she had been so caught up in her own situation that she had forgotten about ChaCha and the others. Surely El Diablo's arrest meant that they too would be rescued. Hadn't the detective even asked her if she knew the address where she had been held? She didn't know exactly, since El Diablo had done everything he could to keep her ignorant of her exact location. But she'd told them what she knew, so maybe they had already found the house and freed the other girls.

How had it happened? Francesca knew so little about what had transpired that day to bring about her rescue. The detective had told her that a woman had seen her going into the clinic with El Diablo and had reported them. She also said the woman had seen them before and suspected what was going on. Who was she? Who had seen her and realized her situation?

Francesca shook her head. She supposed it didn't matter, though she would like to be able to thank the woman. For now it was enough to know that she would soon see her parents, and that she would never again be forced to live as she had as El Diablo's captive.

The Southern California skyline turned various shades of red and purple as the sun sank behind the Pacific. The blue VW Bug was parked at a bird sanctuary near the water, a spot less populated than most tourist areas. Jonathan questioned his wisdom in picking this place, but it seemed one of the few available locations where they could take a break and eat their dinner in peace. He just hoped he hadn't given Sarah any false encouragement by doing so.

He opened the box and placed it in the small space between them. The pizza would still be warm, if not hot, but he remembered she'd said she liked it cold, so he figured it would be fine as it was. "Sorry I forgot napkins," he said, turning toward her. "I'm not used to having anyone with me when I chow down between deliveries."

Her smile was still visible in the fading light of sunset. Why hadn't he noticed how cute she was before? Probably because she'd been around so much that he'd thought of her only in terms of another kid sister. But she was all grown up now, eighteen and on her way to junior college in the fall. And if what Leah had told him was true, she certainly didn't think of him as a big brother.

Suddenly uncomfortable at their locked gaze and prolonged silence, he reached for a slice of pizza. She did the same, and their fingers touched. Jonathan felt his cheeks grow warm, and he was glad for the muted light in the car. He kept his face down for a moment, hoping she wouldn't see his blush. Determined to pretend that he hadn't noticed their accidental touch, he snagged his food and stuffed a large bite into his mouth. At least that would give him an excuse for not talking.

He also pretended to watch out the window, as the sun disappeared completely, leaving streaks of color behind. But from the corner of his eye, he watched Sarah take her own slice

255

of pizza and bite into it, as she too stared out the window. How had he let himself get roped into this? He could have spoken up and said he preferred not to take anyone along when he was working, even though he'd made the one-time exception with Leah. Was it possible he hadn't objected because he actually liked the idea?

It was a new concept, something he'd never considered before, but the lingering fragrance of Sarah's perfume mingled with the aroma of sauce and cheese, as he slowly relaxed and leaned back against the seat. He might as well enjoy his pizza and make the best of the time with Sarah. After all, it wasn't like he was obligated to see her again. It was just two friends, hanging out. Right?

He risked another glance in her direction. This time she was looking straight at him, though she quickly dropped her eyes and concentrated on the half-eaten slice of pizza in her hand, delicately pulling an olive from the cheese and popping it into her mouth. The memory of Mara's alluring hazel eyes teased his senses, but the added memory of her abrupt rejection won out. For now he'd just enjoy spending time with someone who actually wanted to be with him. It felt good, and obviously she was enjoying it, so why not?

When she looked up and smiled at him, he returned the gesture before shoving the last of his pizza slice into his mouth.

———— ✦ ————

The sun had disappeared and darkness was blanketing the blocks near the beach. Jack still wasn't sure he'd done the right thing by planting himself across the street from Mariner's to watch for Mara. Shouldn't she have shown up by now if she was going to work the dinner shift? But he was sure she would because he'd popped in for a quick cup of coffee as soon he arrived in the area, listening carefully until he heard the waitress mention to someone that Mara would be in later.

And so he waited, though it gnawed at him that he wasn't in his room to catch the call from Tom. He wished he'd thought to give his new cell number to his brother and told him to call that one instead of his landline, but he hadn't, so he'd just have to make the best of it. The next time he talked to Tom he'd be sure to correct that oversight.

A car pulled out of the almost steady stream of traffic passing by Alley Cat's position and stopped in front of the café. Jack perked up. The driver wasn't turning off the headlights or getting out of the car, but the passenger door had opened. Jack squinted, focusing on the figure that stepped out and stood beside the car, waving a final farewell before turning to walk toward Mariner's entrance.

He smiled. He hadn't seen her face, but he knew it was her. Mara had arrived for her evening shift, and his waiting had not been in vain. She might have gotten to work safely, but Alley Cat would make sure she didn't make it back home at the end of the night.

257

Chapter 38

Mara's heart felt lighter than it had in quite awhile, despite the fact that she hadn't gotten any extra sleep that afternoon. Once Barbara had assured her that the girl, whose name turned out to be Francesca, and her baby were safe, the two women had spent the remainder of the day together, talking and becoming better acquainted. It was the first time Mara had realized how hungry she had been for female companionship, for someone she could call a friend. She had so shut herself off from human contact since being rescued from the compound that being in Barbara's presence and sharing her thoughts and feelings with her had seemingly opened up a reservoir of longing inside her that greatly surprised Mara.

She smiled as she tied an apron around her waist and slipped the order pad and pen into her pocket. A friend. A real friend! It didn't matter that Barbara was so much older than she and that they had little in common. They were both women, and the one thing they did have in common was huge: they wanted to see modern-day slavery abolished. Barbara, of course, came at it from a nonpersonal approach, while Mara's was as personal as it could get. She hated everything that had to do with human trafficking, and still found herself amazed at the fact that she had not only survived it but escaped.

I'm free, she told herself, wiping down the counter and pouring ice water into glasses to take to the customers who had just sat down at a booth near the door. *I'm actually free of that horrible life. And now Francesca is too. I wonder what she's feeling right now, what she's going through. Does she have a family who cares about her, someone who will come and take her home with them? Or is she alone, like me? Did her own family betray her like mine did?*

She shook her head. The front door continued to open, with customers pouring in and looking for seats. It was time to get to work. There would be time to think about all that had happened that day when her shift was over and she could finally go home to her bed. She imagined sleep would catch up with her then, but right now she was running on adrenaline and not feeling tired at all.

Heading for the booth with a tray full of water glasses, she smiled a welcome to the family sitting there. It was enough to know that her life of bondage was behind her. All she wanted to do now was enjoy her freedom. What a relief it was to know that no one would ever take that away from her again.

260

⁕

Mara had been so sure her rush of adrenaline would last through her shift, but as the last customer paid his bill and left, she felt the last of her energy leave with him. She was thankful she had only a little cleanup work to do before she could leave to go home. Her bed was calling to her, and she couldn't wait to flop down on it.

It had been one of the busiest Friday nights she could remember, with nothing more than a ten-minute break in the midst of it. But she was finished now. She untied her apron and hung it on a hook, then grabbed her purse, waved good night to the cook and busboy who would leave soon after her, and headed for the door. The thought crossed her mind that she could wait a few minutes and catch a ride with one of them, but it was only a short walk to her place and she was anxious to get going. She'd be in bed before Stephen and Julio locked up for the night and headed for the parking lot.

Closing the door behind her, she pushed aside her ever-present uneasiness at walking alone in the dark and set her sights for home. It was only a few blocks. What could happen in that short distance?

Most of the other eateries and businesses along the way were closed for the night, waiting for sunrise to reopen. She was nearly halfway home, moving at a quick clip through the shadows, when a strong arm grabbed her around the waist and a sweet-smelling cloth slipped over her mouth. Terror spiked through her like needles, pricking her arms and even the top of her head. She knew she should run or at least scream, but she couldn't do either. The sweet odor of the rag nearly gagged her, as a darkness deeper than night enveloped her. The desire to fight melted into the need to sleep, and she felt her muscles dissolve as she drifted away.

261

Sarah couldn't believe how well the evening had gone so far. They had made their last deliveries, and now Sarah waited in the car while Jonathan finished up his duties inside. He had offered to let her come in and wait, but she'd declined, wanting to spend as much time as possible in his car, reliving the events of the evening. She wasn't ready to share him with the other people who would be inside right now, cleaning up and joking around as they prepared to go home. This was all too new and exciting to her, and she needed time alone to think about it.

Had she imagined it, or had he warmed up to her as the night progressed? He certainly seemed to relax as they drove around, and especially when they stopped and ate pizza together. And besides, hadn't he been the one to pick such a quiet and secluded spot? He could have stopped anywhere, but he specifically went where there weren't a lot of other people. Wasn't that a good sign?

Sarah dared to hope so, though she didn't go so far as to believe that her dream of many years was at last coming true. Maybe Jonathan was just being nice; then again, maybe—just maybe—he was discovering that he had feelings for her like she did for him.

That would be amazing, she thought. *If Jonathan could just stop thinking of me as his little sister's best friend and think of me as a grown-up, someone worthy of his attentions and feelings, then maybe—*

Her thoughts were interrupted by the squeaking of the driver's door being opened from the outside. "Hey," Jonathan said, sliding into the seat beside her. "I got done quicker than I expected. You ready to go home?"

Sarah opened her mouth, and then closed it again. She swallowed. Did she have the nerve to say what she really felt? And if she didn't, would she ever get another chance?

Taking a deep breath and ignoring the pounding of her heart, she said, "Actually, unless you're really tired and want to get home, I'd like to go somewhere else for a while."

Jonathan cocked his head, and even in the near darkness she could imagine his surprised expression. "Like where?" he asked.

She shrugged, taking another deep breath to try to calm herself before daring to speak again. "Oh, I don't know.

Anywhere, really. I . . . I'm just not ready to go home yet."

Sarah waited, each second dragging out as she wondered what was going through Jonathan's mind. Was he looking for a way to get out of this gracefully? Was he sick of her after all and wishing he could get rid of her?

"I know a place that has great ice-cream sundaes," he said. "Would that work?"

She grinned, barely squelching a yelp of excitement. "Sure," she said, surprised at the level of calm in her voice. "That sounds great. I love ice-cream sundaes. Hot fudge especially."

Jonathan laughed, and the warmth of it zigzagged up Sarah's spine. "I was hoping you'd say that," he said, putting the key in the ignition and starting the engine. "Hot fudge is my favorite too."

They were halfway down the block before Sarah's breathing returned to normal. This night was turning out better than she had ever dreamed.

Chapter 39

At some point Francesca had drifted off because the clock next to her bed said it was nearly midnight when she was awakened by voices outside her room. Was it the people who ran the shelter? The couple who had greeted her when she arrived was very kind, and she was grateful that they spoke Spanish. She had certainly learned to converse in English since being dragged across the border and held captive by El Diablo, but she could relax when others spoke Spanish around her.

She shut her eyes in what she knew was an irrational attempt to hear better, but it helped her concentrate on the words floating through her closed door. Indeed the conversation was in Spanish.

Curious now, Francesca rose from her bed and tiptoed to the door, cracking it slightly and pressing her ear to the opening. It took no more than a few words for her heart to leap with recognition. Throwing the door open, she raced down the hallway and into the main room where her parents stood talking with the couple who had welcomed her earlier.

Her mother saw her first, and a cry burst forth from her lips as Francesca threw herself into the woman's embrace. The familiar feel and smell of the person she loved more than life itself enveloped her, even as she felt her father's arms wrap around them both.

"*Mijita*," her father crooned, as her mother wept, unable to speak. "My little girl! My baby girl."

Francesca thought the joy she felt would explode out of her and fill the room, though she couldn't stop crying, mingling her tears with those of her mother. At some point the couple must have left to give them privacy because when Francesca finally looked up, she discovered that the three of them were alone.

Slowly, haltingly, they made their way to a couch, never letting go of one another along the way. They sank down onto the soft cushions, Francesca in the middle, and began chattering all at once. Her mother continued to stroke her daughter's cheek, her hair, her hand, as if she couldn't believe they were actually together again. Her father kept asking how she was and Francesca kept assuring him she was fine, though she knew none of them really believed that.

And then her mother asked about the woman who had called the police. "Do you know her?"

Francesca shook her head. "No, Mama, I don't, but I wish I did. I want to thank her."

Her mother nodded. "And we will, I'm sure. The *policia* will tell us who she is, and we will go to her and thank her with all our heart."

"But how did she know?" Francesca asked. "I've been wondering that ever since the men came and rescued me. How did the woman know what was going on and that I needed help?"

Her mother's dark eyes, still brimming with tears, softened, and Francesca recognized the wisdom she saw there. It was something she'd grown accustomed to over the years, something born out of her mother's strong faith in God. "God knew," she said. "He knew, and He used her to save you." She paused and patted Francesca's hand. "And now I believe He wants us to pray for her. That is the best way we can thank her, you know."

Francesca closed her eyes. As always, her mother was right. Before she could say a word, she heard her parents begin to pray for God to bless the woman who had helped reunite their family—to bless and protect her always, and to hold her close to His heart.

Amen, Francesca thought. *Yes, please, God. Whoever and wherever she is, bless and protect this wonderful woman. And may I meet her face-to-face so I can thank her very soon.*

Jefe lay on his bottom bunk, staring at the one just a couple of feet above him. It was empty at the moment, but he knew another inmate would occupy it soon. The bunks never stayed empty long, but at least for now he had a little privacy—as much as anyone could have in this place where the lights were never turned off and a handful of prisoners yelled all night long.

But at least he knew that Alley Cat had finally taken the first step in carrying out his assignment. He had nabbed that traitorous girl who had landed Jefe in this rotten place, and now her payback would begin.

He smiled at the thought. His only regret was that he wouldn't be there to witness her suffering or her ultimate demise. But at least he knew it would soon be underway. Jack had made the call to the anonymous number, and from there word had been passed to Jefe, even in prison, that the mouse was in the trap. Jefe prided himself in being so well connected that steel doors and locks and even armed guards

267

could not keep necessary news from him. After all, occasional correctional officers had a price, and he knew how to keep them in his pocket. Now the good news had been delivered; the only thing that still concerned Jefe was that the bad news might reach Alley Cat before he completed his assignment.

Jefe rolled over, punching and rearranging his thin pillow in a vain attempt to make it more comfortable. He didn't really see any way that Jack would find out that Tom had died just hours earlier as a result of the beating that had put him in the prison hospital, but he sure didn't like that tiny risk factor. So long as Tom was alive, Jefe didn't imagine the authorities would try very hard to contact Jack, but the minute he died, it became a distinct possibility. It was only a matter of time.

As long as they can't reach him until he finishes his job, I should be OK, he told himself. And how would they? Jack was supposed to take Mara to a secluded spot, somewhere no one would think to look for them. If he did that, there was no way he'd find out about Tom until Mara was dead.

He smiled again. *I told him to take his time, to make her suffer. If he just drags it out for a couple of days, I'll have my revenge. And then he can find out about his brother. What do I care if he gets mad that he carried out his part of the bargain and I didn't? The beating happened before he caught Mara. If he'd grabbed her sooner, I would have started protecting Tom before this, and he'd still be alive right now. So the way I see it, it's not my fault at all.*

He closed his eyes, refusing to dwell on the issue of Alley Cat and his dead brother. All he wanted to do now was to imagine Mara's terror and pain until she was dead. That would be enough to keep him going for a very long time.

Jack thought he was living up to his name, as he paced like a cat, tense and ready to pounce. He had followed Jefe's directions to the letter, grabbing the girl and getting her to an isolated place before she woke up. She was still knocked out, though he imagined she would come to soon. But even if she did, she'd never escape. He had her tied to a metal chair that was secured with bolts to the floor. She wasn't going anywhere. He hadn't even bothered to put a gag in her mouth, as he knew she could scream all night and no one would hear her.

He'd known the perfect spot for this assignment from the moment he'd received it. Less than an hour inland from San Diego, the old abandoned farmhouse, once owned by Jack's grandfather and now legally his, was broken down and uninhabited. The only thing recognizable was the basement, where Mara was now imprisoned and where she would eventually die. Jack still wasn't crazy about the idea of torturing and killing her, but he had no choice. Tom must be protected at all costs; he was the only family Jack had left.

Maybe, when Tom gets out, we can come back here and fix up the place — at least make it livable, he thought. *Maybe I can even fix it up myself and have it ready for him.* He nodded. Yeah, he liked that idea.

What he didn't like was not knowing how Tom was. Had he tried to call? Jack knew he wouldn't have been able to leave a message because he had to call collect, but at least the number would show up on caller ID and Jack would know his brother was all right. But the only way to know that would be to go back to his room in town and check the phone.

He cursed himself again for not making sure Tom could call him on his cell, but it was too late to worry about that now. Once again he had a decision to make. He either had to ignore Tom and hope for the best so he could get started dealing with

269

the girl, or leave her there and drive back into the city to see if Tom had tried to call.

Why not go check, he wondered. It wasn't like she could go anywhere. She'd be right where he left her when he got back, and he wouldn't have to worry about Tom anymore. He could focus on the job at hand and get it done, once and for all, so he could finally rest easy, knowing that Tom was protected until he got out of that place.

With the decision made, he opened the storm doors that led down the stairs into the basement. He'd better at least check on her before he left.

The musty air nearly gagged him as he descended the shaky wooden steps. He hadn't even reached the last one when he heard a moan. So, she was waking up.

Her head rolled back and her eyes opened and seemed to try to focus on him as he approached. Too bad she was so good looking. What a waste to snuff her. Then he grinned. Who said he couldn't take advantage of her beauty before he finished her off? Didn't Jefe say he wanted her to suffer first anyway? Why not include some enjoyment for himself and make the job a little more pleasant along the way?

Confusion gave way to terror in her hazel eyes, as he stepped up to her, stopping just inches away. He reached toward her face, but she jerked her head back and he laughed. So, she was going to fight him. Good. That would just make the experience that much better.

He leaned down, close to her face, delighting in the fear that he could almost smell. "I'll be back," he said. "I have something to do in town first, but then I'll be back to finish my job."

Her initial confusion seemed to return, and her mouth moved as if she was having trouble forming words. "Job?" she managed at last.

He grinned. "Jefe hired me."

Her eyes widened, and he heard her suck in her breath.

"That's right," he said. "Jefe. Sitting behind bars because of you. But he hasn't forgotten you, pretty lady. In fact, he told me he wanted you to be sure to know that everything I do to you between now and the time I kill you is a present from him." He laughed again, stroking her cheek and delighting to feel her tremble beneath his fingers. "Of course, I may add a touch or two of my own before we're through. No sense wasting our time together now, is there?"

The fear in her eyes darkened to what Jack was sure was anger, but he didn't react quickly enough. Her spit landed between his eyes and dripped down his nose, infuriating him. "So," he said, his voice a low growl now as he moved his hand from her cheek to her throat, exerting just enough pressure to make her gasp for air, "you want to play rough, do you?" He leaned down and planted a kiss on her lips, his hands preventing her from turning her face. "That's just fine with me, pretty lady. We can do this any way you want to, but you might as well know that there's no way you can win. You're stuck here until I get back, and then we'll finish this — slowly but surely — and before you know it, you'll be begging me to kill you."

Tears pooled in her eyes then, and he jerked his hand from her throat. He had succeeded in terrorizing her, and he knew she couldn't escape. There was no reason for him not to leave long enough to ease his concern about Tom. He'd deal with the pretty lady when he got back.

Chapter 40

Mara thought she had seen darkness in her life, but this was the blackest night she could remember. At least before that creep left, there had been a dim overhead bulb to cast a little light on the ancient, dusty room that had become her prison, but before he climbed the stairs and drove away, he had turned out the light. Now she could see absolutely nothing.

The effects of what she imagined was chloroform had worn off, though she still felt a bit nauseated. But who wouldn't, under the circumstances? She still couldn't believe she was a captive again. After more than a decade of slavery, she'd been rescued, and she thought her ordeal was over. But she should have known that Jefe would find and punish her, even from his prison cell.

The man's face loomed in her mind, leering at her as she tried in vain to block it out. How she hated the memory of the sound of her tio's voice, the slimy feel of his hands on her body. He had told her he owned her and would kill her if she ever left or turned on him. Mara thought she had managed to disprove his threat, but now she knew better.

And who was the horrible man who had done her tio's bidding? She didn't recognize him, but then she supposed it didn't matter. Jefe had some sort of hold over him, and the disgusting coward would do whatever was required of him, including killing her.

He said he'd torture me first, she thought, the fresh sting of tears springing to her eyes. *No doubt he'll rape me too. The creep! If he loosens just one of my hands, or even a foot, I'll fight him to the death. I won't let him end my life without paying a price.*

But the words of anger couldn't override the sense of terror that seemed to smother her in the thick darkness. Hopelessness washed over her, and she slumped forward as much as the ropes allowed, allowing her tears to flow freely down her cheeks and splash onto her jeans. Just when she'd thought she would finally have a chance at a decent life, the end she'd always feared the most had returned to finish her off.

No, she decided, *I won't fight after all. Let him kill me and get it over with. It's my destiny, so I may as well just accept it. At least I was able to help rescue that other girl before I died. If there's a God and if there's any justice at all, maybe He'll take that into consideration before sending me to a place that can't be much different than where I've lived most of my life.*

She laughed out loud, the sound startling her. "That's right, God," she whispered. "I'm already well acquainted with hell, so give me Your best shot after I die. It can't be any worse than what I've been through already."

❦

With few cars on the road, Jack made it back to town in just over half an hour. All he needed in order to know his little brother was all right was to see the familiar number on his caller ID. Then he could relax and get back to the task at hand—which, after seeing how attractive this Mara chick really was, might not be so bad after all.

With a smirk on his face, he used the front door key to let

himself into the boarding house and then hurried up the stairs, briefly shifting his focus from Tom to Mara. But the minute he let himself inside, he headed straight for the phone by his bedside, once again thinking only of his brother.

The red message light was blinking. *Strange*, he thought, the first feeling of alarm snaking up his spine. *Tom can only call collect; he can't leave messages. Who else knows this number?*

A sense of relief eased the tension in his shoulders as the obvious answer popped into his head. Jefe, of course! He probably found a way to call and congratulate Jack on his success in snagging Mara.

He frowned. But why would Jefe do that? Jack had already gotten word to him that Mara was caught, and Jefe knew Jack would be busy with her for quite a while after that. There'd be no reason to call. Besides, Jefe would call the cell phone. So who . . . ?

Heart racing, he dialed the number for voice mail. He had one new message, and it was from the prison. But it wasn't Tom. Jack didn't recognize the name, but the official who called left a number for Jack to call "as soon as possible." Jack didn't like the sound of that.

He scrambled for a pen and a piece of paper, and then listened to the message again, this time writing down the information. By the time he punched in the numbers, his hands were trembling. Forcing himself to keep his voice even, he said what was needed to get patched through to the man with the familiar voice, the one who had left the message.

Jack quickly identified himself, adding, "I'm Tom's brother. You said to call right away."

His heart hammered in his chest and his ears as he listened to the words that changed everything. Tom was dead. Just as Jack had feared, his brother had been beaten by other inmates

275

and then succumbed to his wounds while lying alone in a bed at the prison hospital.

The man was still talking when Jack interrupted. "When did this happen?" he demanded.

A slight pause, and then the voice answered, "He died earlier today, but the beating was a couple of days ago. I'm sorry we didn't call sooner, but—"

Jack hung up the phone while the man was still talking. He had heard enough. There was no way Jefe hadn't known about Tom by the time Jack snatched Mara, but the slimy creep had let Alley Cat move ahead with the plan as if everything were just fine.

Ripping the phone from the wall, he hurled it across the room. Everything was *not* fine! His little brother, the only family he had, was dead. When was Jefe going to tell him? After Jack had tortured and murdered Mara, no doubt. Once Jefe had his revenge, he wouldn't care if Jack knew about Tom. But the pervert hadn't counted on Tom finding out *before* he carried out his end of the deal, and now the deal was off. As far as Jack was concerned, he owed Jefe nothing, and nothing was exactly what the two-faced convict would get.

Jonathan and Sara had closed up the ice-cream parlor, but not until they'd shared the biggest banana split, smothered in hot fudge, on the menu. Even then they'd stayed, talking and laughing about instances in the past, things that had happened over the years while Sarah and Leah were such good friends. It had struck Jonathan as they talked that he was seeing an entirely different side of the blonde with the sprinkle of freckles than he'd ever noticed before. And though he wasn't sure he was ready to admit it, even to himself, he thought he liked what he saw.

When he dropped her off in front of her house, he realized she was hesitating, very possibly in hopes that he would kiss her. Confused at the thought, he held back, waiting in his car until he saw that she was safely inside, and then tapped his accelerator a couple of times and drove away. Now he sat in the driveway, in front of his own house, reflecting on the events of the evening.

How could a few short hours make such a difference? He shook his head. Was it because he'd never thought of Sarah as anything but his sister's best friend, and therefore practically another sister? Or was he now imagining his feelings, which were more uncertain than anything else?

I like Sarah. But then, I always have. Do I really feel differently about her, now that I know how she feels about me? Or am I just reading something into it that isn't even there?

The memory of Mara's face, her wide hazel eyes with the dark lashes, interrupted his musings, detouring his heart. Mara was so beautiful. He'd been struck by her beauty from the first time he laid eyes on her, just over two years ago when he was delivering pizzas at the motel.

The motel where she was being forced into sexual slavery, he reminded himself. *The motel where everything in my life seemed to change—what I thought, what I believed, what I wanted. Is that why she has such a hold on me?*

His memory of Mara's face took on a look of rejection now, as she turned from him and went inside the house where she lived, leaving behind the unspoken but clear message that she was not interested in him beyond gratitude for what he'd done to help rescue her. *What else do I want from her?* He shook his head, wishing the action would clear his thoughts. How many times had he told himself that Mara was not the girl for him? They had nothing in common, not to mention the fact that she was probably so emotionally damaged that she'd never be able to have a normal relationship. But despite his repetitions to himself, he knew his heart wasn't convinced.

I should be glad someone as nice as Sarah is interested in me, he thought. *She may not be quite as strong a Christian as I'd like, but at least she doesn't have a ton of emotional baggage as big as the Great Wall of China.*

He sighed and climbed out of the car. He'd enjoyed the evening with Sarah, but the spark he felt when he was around Mara just wasn't there with Leah's friend. Still, did that really matter? Maybe it was all right to just enjoy a few dates with Sarah over the summer and then return to school in the fall. It wasn't like they were going to get married or anything.

Jonathan let himself into the house. He imagined Sarah was lying in bed by now, staring at the ceiling and reliving their time together. That was normal. He knew Leah well enough to know that's what teenage girls did when they had a crush on some guy and had just spent time with him.

But Mara? That was another question entirely. The girl was a mystery, and he wondered if that's what intrigued him most. As he bypassed the kitchen and headed up the stairs, he wondered too what Mara might be doing right about now. Was she too safely home in her bed? Something told him that with Mara, you could never really be sure what was going on with her.

Chapter 41

Alley Cat cursed and fumed the entire way back to the old farm. By the time he got there, the only thing he was certain of was that he wished it was Jefe he had tied up in the basement instead of Mara. Any thoughts he'd had of forcing himself on her before finishing her off had long since vanished. The primary emotion he felt right now was raging hatred at the man who had withheld the news about Tom's death just so he could get Jack to carry out his end of the bargain. He knew too that if he let go of that hatred, he'd be crushed by grief and despair, and he wasn't about to let that happen.

He screeched into the yard and parked near the storm doors that led down to the basement. No doubt she'd heard him arrive and was shaking at the thought of what was about to happen to her. Normally he would take pleasure in that thought; right now it didn't even faze him. He just wanted to get back at Jefe.

He stood beside his truck and looked up at the sky. The moon was a faint sliver of itself, but an occasional star winked at him, as if they were in on his secret.

What secret? he thought, squinting at the spot where the last star had blinked. *What do you know that I don't? I haven't even decided what I'm going to do yet.*

Silence was his only response. Not even a rustling of wind in the trees or the hoot of an owl broke the quiet. He reached into his pocket and pulled out a half-empty pack of cigarettes. Jack didn't smoke regularly or often, but when he was stressed, he reached for what his mother used to call "cancer sticks." Somehow inhaling the burning smoke helped him relax and think more clearly.

He plucked a match from the same pocket and lifted his foot, striking the match on his boot before lighting the cigarette that was already in his mouth and taking a long drag. What should he do? He didn't care about the girl in the basement, had no personal beef with her, and he no longer looked forward to forcing himself on her. Jefe had nullified any duty Jack felt toward him or their previous agreement, and he'd never been keen on torturing or murdering anyone in the first place, so why bother?

280

At the same time, he sure would like to find a way to use the situation with Mara to his advantage. How could he turn this all around to get even with Jefe? For that was what he wanted most of all.

He sucked on the cigarette again, a plan beginning to form in his mind. At last he nodded and threw the stub to the ground, grinding it out with the same boot he'd used to light the match. He had a plan now, and Jefe wasn't going to like it one bit. But Jack had nothing left to lose. His brother was already dead, a fact he refused to allow himself to dwell on. Right now he needed to stay focused on using Mara to exact revenge from that creep in prison who hadn't told him about Tom.

Maybe if he had, Jack mused, taking his first step toward the entrance to the basement, *I'd have followed through with our agreement. But since he didn't, I get to call all the shots now.*

He pulled open the storm doors and heard a frightened whimper echo upwards in response. Jack smiled, liking his plan better by the minute. He might have lost his only brother, but at least Tom wouldn't have died in vain.

❧

When Mara heard tires crunching on gravel and then the screech of brakes, she knew her executioner had returned, and she was no closer to being free of her bonds than when he left.

Trembling, she waited, trying to block out images of how she would suffer before she died. No doubt her torture would involve rape, which she'd certainly experienced many times before. How much worse could it be than in the past? She shivered at the unspoken answer.

"Oh God, if You're real and if You're listening," she whispered, her voice trembling, "please let me die quickly."

The sound of the storm doors opening broke her resolve to be strong, as tears once again sprang to her eyes. The man's heavy footsteps were tentative until he found the string that turned on the overhead bulb, dimly illuminating the room.

He's so big, Mara thought, staring at the man's bulky, six-foot frame. *He could kill me with his bare hands.*

The meanness on his face, which she'd tried to forget, came back into focus as he drew closer. She told herself to turn away, but she couldn't. The blackness in his eyes and the sneer of his lips seemed to hold her captive as surely as the ropes he had fastened around her, securing her to the cold metal chair.

"Still here, eh?" He laughed. "Well, I'm glad you decided to wait for me, pretty lady. You must be looking forward to this nearly as much as I am."

Mara cringed, fighting a wave of nausea. She wondered if he could smell her fear.

The man turned then and reached to pull something down from a nearby shelf. As he unwrapped it from its dark cloth covering, she realized it was a video camera. So, he wasn't satisfied just to torture and kill her; he planned to tape the ordeal and relive it later.

Or give it to Jefe.

The thought would have knocked her from the chair if she hadn't been secured to it. Of course, that was the plan. Her *tio* not only wanted proof that she was dead, but he wanted to watch it happen. How he would make that a reality in prison, she couldn't imagine, but she knew he'd find a way. She also knew he would have preferred to be here and watch the entire event as it unfolded, but he would settle for the next best thing. Mara had always thought she couldn't hate her uncle anymore than she already did, but now she knew otherwise.

The man dragged an old wooden crate over in front of her and set up the camera on top of it. At least she knew where all the action would take place — right where she was. And from the look of things, her tormentor was about ready to begin.

"There," he announced, turning to her with a self-satisfied smile. "We're all set. Jefe won't have to miss a thing."

Hot tears flowed freely down her cheeks then. She didn't even try to hold them back, but she did squeeze her eyes shut. There was nothing she could do to stop what was about to happen, but at least she didn't have to look at her murderer's disgusting face during the process.

She felt him step near her, as he reached out a rough hand to stroke her cheek. "What's the matter, pretty lady? You don't want to watch?" He laughed. "No matter. Jefe's the only one who really needs to see it all."

He moved his hand then, from her cheek to below her neck, where he grabbed her shirt and, with one powerful jerk, ripped it open, sending her buttons scattering to the floor.

"How'd you like that one, Jefe?" the man growled, as Mara's weeping increased.

He laughed then, as she yielded to the impulse to open her eyes to see what he would do next. She was just in time to see him flip open a large pocketknife and hold it up to her face.

"What do you think I'm going to do with this?" he asked, leaning close enough that she could feel his breath against her skin.

When she didn't answer, he pressed the knife against her cheek. "I asked you a question," he snarled. "You'd better answer me, you understand?"

Mara nodded, fighting to control her sobs so she could speak. "Yes," she gulped. "I understand. But I don't know what you're going to do with it."

He grinned and then turned to face the camera, though he didn't remove the blade from the side of her face. "I'll bet you have a couple of good ideas about what I should do with this knife, don't you, Jefe?"

He laughed again and turned back to Mara. "Let's see. I could carve my initials into your face." He slid the tip of the knife downward, slowly and just close enough that she could feel it without getting nicked. He stopped when he came to her chest. "Better yet, I'd have more room here. I could carve my entire name. What do you think, pretty lady? How'd you like to have my name carved into your skin?"

Mara sobbed hysterically, no longer able to think or speak coherently, though she frantically shook her head from side to side. "No," she cried, using the only words that came to mind. "No, please! No! No!"

The man paused. "No? You don't want me to do that?" He swiveled back toward the camera. "What do you think, Jefe?

Mara doesn't want me to use this knife on her. But I'll bet you do, don't you? You'd like me to cut her into little pieces until there's nothing left, wouldn't you?"

He stood up then, pulling the knife away from Mara. "Well, now, Jefe, I tell you what. You knew from the beginning that I really didn't want to do this job, but you had old Alley Cat over a barrel, didn't you? You promised that if I got revenge on this girl for you that you'd make sure my brother was protected in prison. But we all know you can't keep your end of the promise now, don't we?"

He looked back at Mara and grabbed her by the hair with his free hand, yanking her head forward as she yelped in pain. "You see this girl, Jefe?" he said, still holding onto her as he turned back to face the camera. "Look at her real good because I don't want you to miss this. If you'd just been honest with me about what happened to Tom, I might have followed through on my end of the bargain. But you held out on me, and I don't like that one bit."

With one quick movement, the man swiveled toward her and bent down, using the knife to cut the ropes that held her feet. Then he moved behind her and did the same to the ropes around her wrists.

Too stunned and terrified to move, Mara sat motionless as the man laughed and stepped between her and the camera. "When I found out about Tom and realized what you'd done, I asked myself how I could get even with you. I realized there was nothing that would hurt you more than to see me cut this girl loose just when you thought you were finally going to get your revenge. So that, *amigo*, is what I just did. Mara is free. What do you think of that, Jefe?"

He laughed and turned to look down at Mara. "You still there?" he said, raising his eyebrows. "If I was you, I'd be running like crazy before I decide to change my mind."

Mara, trying to absorb the man's words, felt paralyzed, welded to the metal chair.

The man leaned down again, his face just inches from hers. "Are you deaf? Didn't you hear what I said? I'm letting you go—right in front of Jefe's eyes. Now get out of here while you still can. Go on. Get out!"

Mara gasped, as reality seemed to smack her in the face. Without another moment's hesitation, she jumped up from the chair where she'd sat for several hours now, and scrambled on nearly numb legs to the stairway, praying it wasn't a trick. What if he was just playing her, letting her think she was going to escape, only to recapture and torture her as he'd threatened to do?

Expecting his grasp to stop her at any moment, she forced her legs to carry her to the top of the stairs and to hold her steady while she pushed the storm doors open. The whoosh of cool night air brought fresh tears to her eyes, as she pulled herself from the basement and out onto solid ground. Without a glance backward and with nothing but the faint light of a sliver of moon and a few scattered stars above her, she gulped great swallows of sweet oxygen as she ran, praying all the way that someone would come along and help her before the crazy man in the basement caught up with her.

285

Another misty morning had broken over the thick bamboo-forested Mekong River valley. Mynah birds issued wake-up calls from treetops as elephants trumpeted a welcome to the new day and Lawan opened sleepy eyes to a sight that was becoming at least slightly familiar.

I like it here, she thought, as understanding seeped into her mind. *The woman named Joan and her husband are very nice to me — the others too, but especially her.* She smiled, though a tinge of sadness marred her joy. *Many of the girls call her Maae. She is a good lady, but I do miss my own maae and phor very much. And my baby sister, Mali, too. Will I ever see any of them again?*

She refused to let her thoughts drift to her older sister, Chanthra. The memory of the girl's death was still too fresh, but at least she knew she was now with *phra yaeh suu*. Was the rest of her family with Him too?

"Good morning, Lawan."

286

The shy greeting came from five-year-old BanChuen on the next sleeping mat. Lawan banished her memories and wonderings, turning her head to answer the little girl who had quickly become her friend. The child's smile was warm, and Lawan's heart soared at the reminder that she no longer lived or worked in a brothel. She was free! For however long she was allowed to stay in this wonderful place and regardless of whether or not she ever saw her family again, she would be grateful for this moment, this day, here in the middle of the Thai jungle.

Chapter 42

The young couple had scarcely been married a month as they rolled along the back road toward home. They'd driven into town for dinner and a movie, staying out later than they normally would on a week night.

Christine yawned, leaning her head against Steve's shoulder, while he steered with his left hand, his right arm around his wife, holding her close. "You're going to be dragging at work tomorrow," she mumbled, nearly lulled to sleep by the steady thrum of the pickup's engine and the warmth of her husband's presence. "We're going to have to reserve these late nights for the weekends."

Steve chuckled. "Hey, we're still in our twenties, OK? I think we can still handle a night or two like this once in awhile."

Christine giggled. She supposed he was right. After all, they didn't want to start acting like her grandparents, who had supper at 4:00 P.M. and went to bed before sundown. But she sure was glad those same grandparents had offered to let her and Steve come and live with them on the farm in exchange for some help around the place. It was the only way they could get enough money saved to buy a place of their own anytime soon.

"It's nice out here, away from the city," Steve commented, pulling Christine back from her thoughts about her grandparents. "I'm glad we agreed to move out here, at least for a while."

Christine nodded, pleased once again to realize how often their thoughts seemed to run in similar directions. She'd loved Steve since they were kids, and she still had trouble believing they were actually married. One of these days they'd have children of their own and —

The jolt of their screeching tires nearly catapulted Christine into the windshield, but Steve held her tight as they fishtailed to a stop.

"What's wrong?" she cried. "What happened?"

"There," Steve said, staring out the front window. "Look! There's a woman standing by the side of road, waving at us."

Christine felt her eyes widen and her mouth drop open as she caught sight of the disheveled, wild-looking young woman. "Her clothes are nearly ripped off," she said. "She looks half crazy."

288

"She looks like she needs help," Steve said. "Wait here."

Christine grabbed his arm. "No, don't go," she begged. "She might be dangerous."

He looked down at her, his eyes convicting her heart. "Would Jesus leave her there?"

Christine felt her cheeks flame, and she slowly shook her head. "No," she admitted. "But be careful."

Steve nodded. "I'll be careful. You pray."

And he stepped out of the truck and walked toward the woman, who fell sobbing into his arms.

❦

Leah's cell phone jangled her awake with one of her favorite songs that she'd downloaded from the Internet. She willed herself to clarity as she squinted at the name on the screen.

Sarah. That part wasn't surprising, but the screen also informed her it was only 8:30 on Saturday morning. She frowned. What was her friend doing up so early, particularly after being out late with Jonathan the night before?

Leah's frown turned to a grin; she had just answered her own question.

She punched the Receive button and purred a teasing hello.

"Leah, it's me, Sarah."

"No kidding." Leah laughed. "Let me guess. You want to talk about last night."

Sarah's pause brought a stab of guilt to Leah's heart. She hadn't meant to be sarcastic or catty. Had she come across that way?

"Sorry," she said. "I just know you. Tell me what happened."

Her friend's enthusiastic tone was back. "Well, nothing really happened — I mean, well, not really. I guess. But . . . well, we did have a really good time. We even went out for ice cream after Jonathan got off. We shared a huge banana split."

Leah smiled. "Sounds romantic."

"It was." Leah heard the sigh in Sarah's voice. "Well, to me it was anyway. I have no idea if it meant anything to Jonathan other than just spending a little time with his sister's friend." She sighed again. "Leah, do you think he'll ever see me as anything but just another annoying little sister?"

"Hey," Leah joked, "watch who you're calling an annoying little sister! That would be me, you know."

Sarah giggled. "You know what I mean. Do I at least have a chance with him?"

Leah resisted the urge to shrug, reminding herself that Sarah couldn't see her. "Who knows? I can't really say one way or the other, but stranger things have happened. For all we know, he's been thinking about this very thing since he brought you home last night."

"Do you really think so?" Sarah's voice scarcely concealed her excitement. "Do you think I should call him—you know, just to say good morning or something?"

"I wouldn't go that far," Leah cautioned. "Especially not this early." She hesitated, wanting to offer a nugget of encouragement but not wanting to give her friend false hope. "Tell you what. When he gets up, I'll get him alone and start a conversation—about different things, not just you—and then I'll drop your name into the middle of it and ask how things went last night. I know my brother well enough to read between the lines, even if he doesn't come out and tell me what he feels."

"Oh, Leah, that would be great! Thank you so much."

Leah smiled again. "My pleasure. Now how about if you hang up and let me catch a little more sleep? Knowing Jonathan, he won't be up for at least a couple of hours yet anyway."

"OK. But don't forget to talk to him . . . and let me know what he says!"

"I won't forget," she promised, and clicked off.

Barbara's heart hammered as she drove as fast as she safely or legally dared, headed for the police station. She wished Mara had called her immediately after the couple that rescued her used their cell phone to alert the authorities. But she understood that the girl was too traumatized to think straight and that the police had wanted her to be checked out by a physician and questioned by a detective. Mara had complied without considering the need to call a friend to be with her during the ordeal.

A friend. The entire concept is undoubtedly foreign to her. It's a wonder the poor girl trusts anyone after all the betrayals and abuse she's suffered in her lifetime. Barbara shook her head as she turned into the public parking lot near the station. That Mara trusted her enough to call her at all was encouraging.

She shut off her car, grabbed her purse, and made a beeline for the front entrance. She knew enough people here that she could bypass some of the delays and protocol that might otherwise hold her back from getting to Mara. Sure enough, a longtime acquaintance sat at the front desk and offered her a warm smile as soon as she looked up and spotted her.

"Barbara, good to see you again. How can I help you this morning?"

Barbara gave a quick summary of the situation, and in minutes she was being ushered into a small, windowless room down the hall. The sight of Mara broke her heart. The young woman looked like a helpless little girl, as she raised her head and focused on Barbara. Mara's eyes were red, no doubt from crying and lack of sleep, and she wore a man's suit jacket over her shoulders, though it didn't completely hide her torn clothing. Barbara was grateful for the nameless gentleman who had covered her.

Mara's mouth opened and a cry escaped, sounding somewhat like Barbara's name. The older woman rushed to her side and knelt down beside her, gathering her into her arms.

"Oh, Mara," she crooned, "thank God you're alive! I can't even imagine how terrifying all this has been for you, but thank you, thank you for calling me."

Mara's tears seemed to burst from her eyes, as sobs rolled up from deep within, nearly choking the girl with their intensity.

As long as Barbara had been involved in the ministry of rescuing human-trafficking victims and as much of the depraved side of life that she had witnessed, she would never grow accustomed to the level of evil that human beings inflicted upon one another. And the fallout for the victims seemed never-ending.

Holding Mara tightly against her shoulder, Barbara rocked her as if she were her very own daughter, imagining that she couldn't hurt for her any more if she truly were.

Chapter 43

Jonathan pulled himself from bed a little after 10:00 and headed for the shower. It was Saturday and he wasn't working tonight, meaning that his usual first thought would be to try to rustle up a baseball game for the afternoon. But today was different. His heart just wasn't in it. Confused thoughts of Sarah and Mara had tumbled about in his mind the night before, keeping him awake until the early morning hours, and had then teased him even in his sleep. When he awoke, he hadn't felt anymore rested than when he'd first gone to bed, and his feeling of confusion had grown. Even the soothing hot water from the shower didn't ease his tensions as it normally did.

He trudged down the stairs, his slow steps a far cry from the bounce that otherwise marked his daily descent in search of breakfast. He just hoped his parents and sister were occupied somewhere else so he could have the kitchen to himself and not be forced to smile and participate in a family conversation, which sooner or later would lead to his evening with Sarah.

The room was empty as he stepped inside, and he sighed with relief as he headed for the refrigerator to snag a glass of orange juice. He'd scarcely poured it before he was interrupted by a familiar voice behind him.

"Hey, Bro."

He froze, his hand clasping the glass midway between the counter and his lips. So much for avoiding conversation.

"Hey, yourself," he said, purposely not turning around as he brought the glass to his mouth, drinking it down without stopping for air. Maybe Leah would take the hint and leave him alone.

"So," she said, her voice closer now, as he realized she was standing nearly at his elbow. "What's new?"

He sighed and turned to face her, forcing a smile that he knew didn't reach his eyes and that she'd never buy. "Not much," he said. "How about you?"

Leah's perfectly matched eyebrows shot upward. "Seriously? You went out with my best friend last night, and there's not much new?" Her thick red curls were piled on top of her head, held somewhat in place by a brown plastic clip. Her hands were perched on her hips, and her green eyes bored into his. It was obvious she wasn't going anywhere without a blow-by-blow account of his time with Sarah.

He shrugged and feigned nonchalance as he turned back to the counter to grab a mug from the cupboard and pour some coffee from the still-warm carafe, no doubt left there by his ever-efficient mother. "It's not like we were out on a date or anything," he said, his back to her. "She just rode along with me while I made my deliveries—like you did that time."

"Except you and I didn't go out afterward or share a banana split together."

This time it was Jonathan's turn to raise his eyebrows, as he turned back around. The teasing smile on his sister's face lit up her green eyes.

"How did you know about that?" he asked. "You talk to Sarah already today?"

Leah nodded, a self-satisfied expression replacing her tease. "She called me at 8:30 and told me all about it."

All about it? Jonathan thought. *All about what? It's not like anything happened. We just talked.* But somehow he knew he wasn't going to get away with so simple an answer. He loved his little sister, but she could be a real pain at times.

His thoughts raced and Leah waited, as Jonathan tried to formulate an answer that would be honest and yet satisfy Leah's curiosity. No doubt whatever he told her would quickly be passed on to Sarah, and he didn't want to give either girl a false impression. He'd enjoyed the evening with Sarah, but it's not like he was attracted to her . . . was he?

Before he could answer, the landline rang, drawing their attention to the cordless phone on the counter by the stove.

"You want to get it?" Leah asked. "Mom and Dad went out for breakfast, so we're the only ones here."

Jonathan shook his head, hoping Leah would answer and he could make a quick escape before she hung up. "Nah. You go ahead. Like you said, it's probably for Mom or Dad anyway. If it was for one of us, they'd call on our cell."

295

Leah nodded. "True. I'll just check caller ID."

She picked up the phone and studied it, as Jonathan made his break. "Wait," she said, stopping him in his tracks. "It's Barbara Whiting. I wonder what she wants." She punched the receive button and pressed the phone to her ear. "Hello?"

Jonathan hovered in the doorway, wondering why he didn't just make a mad dash for freedom but held in place by curiosity. Barbara seldom called unless it had something to do with the human-trafficking ministry they were all involved in or had something to do with Mara. The thought started Jonathan's heart hammering.

"You're kidding," Leah exclaimed, her voice hushed. "Mara? Is she OK?"

Jonathan nearly dropped his coffee mug as he stepped closer to his sister. What had happened to Mara—and why did news of her affect him in a way that being near Sarah never could?

Alley Cat knew it was just a matter of time until they caught up with him, but he didn't care. Tom was dead, and Jack didn't have anyone else. Since their parents died, the two of them had been family—the only family either of them wanted or needed. Jack just regretted that he hadn't set a better example for his little brother. Maybe Tom wouldn't have ended up in the slammer if Jack had done something decent with his own life.

But it was too late now. He lit a cigarette and took a long puff. With Tom gone, there was nothing or no one left to live for. The only halfway decent thing Jack figured he'd ever done was to let that girl go. And his motives for doing that had been none too pure. All he'd really cared about at that point was making sure old Jefe got what was coming to him—a video of Mara being set free. It was the best spit-in-the-face Jack could come up with for the no-good skunk who had betrayed him and let his baby brother die.

The best way to get revenge on Jefe was to make sure he didn't get the revenge he wanted on Mara, Jack thought, as he sat alone in his pickup truck, parked on a lonely edge by a drop-off into a rocky canyon. It was nearly noon now, with the Southern California sun directly overhead. He'd been there for several hours, ever since he'd done what he needed to do to make sure the video got delivered to Jefe.

Amazing what you can get in and out of prisons when you have the right connections, he mused. *And Jefe sure has them, though they won't do him any good once he sees that video.*

He smirked and took another drag. *He thought he had it all figured out, even down to how he could keep me from finding out about what happened to Tom until it was too late. But he hadn't figured on me heading back to check my phone last night. If I hadn't, Mara would be close to dead by now — and begging for me to end it. And then what? I'd finally finish her off and send the tape to Jefe, only to find out Tom was already dead.* He shook his head. *It would have been too late. I could never have gotten even with him then. But this way . . .*

He thought again, as he had several times throughout the last few hours, what Jefe would feel when he saw that footage of what he thought would be Mara's torture and death but instead showed her release. "In your face, you slimeball," Jack muttered.

He flicked the cigarette to the ground and stomped it with his boot, then spun around and nearly threw himself into the cab of his pickup. The thought that cats — even alley cats — had nine lives flitted through his mind, but he cursed it away. With shaking hands he thrust the keys into the ignition and gunned the truck to life. He had to do this thing before he chickened out.

With a scream that came from somewhere below his lungs, he stomped on the gas and closed his eyes, hurling the truck over the cliff and his soul into what he hoped would not be a worse hell than what he falsely believed he would have to endure if he remained on earth.

297

❦

Francesca still couldn't believe she was finally free. Though the US officials had explained to her and her parents that they would have to return to San Diego so Francesca could testify against the man who had kidnapped and held her, forcing her into sexual slavery, for now they were headed back to their home in Juarez. Even with all the drug wars and violence that went on in their once peaceful hometown just across the border from El Paso, Texas, Francesca couldn't wait to see it again.

She closed her eyes as she sat in the back seat of her parents' old car, allowing the early afternoon sun to warm her through the window and envisioning the little house where she had grown up with her siblings and which she'd come to think she would never see again. She still had trouble believing her rescue had truly happened and that she wouldn't suddenly wake up and find herself back in the small room on one side of the adjoining bathroom with ChaCha's room on the other.

ChaCha, she thought. *The* policia *told me she has been rescued — and the others too. What will happen to them now? ChaCha always told me she didn't have a* familia *to go back to, no one who would want her anyway. How is that possible? What* familia *would not want their child back? It wasn't her fault she ended up in that awful place.*

El Diablo's evil face swam into her memory then, sneering at her as he called her "mi amor," and she quickly shoved the image away. She knew she would have to face him again when she and her parents returned to the United States for the trial, but for now she just wanted to think about going home, where her brothers and sisters waited for her, watched over by their grandparents who also longed to see her again.

I am so blessed, she thought. *I have a family who loves me and wants me home. But what will they all say about the baby — my baby? My parents know now, but Papa says we will talk about it later. What does that mean? What will happen when my stomach begins to grow and I bring shame on our family?*

Once again she pushed away the thoughts that brought her pain. There were so many of them, and they overwhelmed the young girl. For now it was enough that she had broken free of El Diablo—thanks to the person she had come to know was named Mara. She hoped she would meet this Mara one day so she could thank her personally. Meanwhile, she would continue to pray for her, as she and her parents had done the night before.

Chapter 44

Mara thought evening would never come. There was something about the day's sunlight that had seemed to peer deep inside her, exposing her in a way she couldn't understand. But she was home now—or nearly so, as Barbara steered her car toward the sidewalk and parked in front of the large house where Mara's empty room waited for her.

Barbara turned off the engine and reached over to lay a hand on Mara's arm. "I'm coming in with you for a while," she said. "And I'll stay until you're asleep."

Mara shook her head. "I don't think I can sleep, at least not yet."

"Then I'll stay and keep you company until you can."

What was beginning to feel like a never-ending supply of tears once again pricked Mara's eyelids. How grateful she was for this woman who scarcely knew her and yet was the closest thing Mara could imagine to a mother. Would she ever have developed such a close and trusting relationship with her own mother if her parents hadn't sold her to her *tio* when she was just a little girl?

No. The very fact that her parents had sold her, even if they didn't realize exactly what horror lay ahead for their only daughter, precluded a close relationship of any kind. What kind of mother sold her child for any reason? Not the kind

Mara wanted anything to do with. She was better off with this near stranger who sat at her side.

"Thank you," was all she could say, as she opened the door and stepped out onto the sidewalk, grateful to know that Barbara would follow. She really did not want to be alone right now, and she'd never allowed herself to become acquainted with any of the other renters who shared the building. She was glad she wasn't scheduled to work that evening, since she hadn't even thought until now of the need to call Mariner's and let someone know what was going on. Perhaps she'd be able to face them by the time she was supposed to report for work tomorrow afternoon, though she imagined that the news of what had happened would have reached her fellow employees by then. After all, she couldn't hope to keep something like this a secret forever, though she could certainly try.

She pulled herself up the steps to the porch, her feet feeling leaden as she flashed back to her recent encounter on this very spot when Jonathan had stopped by. She had been rude and she regretted that, but she simply hadn't been able to allow herself to think positively and certainly not romantically about any man, regardless of how attractive he was or how he had intervened to save her life.

Gratitude, that's all it is, she told herself, pulling open the front door and heading for the stairway. All she wanted to do was go upstairs to her room, take a shower, put on fresh clothes, and sit outside in the cool of the evening with Barbara, knowing that she could talk about her recent experience if she wanted to . . . or not. Barbara would understand.

She grabbed hold of the railing and began the ascent, taking comfort in hearing Barbara's steps echoing her own.

Jonathan had scarcely been able to stop himself from trying to go to Mara ever since Leah told him what had happened. But Barbara had cautioned Leah that Mara was too fragile for company, at least not right away. Besides, hadn't Mara practically sent him packing the last time he stopped by to see her, and she wasn't even in such an emotional state then as she no doubt was now. His visit would be about as welcome as the proverbial plague. Still . . .

It would have been easier if he were working tonight, he thought. At least it would give him something to do but drive around town, trying to steer clear of Mara's street but not doing very well at it. For the third time he came within a block of it and nearly turned toward her house, but for the third time he stopped. Would she even be there? Barbara had told Leah she didn't know how long they'd be at the police station or where they would go when they left. Barbara would either take Mara to her own place or back home with her, whichever the girl preferred. And even if they'd gone to Mara's, that didn't mean she wanted to see him.

But I want to see her!

He pounded the steering wheel, frustrated with himself for the feelings he couldn't seem to banish. At least his time with Sarah the night before had been pleasant if not exciting, and she welcomed his company. Mara appeared not to be able to stand the sight of him.

Was it because he reminded her of where she had been, what she had been forced to do before he helped her escape? He wanted to believe that's all it was and that it wasn't a personal rejection, but how could he know if he couldn't get close enough to her to find out?

Now he was being selfish, adding guilt to his frustration and concern. Yes, at least there was concern in the mix. In fact, he decided, concern truly was the strongest emotion, overshadowing the others. He wanted above all to know that she was all right, though he couldn't imagine how she could be. How did one young woman survive so much pain and danger and still end up all right? Could she ever *really* be all right?

It was a thought that had concerned him even before she turned away from him the last time he stopped by her house. Over and over, he had asked himself why he would want to get involved with someone who was so obviously damaged. Though he realized it wasn't her fault, that the damage was done *to* her and not *by* her, he questioned the wisdom of even trying to initiate a relationship with someone who might never be able to have a serious or healthy relationship. Wasn't he just setting himself up for failure and heartache?

He smacked the steering wheel again. Yes, he was, but it just didn't matter. She could reject him again or break his heart or just tell him to go fly a kite, but he couldn't stay away. He had to see her for himself, make sure she was OK, try to break through that wall.

This time he followed his instincts and turned the car down the street toward her home. For some reason, when he pulled up in front and saw Mara and Barbara sitting under the dim light on the porch, he wasn't surprised. But he was nervous. As he parked the car and opened the door, he prayed the butterflies in his stomach would settle down so he could at least carry on a sensible conversation with the two ladies who now watched his every move.

Sarah's insides quivered like a gelatin dessert on a shaky kitchen table. Why had she agreed to come with Leah to see Mara? True, Sarah had met her at the mall once and hadn't thought much about it, but now Leah had told her just a little of Mara's past, and it made the younger girl very uncomfortable.

I shouldn't have borrowed my mom's car, Sarah thought. *Should have told Leah I couldn't get it. Or at least, after we went out and ate, I should have told her I had to get right back home. Why did I let her talk me into driving to Mara's house? Just because Leah wants to see her doesn't mean I do.*

But despite her misgivings, Sarah kept driving, following Leah's instructions to "turn left" or "veer right" or "go straight through this intersection." Along the way, Leah told her just a little more about what had happened to Mara the previous night, and Sarah was now caught between sympathy and revulsion. What kind of girl was this Mara person to be involved in such things?

And then, suddenly, they were there, pulling up in front of a house that scarcely registered in Sarah's line of vision; all she could see was the old blue VW parked out front.

Pulling up behind the familiar blue Beetle, Sarah turned off the engine. "I'm not so sure I should go with you," she said, her glance darting from Leah beside her to the three gathered on the porch — two women in chairs and one tall male standing in front of them. "Why don't I just wait in the car while you go talk to them? Mara doesn't really know me."

"I don't think that's a good idea," Leah said, eyeing the trio on the porch. "They've all stopped talking to watch us now. They know you're here. Maybe I was wrong to come, but I've been thinking about Mara, and I just want to know she's OK."

"Seems you're not the only one," Sarah remarked. "Did you know Jonathan would be here?"

Leah shook her head. "No, but I'm not surprised. He was there when Barbara called me and told me the news. She must think we're terrible. She specifically said Mara probably wasn't up to company yet, but here we all are."

Sarah felt her cheeks color. "Yeah, here we all are. I knew this wasn't a good idea."

Leah shrugged. "Probably not. But we're here now, so let's get out and go say hello. We don't have to discuss what happened unless she mentions it. We can just say we wanted to make sure she was OK and offer our support. We'll keep it short, I promise."

"That's for sure," Sarah agreed. "The shorter, the better."

Taking a deep breath, she opened the driver's door and stepped out, ready to follow Leah who was already making her way toward the porch. She tried to convince herself that it was worth the stop, just to see Jonathan again, but she really would rather have done so in a different place and under different circumstances.

"Hey," Jonathan said as the girls joined them on the porch. "I didn't expect to see you two here."

"We didn't expect to see you either," Leah said before turning her attention to Mara. "We can only stay a minute," she said, stepping toward the girl who was still seated, her face upturned quizzically.

Barbara started to stand up. "Here," she said. "Why don't one of you take my chair? I've been sitting all evening."

"Oh no," Leah responded, waving away the offer. "Really. We can't stay. We just happened to be . . ." Her voice faltered, and her cheeks showed a faint blush, even in the dim light. "We were passing by on our way to the mall, and I asked Sarah to stop for a minute so we could see how you were." She ducked her head briefly before looking toward Barbara. "I know you suggested we not come by yet, but I just needed to see Mara and know she was OK."

She turned back to Mara then, and Sarah watched as the beautiful young woman with the large, sad eyes moved her gaze from Leah to Jonathan and back again. But in that brief moment when Mara's eyes connected with Jonathan's, Sarah knew. There was a spark between them that she could never ignite in the tall, handsome young man who stood so close to her.

"I'm fine," Mara said, her smile forced. "Really. But right now I'm just tired." She glanced at her friend, who sat in the chair nearby. "Barbara and I were just about to go inside." Mara smiled, and this time Sarah thought her smile was more genuine. "Barbara promised to stay with me until I fell asleep—longer if I need her. I think I'm ready to take her up on that offer now."

Barbara nodded and rose from her chair, as Leah and Jonathan pulled themselves together and excused themselves, saying they had to go anyway. Sarah said nothing, realizing that no one would notice even if she did.

Raising her gaze to Jonathan's face, Sarah saw the longing in his brown eyes as he watched Mara, and the thin thread of hope Sarah held out that he might feel as she did vanished. Mara might not know it yet, but Sarah did: Jonathan was in love with Mara, whether she returned that love or not. And that was that.

Sarah turned and walked toward her mother's car, as Jonathan and Leah followed close behind and the front door banged shut behind Mara and Barbara. The lines had been drawn, and Sarah's childhood crush had evaporated into the night air, leaving a sting of tears behind. She climbed into the car and waited.

307

Epilogue

Logs crackled in the fireplace, sending sparks shooting upward as Nyesha snuggled close to Kyle on the reclining loveseat, enjoying some rare alone time now that their five-year-old Anna was asleep in her room.

"First fire of the year," she commented. "I love it."

"Me too. I kind of hope it'll be a cooler than usual winter so we can have plenty of them."

Nyesha chuckled. "You mean, you hope it might actually get down close to freezing a night or two? Because that's about as cold as it's going to get in San Diego."

"True. But anything below 50 is fireplace weather, as far as I'm concerned."

She sighed, her mind taking a turn to a faraway place that had only this very day come back into play in their lives.

"What do you think about Lawan?" she asked. "They've approved and expedited our application; and before you know it, Anna is going to have the surprise of her life."

She felt Kyle nod. "So much has happened so fast," he said. "Just a few months ago we were talking about maybe contacting the agency to see if they knew anything about Anna's remaining family, and now, just weeks before the holidays, we get word that the adoption is approved and Anna's sister is coming to live with us." He squeezed her shoulder. "Not to mention all the stuff that went down in between."

Nyesha knew what he meant. First the young woman named Mara helped rescue a teenager from sexual slavery. The girl's release then led to the freeing of several others who had been held at the same house and eventually the conviction of a man known as El Diablo, apparently the head of a ring that kidnapped young girls and forced them into an unimaginably horrible life. And within days of Mara's initial involvement in that situation, she had been kidnapped and nearly killed herself, seemingly in some botched revenge plot by her former owner who was serving a life sentence. That situation had culminated in a suicide by the man known as Alley Cat who had been contracted to kill Mara but had changed his mind when he learned of his brother's death. It was all nearly too much to take in, even with the passing of time.

"Yes," Nyesha said, forcing her mind back to the good news of Lawan's imminent arrival, though the sad news that her natural parents were both dead cast a shadow over the event. "Ever since that special delivery letter came this morning with Lawan's picture and the approval notification, I haven't been able to stop picturing the reunion those two sisters will have. And that we get to be part of it is almost too good to be true. Do you think we should tell Anna soon?"

"Tell me what?"

The sleepy voice interrupted their conversation, and they sat forward, turning their eyes toward the tousle-haired girl standing in the doorway, her innocent face illuminated by the firelight.

Nyesha glanced up at Kyle. "Well, what do you think?"

He smiled. "I suppose now's as good a time as any."

"Come here, sweet girl," Nyesha said, holding out her arms. "Your daddy and I have something to tell you."

"Will I like it?" she asked, crawling up on her mother's lap.

Nyesha laughed. "Oh, I think you're going to like this news very, very much." She reached to the end table beside the couch and lifted a large envelope into the air. "You see, we got a special delivery letter today, and it says that our little rainbow family is going to grow just a little bit bigger."

The End

THE DELIVERER

Kathi Macias

Prologue

The sun set early in late November, and though a pleasant warm spell had kept San Diego's daytime temperatures in the lower 80s for the past week or so, the air cooled quickly as darkness approached.

Mara didn't mind. She loved watching the sun go down over the Pacific at any time of year and in any sort of weather. Just being able to sit on the seawall and watch the colorful streaks in the broad expanse of sky, seeming to frame the dark and restless ocean, reminded her of how precious her freedom was and how much she'd endured before obtaining it.

Zipping her windbreaker against the encroaching dampness, she gazed down at the envelope in her hand, postmarked Juarez, Mexico. She'd nearly memorized the words in the one-page letter handwritten by the fifteen-year-old girl Mara had helped to rescue just months earlier. Mara had been working at her waitressing job when she spotted Francesca with her owner and immediately recognized the signs of a girl caught up in human trafficking. The situation had dredged up many of her own dark memories, but Mara was glad she'd been in the right place at the right time to assist the girl's release and eventual return to her family.

I'm just glad she had a family and a home to go back to, Mara thought, resisting the tears that bit her eyes as she compared Francesca's situation to her own. At least Francesca had been kidnapped, not sold into slavery by her own parents.

Mara shook her head. She had to stop this constant slipping back into self-pity about her past and just enjoy the present. She was free now, working and hoping to start classes at the local college after the first of the year. It was more than she had ever dreamed of during her ten years of captivity.

She pulled the letter from the envelope and squinted to reread portions of it in the fading light. *The baby will come soon . . . not sure yet about adoption . . . praying for the right answer.* Mara, too, had become pregnant during the years she lived as a sex slave—several times, actually—but she'd never even had the chance to choose to carry her babies to term. Always there was a forced abortion, and always she had to suppress her grief and go right back to the life she despised.

Never again, she told herself. *And never again for Francesca. But what about all the others?*

The tears won over at that point, dripping onto her cheeks as she thought of Jasmine and others who had died at the hands of their abusers. She thought, too, of what she'd heard about a young Thai girl named Lawan, rescued from a brothel in the Golden Triangle and even now winging her way across the ocean to join her adoptive family right here in the San Diego area.

One more set free . . . so many left behind. No matter how hard she tried, Mara could not banish that truth from her thoughts. She'd often talked about that very thing to her friend Barbara Whiting, the lady involved with an outreach to human-trafficking victims, and Barbara too had lamented the many who never escaped. "But that doesn't mean we quit trying to help them," she'd said. "We may save only a small percentage of them, but each life we save is precious and makes our efforts worthwhile."

Each life? Even mine? Mara wasn't so sure, though she wanted desperately to believe it. The reminder that she had also discussed this topic with Jonathan, the handsome Bible college student who had helped rescue her more than two years earlier, brought a rush of heat to her cheeks, and she was glad for the near darkness that hid her emotions. She had tried to deny her feelings for Jonathan and to hide them from him, but he'd faithfully kept in touch with her through letters since going back to school this past fall. One of the things he said to her over and over again was that her life was precious to God and that He loved her and had a purpose for her. At times she dared to believe it, but most of the time . . .

A taunting male voice from a passing car interrupted her thoughts as he called out a suggestive comment to her and then laughed as the vehicle sped away. Mara recoiled at the sound and shoved the letter back into the envelope. She stood up from the seawall, brushed the sand off the back of her jeans, and turned toward home. She had to work the breakfast shift in the morning, so she'd better get to bed early. Tomorrow was Saturday, and Mariner's would be busy. She just hoped that meant some good tips because she could sure use the money.

New Hope® Publishers is a division of WMU®, an international organization that challenges Christian believers to understand and be radically involved in God's mission. For more information about WMU, go to www.wmu.com. More information about New Hope books may be found at www.newhopedigital.com. New Hope books may be purchased at your local bookstore.

Use the QR reader on your
smartphone to visit us online at
www.newhopedigital.com

If you've been blessed by this book, we would like to hear your story.
The publisher and author welcome your comments and
suggestions at: newhopereader@wmu.org.

FREEDOM SERIES BOOK #1

Deliver Me From Evil
ISBN-13: 978-1-59669-306-7
$14.99

Praise for Deliver Me From Evil...

"Macias tackles one of our world's most perplexing social issues with intense realism and hope. *Deliver Us from Evil* reveals depth, honesty, and grace to guide readers toward a deeper faith and a heart challenged to make a difference in our world."
—**Dillon Burroughs**, activist and coauthor of *Not in My Town*

"*Deliver Me from Evil* will grip your mind and heart from the opening chapter and refuse to let go till you reluctantly close the back cover. Kathi Macias tackles a dark and difficult issue with compelling, complex characters and vivid prose. This novel will change you."—**James L. Rubart**, best-selling author of *Rooms, Book of Days,* and *The Chair*

Available in bookstores everywhere.

For information about these books or any New Hope product,
Visit www.newhopedigital.com